Prais_ ___

The Mountains Under Her Feet

Isabel possesses that relatable yet paradoxical spirit of resilience and strength, naivete, and intuitive wisdom that all of us have experienced as we journey through our lives. We wince when she missteps, applaud when she stands up to her oppressors, and smile in recognition of those small yet precious moments that mark our place in this world.

—**Georgina Key**
Author, *Shiny Bits in Between*

The Mountains Under Her Feet encompasses a broad range of emotions using wit, warmth, and overcoming. The pages weave in labor, motherhood, abuse, and privilege with doses of warmth and intelligence. The threads of abuse that were normal and never spoken of are here on these pages. A fabulous tapestry!

—**Marie Posthumous**
Editor, *Our Silent Voice*

With sensitive observation and crystalline prose, Vance tells the story of a strong girl who becomes a stronger woman, struggling through difficult family dynamics to find her place in a constantly shifting world. Isabel is a protagonist who won my heart.

—**Vicki Lane**
Author, *And the Crows Took Their Eyes* and the Elizabeth Goodweather Appalachian Mystery series

The
Mountains
Under Her Feet

The
Mountains
Under Her Feet

a novel

Catherine Vance

BALANCE OF SEVEN
Dallas

For information, contact:
Balance of Seven, www.balanceofseven.com
Managing Director: nyri.b@balanceofseven.com
Book Production Manager: tntinker@balanceofseven.com

Cover Design by Eben Schumacher Art
ebenschumacherart.artstation.com

Developmental Editing by Nyri A. Bakkalian, PhD
nyri.b@balanceofseven.com

Line Editing by Georgina Key

Copyediting by D. Ynes Freeman

Formatting and Proofreading by TNT Editing
www.theodorentinker.com/TNTEditing

Proofreading by Amanda Mills Woodlee

Publisher's Cataloging-in-Publication Data

Names: Vance, Catherine.
Title: The mountains under her feet / Catherine Vance.
Description: Dallas, TX : Balance of Seven, 2023.
Identifiers: LCCN 2023931042 | ISBN 9781947012462 (pbk.) | ISBN 9781947012479
    (ebook) | ISBN 9781947012554 (itch.io ebook)
Subjects: LCSH: Appalachian Region – Fiction. | Families – Fiction. | Family violence
    – Fiction. | Internally displaced persons – Fiction. | Mothers and daughters –
    Fiction. | BISAC: FICTION / Family Life / General. | FICTION / Historical
    / 20th Century / World War II. | FICTION / Women.
Classification: LCC PS3622.A53 2023 (print) | PS3622.A53 (ebook) | DDC 813 V36--
    dc23
LC record available at https://lccn.loc.gov/2023931042

27 26 25 24 23   1 2 3 4 5

To the strong women of my family,
past and present.

"You don't know how strong you are until being strong is the only choice you have."
—Isabel King

Contents

Contents

One

Second Husband

1936

It was getting dark, but a scrap of sky was caught in the middle of the chinaberry tree. I looked again, and it was my daughter, her skinny legs trembling. She was wearing her pale-blue cotton dress that came just past her knees.

I was only a few feet away from the front porch when I heard her sobbing. I was returning from the grocery store. I always made the trip on foot, and it was chilly, so I had on my ancient winter coat, its color drab as the paper bags I was carrying.

"Mother! I'm up here, Mother." Janey's voice seemed to come from over my head, so my chin went straight up, and that's when I thought I saw the sky.

"Whatever's the matter, honey? Why are you up there?" I let my bags slide to the ground as I reached the base of the tree. Apples and cans rolled away in slow motion.

"I think I might fall," she said, as if thinking about

1

doing it on purpose. She was twelve years old. The limb she was balanced on was a thin one, and it flexed like a whip.

"Good Lord! Listen to me now. Crawl backwards, slow," I said, and inch by inch, I encouraged her as she moved inward to the trunk. I lifted my arms like a preacher, like I believed I could save something.

"All right, bring your left foot down. That's it; now reach a little to the side. Don't be afraid. I'm going to catch you."

Somehow, I talked her within reach.

"I got you; come on," I said, and she leaped to me like a cat. I wrapped her in my arms. As soon as I set her down on the earth, her bladder released, drenching her shoes.

She spread her legs wide and started to cry harder. I tried to lead her to the house, but she pulled against me.

"I won't go back in there. I'm scared; he—he put his hands on me." She reached to cup her tiny breasts but stopped and shook her fingers like she was flinging off water.

"What do you mean, he put his hands on you?" My mind flashed, *No, that can't be.* But I registered what she said. I knew exactly what she meant.

John L. My husband, her stepfather.

Jane saw my look of horror and drew a deep breath. Her eyes darted to the front door of our four-room bungalow. It needed a new coat of red paint.

"Mother, please, let's not go in there. We can sit out here and have us a picnic for supper." She picked up an apple.

A gear in my brain started a slow turn, and calm floated through me like a current of cold air. Other things that had happened recently started to make sense. "We got to go in there, Janey. Our clothes is in there."

The words were no sooner out of my mouth than I realized I had not corrected my grammar to proper English, as I usually tried to do.

"Look at you; you need clean clothes. I won't let anything happen. Come on; don't worry now, I'm here."

We began to pick up the fallen groceries and put them back in the sacks. We moved slowly, as if our arms were in restraints.

She clutched my coat as we mounted the steps. It was a clean and respectable home, not grown over and cluttered, like some of the neighbors' places here on the outskirts of Knoxville. I looked at the empty geranium pots by the front window and realized a shift was happening. Those pots *had been* mine. I was already seeing things in past tense.

When I opened the door and peered around the edge, there was John L., snoring on the sofa. *What would he do if he woke up? What would I do?* The sound of my heart bumping filled my ears. We went past him fast, as if he were a dangerous dog. I hustled Jane through the living room to her bedroom and shut the door. I put a chair under the knob.

"Where is your underwear?" I asked, noticing the absence as we wiped her up. She was covered in gooseflesh and shaking so much that her teeth chattered.

"I don't know."

Her eyes widened, and a thousand ugly pictures flashed in my mind.

"Well, here, then," I said, acting as matter of fact as I could. I took a clean pair out of her dresser and helped her step in. When she was fresher, we sat side by side on her bed.

"Okay, tell me. Can you tell me, sweetheart?" We were always close. I cuddled her and stroked her hair. That had always helped her to settle when she was upset. "I'm so sorry I wasn't here, but I am now, and I will make sure you're safe."

There was a long silence. She could not look at me, but I kept massaging her shoulder and matching her breathing: inhale and exhale. Finally, she started talking to the floorboards.

"John L., well, he was more restless than ordinary this evening. He must have gone to Wing Key's," she said. Her voice was breaking again. She was referring to the Chinese restaurant where he gambled in a back room. "He kept looking in his wallet. I figured either he lost money in a game or it was stolen from him."

She continued. "He was getting up and pacing around the house. He had kicked his boots off and was drinking. I could hear the liquor settling back into his bottle after each swig. I went on in the kitchen and tried to ignore him. I laid my schoolbooks on the table and sat down to do my homework. He came stumbling in and stood right behind my chair. Put his arm over my shoulder and around my chest. I couldn't get out of the chair, and the next thing I knew, he was kissing my ear."

Jane began to tremble harder.

"When he did that, I screamed for him to stop it." She twisted her head to avert her gaze, like the scene was visible in front of her. "He was saying I don't know what all. I don't remember."

"Oh, honey." I was suddenly weak all over, and I panted open-mouthed like a wild animal. I pressed her head into my arms, then examined her some more. She had a few scrapes and bruises from being thrown on the ground and from her foray into the tree. She wasn't bleeding anywhere, thankfully.

"Where do you hurt?" I asked.

"I'm okay," she said. "I think I got away from him fast enough."

I thanked the Lord for John L.'s drunkenness at that moment.

"How did you get away from him, honey?"

"I slid down the chair and crawled away under the table and out the other side. He was so drunk, he relaxed his grip. I don't remember. I was running across the porch. I heard my feet and his feet pounding on the boards. He came after me, calling me a little bitch."

Her shoulders started to heave, and the tears poured.

"He came after me and caught me by my arms and pulled me into the front hedge and was dragging down my pants. And that's when I saw this bird. It was a red bird, sitting on top of the bushes, and it started to fly away, and I thought, 'No, don't leave,' and it was like it heard me and came back. Somehow, I don't know how, the bird showed me how to struggle away, then climb up, fly up, to get away from John L. It was like I sleepwalked and woke up in the tree, higher than I ever remember being."

The phrase rang in my head: *higher than I remember being.* A couple of years ago, Jane had a playmate who had cerebral palsy. A group of kids, including Jane herself, coaxed that child up into a tree. The little girl got up there and then panicked, wrapped herself around the trunk, and cried and called for her mama, so similar to what had just happened. She wet her pants too, but she didn't wait until she was out of the tree. The fire department had to come and pry her out of the branches. I punished Jane for that, for the way she'd treated another person. It mattered; it had always mattered to me, to be proud of your behavior.

My God, I thought now, *what about my own behavior? What*

have I done? To have mixed myself up with such a man and have Jane suffer the consequences? I felt something bitter at the back of my throat and recognized it as shame. We had been married only a few years, and I knew well why I had done it and why I had stayed.

"Has anything like this ever happened before?" I asked. "With John L.?" My own body had begun to wrack as if I was freezing cold.

"Well, not exactly," she said. "But there were some times he walked around . . . walked around naked. I tried not to see him, but then I thought—maybe he wanted me to!" She threw her face into the bed pillow and sobbed.

"Why didn't you tell me this?" I could barely pronounce the words. The muscles of my face seemed paralyzed.

"I don't know," she said. She sat up and put her face onto my shoulder. Her voice was muffled. "I thought you might be angry at me. And I didn't want to believe anything was wrong."

"Angry at you? Honey, no—never. Never think that."

I eased away from her and, removing the chair, pried the bedroom door open a crack. There was a man in the next room still lying inert on the sofa, but I didn't know who the hell he was.

"Stay right here," I said to Jane. I went past John L. without fear for myself. Some things I just had to find out, despite the dread. Something in my chest seemed to be hanging in shreds. I opened the front door and went outside to look in the hedges. Jane's underwear was there under the bushes, rolled in a figure eight.

I could have strangled John L. with my bare hands.

I had to go past him again to rejoin my daughter in her bedroom. It was all I could do to not spit on him. The gob rose in my mouth, and I gathered it with a terrible pleasure. But I swallowed it back.

Jane followed me with her eyes as I stuffed her underwear in my pocket.

"How do you feel, honey? Tell me if you can." I was staying contained, though I was nearly choking.

"I'm okay now. While I was up in the tree, John L. came and stood right where you did. He was swinging his arms through the air and hollering, 'Git down from there. You are going to get beat if you don't mind me.' He managed to climb up to the first notch before he got too dizzy. I thought he was going to kill me and himself both, but finally he got tired and went back in the house."

She added, "I never really looked at things from up that high. It was like I became the red bird, looking down. But finally, I saw you walking up to the house. You looked so small and thin, all shoulders and knees. And I saw the roof and the chimney below me too. I could feel the breeze swirling around me. My hands and feet were tingling." She talked as if retelling a dream.

I had brought the groceries in the bedroom with us and hadn't stopped to put them on the kitchen table. I picked up a bottle of cider vinegar out of one of the sacks and let out a laugh. I imagined what I could do to him. I hefted the bottle up and down by its neck, tempted to go right then and smash it into his head, but I set it down.

I saw John L. starting to stir.

"Just stay in here," I warned, with an outstretched arm.

John L. looked up at me from his prone position on the sofa, as if he had no memory of what he had done.

He might not have.

"What's for supper?"

I went to him and grabbed his hair with one hand, then

pounded his chest as hard as I could with the other fist. His dark bangs, which at one time I loved to sweep back with my hand, seemed greasy and disgusting. I wanted to rip them from his head. His skin, so pretty it was like a choir boy's, had attracted me when we met. Now it was red and mottled, and I grimaced from his stinking breath. I was filled with loathing for him and for myself.

"How dare you! How dare you!" I kept hitting him and hitting him with my fist, my knuckles chafing against the rough tweed of his jacket. I opened my palm and slapped him five or six times. It satisfied me to see the welts, the outlines of my fingers. My lip curled.

"You are pathetic—a worthless excuse for a man!"

He cowered, too drunk to sit up, and fended me off weakly.

"Stop, stop! I'm just lying here!" He rolled back and forth. "Aah! Son of a bitch!" He slurred and rubbed his jaw.

"Yes, you are! Just lying there, a lying son of a bitch, and you've been one as long as I have known you!"

Shaking, I bared my fingernails. It was a primitive instinct I didn't even know I had, and I pressed them to the sides of his face. I wanted with all my heart to scratch him, but I halted before I could score his cheeks and draw lines of blood. I was proud of my restraint. But as I stood up, I felt unsatisfied that I had not released all the rage and scorn I felt onto his body. John L. didn't move.

It took me no time at all to decide. As quick as ever my passion for him had appeared three years ago, that's how fast it went away. Just this one moment and it was gone, like water that had drained, with nothing left except a black rim, a residue of dirt.

Dirt. I had worked in a laundry, and John L. had saved me from that. But at what price? I knew, or knew of, women who stayed with abusive men, men who did bad things to them and to their children. I used to judge them for that, compliment myself for not having that kind of situation. But my life with John L. had progressed in a direction I had not foreseen. I could dissect it all later. Maybe I knew more than I admitted. But now I saw I had become a person I didn't want to be, like one of those women I worked with who'd say, "He treats me good. He never laid a hand on me but the once, and I deserved it that time." As if not being beaten was all it took to call a marriage good. I had not cared enough for myself, and now it had affected Jane as well.

Well, I thought. *No more*.

A person doesn't know how strong they are until being strong is the only choice they have. I was about to find out what I was made of.

I pictured my old suitcase sitting on a high shelf in the bedroom closet for the past few years.

I went to get it, gather Jane, and go.

Two

My Mama

1911

I saw my arm swinging a bucket of food, the undamaged springy smoothness of my child skin. I was nine years old, walking up the hill to my mama, to where she was plowing. It was maybe my last innocent moment.

"I'll take your brothers' lunch out to the barn, you take your mother's to the field, then we can get back to making mud pies," my friend Queenie had said. Her real name was Elizabeth. Everyone thought she was adorable, a cute little blonde. But she was powerful in her personality. We all called her Queenie because she was the kind to take royal charge, even at someone else's house. I was her opposite—shy and dark-headed, rawboned, and tall for my age.

We had been preparing for our tea party, which centered around some corncob dolls wrapped in scraps of fabric for clothes, with corn silk tucked in for hair. They did not even have faces. Mine was named Delydia and hers was called Rosa June. We had ten other little corncob stubs wrapped in bits of cloth, and they were the babies. The tea table was a large flat stone that was a fixture in our yard, and we were using old pieces of broken crockery for plates and big acorn caps for cups. We had some wooden spoons and a couple of my mama's pie pans as well. We lined everybody up at the table.

"Look," said Queenie. "It's twelve of them. All sitting there in a row. Like the Last Supper, sort of."

"Let's make 'em say a prayer before they eat, then. But mine are all girls; they can't be disciples."

In the dirt nearby, an old baseball without its cover was waiting, as well as a bat my brother Avery had carved. When we were through with the doll picnic, we would have batting practice.

Suddenly, Daddy called to us from the doorway, "Girls, get in here, now!" He was so tall, his head nearly brushed the top of the frame. He raked his hand through his thick head of hair. "I need some help with this food," he said. "You got to take some lunch to your mama and the boys."

My brothers, Walker and Avery, were in the barn with a cow who was birthing her calf.

"Just a minute, Daddy," I started.

"Right now! No backtalking me!" He lobbed a chaw of tobacco out of his mouth and over the side of the porch rail, then turned on his heel. He slammed the screen door as he retreated inside.

Queenie and I looked at each other.

"Okay," she said. "The sooner we get it done, the sooner we can play. Let's go."

Soon the kitchen table was covered with ham biscuits, boiled eggs, pickles, fried apple pies, and jars of iced tea. We found an excellent opportunity to practice our double-talk while we worked.

"All-fapple pile-fies," Queenie said.

"Bo-foiled el-feggs," I replied.

My friend propped a curl behind her ear, took a berry basket off a shelf, and began to set the eggs in with gentle fingers. "Here," she said, handing the tin lunch bucket to me. "Go, and come back fast, okay?"

I started walking to where my mama was. I felt the weather breathing on me. It was a cool day: overcast, but warming toward the breakout of new green. Late March in East Tennessee. Air sharp, but with the promise of release. I took big steps through the clods, and the wind carried the weighted scent of wet dirt.

In the distance, my mama rough-handled the plow, her knees spraddled for balance, her sleeves rolled up. The strap of the reins was around her hips, and she was trying to get our mule, Maisie, to haw and turn around at the end of a row.

"Come on, Maisie!" Mama pleaded. I watched her beat on the mule's rump with a little switch. Maisie just stood there, stoic.

Then, across the distance, I heard Mama start sobbing. This was not like her at all. Again, she struck Maisie, who just turned her head over her shoulder, then flicked her ears as if asking, *Do I deserve this?*

Oh, the look of my mama—stained pinafore apron, boots clay caked to the ankle, falling strands of hair. Tears streaming down her cheeks. I wondered, was she just over-tired, or was it something else? She hated to plow, not because she wasn't strong enough to do it—she was—but because it was back and forth all day long, tedious work, and lonely. My daddy, on the other hand, said he liked it, that it could even be sort of restful for a poor son of a bitch like himself, who had a family harping on him most of the time.

I waved the tin bucket I was carrying. I could see her, a silhouette at the top of the rise.

"Hey, Mama! You can stop awhile now. I've got your lunch!" I thought of Queenie waiting for me back at the front porch. Remembered how the men of my family were assisting the cow.

Mama had a stick in her fist and some skewed, frantic look in her eye. She was half Cherokee but tall like her Irish father. She had freckles, but her skin was dark, and she wore her hair in one long braid down her back. Her face was broad and high across the cheekbones, and her full mouth showed nice, white teeth.

She was breathing hard, and it frightened me. She stared beyond me like there was something horrible coming up behind.

"You're scaring me! What's wrong?" I said, but I went toward her anyway.

"You, Isabel! You stop now! I don't want you out here," Mama said. She wiped her eyes, then walked around and unhitched Maisie. She left the bridle on and clicked against her teeth, *tht-tht*, to get the mule to step free from the plow. "Go on back now, honey. I hope never to see you out here. This work will kill you."

What is this? I waited as the day went strange. I felt my tea party with its acorn cups and twelve dolls fall away, like a cardboard picture. The world was leaning, some dark tear in the order of the universe making things topple into some new shape.

Mama pulled her dress up above her knees. She grabbed Maisie's stubby mane, then flung her right leg up over the mule's back. I turned around, hoping somebody would come up from the house and explain. But it was just me.

"I warmed up the biscuit and the apple pie for you," I offered, still assuming some part of this was normal.

Mama shook her head. "I got to go, honey. You eat it." She kicked Maisie in the sides. The mule stepped forward toward the line of trees down at the western edge of the field.

"Where are you going? What's the matter? Do you want me to get Daddy?" Mama wasn't headed toward the barn, and the road to our little community, Wheat, ran the other way. The only thing to the west was the train tracks.

Mama turned her ear and listened through the wind for the Clinchfield engine huffing up the grade—but she stopped to say one more thing. She did not answer my questions, not exactly.

"I am going crazy here," she said, as if musing to herself. "All this plowing, plowing, and nothing to do except think and think. I have thought my way to this moment. I have tried to stay, but *he* makes it intolerable. I am plain going crazy here," she repeated, twisting the mule's mane in her hand.

I realized *he* had to be Daddy. She wasn't really talking to me, but then her mouth began to tremble.

"I love you," she said. "Don't never forget that. The boys will be all right; they love the farm. Don't do what you don't love, Isabel. Never do." She turned Maisie toward me, then checked her, hard. "I want to stay for you, honey, I do. But I'm worthless like this. You're better off without me."

With a yank to the reins, she wheeled Maisie, who bolted and broke into a lope, not stubborn at all now.

I ran after her, calling, "What do you mean? Stop! Wait . . . Mama!"

I stumbled in the furrows. The moist smell of the new-turned ground was so strong, you could almost get hold of it, like something you wanted to pick up and eat.

"Don't follow me!" she ordered, screaming straight ahead into the trees. She kicked her heels into Maisie's ribs and didn't look back.

"Take me too!"

". . . *too.*" There was a little echo from my wail. Suddenly, my head buzzed, and the mountain field with the empty equipment stuck in a mound of earth looked off kilter and unfamiliar. I needed something to steady myself, but there was only blowing wind to lean on.

I dropped the lunch bucket and fled back to the house. I did not know how I was able to move. I had seen a chicken get her head chopped off and keep on her feet, unable to comprehend or admit the thing has happened.

Queenie was waiting for me in the yard. She had collected flat pieces of bark for doll saucers and pieces of mica, quartz, and pebbles to decorate the mud pies. She was pumping some water in a pail.

"Calf came," she said. "It's a heifer. I'm taking this to the barn."

"My mama unhitched Maisie and rode away on her," I reported, panting and dizzy. "She said she was leaving, went toward the Clinchfield grade. Where's my daddy?"

Queenie stopped pumping and ran to me with her wet hand out. "He's in the kitchen, drinking coffee." She started leading me toward the door. "He was just getting ready to go out to the field and take over from your mama. What are you saying?"

I staggered like a blind person with Queenie. I felt weak, held tight to her hand. "I'm right here," she said.

Daddy was sitting at the kitchen table with a cup in his

hand. I could tell he was worn out from the calving. He had rinsed his hair and face but had not changed his clothes, and he smelled like manure and well water.

"Mama did about twenty rows," I told him. My voice was not sounding right to me. I swayed, and Queenie squeezed my shoulder.

"That's good progress," he said. "I think I can get at least that many this afternoon before dark sets in, if I don't fall asleep first." He filled his mouth with some lukewarm black coffee and held it in his cheeks a moment before swallowing.

"Daddy," I said. My voice faltered. "Mama rode off on Maisie going into the trees. She said she had to or she would go crazy."

Daddy looked at me down his long nose and drew his eyes narrow. Slowly, he stood. His chair clattered back but did not fall over.

"What do you mean, 'rode off'?"

"She went down into the trees, toward the railroad tracks, and said not to come after her."

Daddy pursed his mouth and looked angry. He was not the kind of man to ask too much *why*. He looked to the future and did what was needed: seeded a field, nailed back loose boards, threw water on a fire, fixed whatever got broke.

When Daddy stood up from the table, he took up the room. He grabbed hold of the back rung of his chair, and I saw his knuckles whiten.

"You and Queenie," he said, each word hard and separate, "go on to Queenie's house and stay there until I come for you. It may be tomorrow. I'm going after your mama to see what is this nonsense. But first, I got to go tell the boys."

"Not go to Molly's house? Tell her?" I wanted to know.

My sister Molly, who had been married just a couple of months, was only sixteen. I thought we might want to keep this in the family, though others would know soon enough.

"Less not bother Molly," Daddy said. "Not yet."

We followed Daddy out of the house. At the barn, in the half-light of a stall, Walker and Avery were tending the weary cow and her new baby.

Avery knelt, petting the cow's nose and whispering something soothing only she could hear. Walker stood against the window, watching them, the bucket with the afterbirth at his feet. I smelled the dusted starch of hay, the slick copper of blood.

Walker and Avery were just ten months apart in age, more fraternal twins than brothers. Avery, the older, had been premature, barely four pounds at birth. He was still small and looked eleven instead of fourteen. At two, he'd still been holding on to pant legs. Walker, on the other hand, had been strapping: a nine-pounder "that like to killed me," Mama always recounted, smiling. He was confident on his feet at one year, so he was called Walker (his real name was Franklin). Now, at thirteen, he was nearly a man, and certainly the leader. Daddy saddled his horse.

"Life can't never be simple," he said. "Boys, your mama's took a notion, and I have to see can I catch her before it gets dark."

Avery wasn't much for talk. He just knotted his forehead and watched the new baby nurse on its mother. The calf had a sweet white face and long lashes, but with my mama running off, I could take no joy in it.

"Daddy," said Walker. He tucked in his shirt and moved forward. "Are you sure? I'll go with you."

Daddy shook his head.

"Girls, now!" Daddy repeated. "Go on!" He looked at

Queenie. "See can you explain this mess to your mother and tell her I'm sorry to have to ask her to keep Isabel."

"Come on, then," said Queenie. "Forget mud pies." She looked a little sad, but she rallied and put her arm around me. "Isabel, I have a new storybook at home. Mama can help us read it." Queenie's mother, Nancy, and their family had the most books out of anybody we knew.

Queenie tugged me toward the footbridge, and we began to cross single file.

"The lunch tin is still thrown down in the field," I said. "And the plow's lying out there sideways. If it rains, it might rust." Suddenly, I was focused on those small details, maybe because they were things I could set to right quickly when everything else had gone to hell in a handbasket.

I held on to the ropes of the footbridge and stared over the edge into the clear brown water of the Clinch. I shivered. The sun, which had felt so good just an hour before, had gone in, and the cold pressed into the top of my head like the sky had an awful hand.

"What do you think happened?" Queenie wanted to know. She stopped in the middle of the bridge and turned around. She was serious. The footboards swung slightly. "Do you think it's another man?"

We knew about lovers. People think children don't have sense to figure things out, that we don't have ears to hear adults gossip, or eyes to see. But Queenie and I had once seen a neighbor woman, a married woman, kissing a peddler in the woods. They were down on their knees face to face in the leaves, eyes closed, hands moving everywhere. We could have been bears and they wouldn't have noticed. It made us afraid that we knew, and afraid for a month after that if the woman saw us at church, she might read our faces and put two and two together.

I had never seen my mama flirting or smiling like a girl at anyone, and no man's grin flashed into my mind, nobody from church or town.

"No-o!"

"Did they fight, then? Did he hit her?"

"Everybody fights sometimes, don't they?" I said, then paused. "Yelling, but not hitting," I confessed. Such questions! I didn't want to get mad at Queenie. I knew I would forgive Mama for any reason she had for leaving, as long as she came back.

We trooped up to Queenie's porch and found her mother in the kitchen, peeling pears. I hung back while Queenie explained, breathless.

"Mrs. King's run off on the mule and left the plow in the field and Mr. King's gone after her, so Isabel's got to stay here."

Nancy kept her eyes on the long spiral of pear skin coming off her knife. Her face did not change, except I saw her chin move a little and jut forward, hardening. When the curl, green on one side, white on the other, fell to the table, she cut some slices off the fruit and handed them to me. It was not the season for fresh pears, but if anyone could work a miracle and manage to have them, it was Nancy. To please her, I put a bite on my tongue. For a moment, it was sweet, but then it felt like a rock in my mouth and I could not swallow it. Nancy looked up then, and her eyes were soft.

"Why, honey, you know you can stay here as long as you want. You are like one of my own. And because you are like one of my own, you can help Queenie bring in the sheets and fold them before you all set the table for dinner."

All afternoon, Nancy kept us busy. If there came a minute our hands were not moving, she found another chore. As long as my hands moved, my stomach did not twist and my brain kept me from framing any questions that might repeat and repeat, begging for an answer.

The next day, Daddy came to see me at Queenie's and tell Nancy what was going on. Nancy went out on the porch to meet him. She stood wiping her hands on a flour-sack towel, worrying the cloth.

"No luck at all." Daddy spoke to Nancy and barely glanced at me. It was like he wished I wasn't there. "Maisie came back to the field, but there's no sign of Martha. I reckon she got on the train. Soon as I can, I'll go into Knoxville and see did anybody see her. She would have been a sight, filthy as she was in her plowing clothes," he added.

Daddy looked at me, finally, like maybe I knew something I should be telling. I dropped my eyes. Was he trying to hold me accountable somehow? I felt responsible for something I had not done.

I thought my Daddy was kindly handsome—very tall and lanky, with his head of light-brown hair just getting some gray, and a bristly mustache. But he had edges, never was what you'd call a sentimental or an affectionate person.

I thought about what Queenie had asked. My mama hadn't run off to another man. I was sure of that. But she might have done it to just not feel so . . . managed. Mama was quiet—quiet most of the time—and I'd thought that was her natural way. But maybe it wasn't. Sometimes, she would laugh and dance around the front room when Daddy wasn't there. If she did it in front of him, he would tell her to quit that nonsense. He just believed in work. I couldn't explain it to anyone, but somehow, I felt how it was for her. Daddy could make you guilty over acting happy. If you press gladness down in you, it sours awful bad.

"Oh, Will, I'm so sorry," Nancy said. "Well, you just

go on and do whatever you need to do, and Isabel can stay with us. Do the boys need anything?"

"No, they'll be fine. I won't be gone but a day."

Daddy regarded me, his face full of low expectations. "You behave now and help out."

"Please find her, Daddy," I said. Queenie came and stood beside me and put her arm around my waist.

Daddy didn't answer me. He looked out toward the creek. He shifted his weight from one hip to the other and touched his ring finger to the corner of his eye.

"She was always high strung," he said to nobody in particular.

"Don't you worry now. Isabel will be fine with us, and I will get that husband of mine to go over and check on the boys," Nancy said.

"Get Tate to look at my cow, will you?" Daddy said. "She was a little tore up. That calf was a big 'un. And thank you." He turned and walked out without another glance at me.

I stayed up at Queenie's house for three days. Finally, Daddy sent Avery after me, and he stood by the well until Nancy, kneading bread by the kitchen window, noticed him. She went to the door.

"Avery, come on up, for heaven's sakes."

"That's all right. I don't need to come in. My daddy says to thank you. You can send her home now." He beckoned me, then turned and headed down toward the bridge.

"Isabel," said Nancy. "Come here. Take this with you so you can finish reading it." She pressed a new copy of *Grimm's Fairy Tales* into my hand. It was a big, special book, with embossed gilded designs on the cover and gold-edged pages. Queenie and I had been lying on her bed reading one story after another to each other. That was another way we'd found to keep me from crying, to keep my stomach from twisting.

"It might get dirty," I said.

"You won't let it," Nancy said. "Take this too." She gave me a flour sack with a jar of beef stew in it.

"Did they get her?" I asked Avery.

"No, honey, they didn't." There were lavender circles under his eyes. I took his hand and felt—really paid attention to—the feel of his skin for the first time. It was hard as leather and laced with scratches and scars. It seemed important for us to touch.

We walked home. I ran in the house, threw myself on my bed, and opened *Grimm's*. What an odd balance, the joy of that book laid side by side with my anxiousness over Mama's leaving. Fairy tales are full of sadness and loss, but all of it turns out to have a purpose—and that brought me a sort of comfort. Snow White's mother was dead; she and I were in the woods together. And there were little helpers who would support you.

Some of the words were hard, like *vagabond* and *dazzle*. Queenie had gotten the dictionary when we read the stories at her house. Sometimes, we had to ask Nancy, who had been a teacher, to frame some other sentences so it all became clear.

There was not a dictionary at my house. But many things I could sound out, then figure the meanings from the story around the mystery word. There were many black-and-white drawings, and I lay there daydreaming about Little Red Cap or the Frog King.

I got lost in the pages. Or tried to. Meanwhile, Daddy told the sheriff to keep an eye out for my mama, and her description was sent around. We did not discuss her leaving.

Daddy just wanted to see his wife's work get done. *Who could possibly do it?*

Nancy showed me how to make cat-head biscuits and cornbread, and I knelt up on a chair and did it, sometimes with tears salting the dough. Everywhere I turned, I hoped my mama would be waiting. At the foot of the bed to say good night. In her rocker, where she sat and sewed in the evening. Every day, I hoped she would walk in the door and life would reel back and erase the nightmare of her absence. In the morning, when I went to gather eggs, there were crows stalking the yard. When I listened to them, they said, *Why? Why?*

Daddy stayed silent until Mama was located. Four months after her disappearance, she was found living down in Tellico Plains with some Cherokee people. Mama's uncle John was full-blooded Indian.

"What kind of a woman leaves her husband and her children and all her responsibilities?" Daddy asked the thin air. I was serving him coffee at the time. "I want nothing more to do with her."

The next Sunday, Nancy spoke to us on the side after church.

"It's a shame, a shame this happened, but truth be known, I have heard of similar incidents. These women are not—Martha was not—crazy. It is just The Change. If only men could understand that and forgive."

Daddy turned red and looked away.

"There is nothing I can think of nor nothing you can say that will justify this running away," he said.

Nancy looked at me. "It doesn't mean she doesn't love you, Isabel."

"I know," I said, my voice small. "That's what she told me." I believed she did love me, though how could she need to get away from Daddy, or the work, more than she needed to be with me? The pain cut me under my ribs, and I thought of Nancy's spiraling twist of pear skin, something coming loose. What was wrong with me that I didn't have enough to hold her?

I envied Queenie and Nancy quite a bit.

I understood that because my mama was Cherokee, well—people did not have a high valuation of her behavior, even before. I appreciated that Nancy and Queenie did not suggest that being Indian had anything to do with it.

Several days passed, and I learned from Walker that Daddy did try to get her to come home. I had collected three eggs in my apron, and he met me coming up the back steps.

"I thought Daddy went to Knoxville for supplies, but he had gone to Tellico Plains and confronted Uncle John, argued with him till he told where Mama was hid. Then he went to the house where she was, but she wouldn't go with Daddy," my brother said.

"Then," Walker said, "it was like Daddy decided he had made a mistake to marry Mama." He pulled a coin out of his trousers and flipped it head to tail, tail to head as he spoke. "Daddy consulted with the sheriff, then with a doctor. He consulted with the pastor too. The end of it was, the authorities went to get her and they collected her by force."

I tried to digest the words *by force*. A corner of my apron slipped, and one egg fell on the planks and broke.

"And?" I whispered.

"Well," Walker went on, "she told them if she had to go back, it would be against her will. She screamed and fought. Daddy said the sheriff threw her over his shoulder and carried her out of the Cherokee house while she beat his back with her fists."

I struggled to breathe.

"Walker, where is she? What did they do with her?"

He reached out and gripped my hand before he told me.

"Honey, they took her to the mental institution—the mental institution in Knoxville."

Three

My Daddy

1913

*A*nd so that's how it was. Two years went by. And then one morning, Nancy came to our front door looking formal, her apron off and her hair in a fresh twist.

"I want Isabel to hear it," she said to Daddy. She took a folded piece of paper out of her pocket; it was the cheapest kind of rough stationery, with writing done in pencil.

"I'll just tell you right now," Nancy said. "This will probably open some old wounds. Martha's been in that insane asylum for a while now. And this is the first letter I've gotten from her. Have you gotten any?"

"I haven't heard a thing," Daddy said. "The woman is so crazy, she probably can't string two good words together."

Queenie and I looked up from our math homework as Daddy's nasty attitude drifted through the room like smoke. Queenie tutored me whenever Daddy would allow. I had laid aside his shirts that needed mending. She had brought an arithmetic book and was trying to explain to me about long division.

"Try this next one now," she said. I had printed 1,365 divided by 7, but suddenly, all I could think about was the paper in Nancy's hand.

Every now and then, I'd been having this dream where I'd have this gun and I'd shoot Maisie so her legs buckled and she fell. My mama couldn't ride away from me then. I loved Maisie, so I'd wake up in tears.

"Just remember your times tables. You memorized them." Queenie again tried to capture my attention, steal it away from what my daddy had said. She took a moment to hand me an eraser, just in case, then pushed the paper over to me.

"Bring down the six?" I asked, but my mind had split and couldn't focus. I cooked and sewed, could read a yard-stick's fractions and measure quarter, half, and thirds of a cup. I could count up money and even knew about percentages. What else was necessary? Daily useful math. I was trying not to keep thinking about what had happened in my life.

My mama and her reasons for leaving. Explanations, just as locked up as the mysteries of geometry and algebra. Any equation with a letter in it was a mystery I probably didn't care to solve. I looked up from the problem and waited to see what this letter—my mama's letter—said.

Daddy set his mouth in a line, which meant he didn't like Nancy sharing whatever it was out loud. But she was not afraid of him. She cleared her throat and read:

Dear Nancy,

I am writing you after all this trouble to ask if you can get William to let the children come to visit me. I have

*missed them something terrible, especially Isabel. Some say
any woman that did what I did does not deserve to have her
children, and William might agree, which is why he swore
out a writ of lunacy against me and has not brought them
to see me. But there is a doctor here who has been very good,
and I have come to understand that nervous prostration
caused me to do as I did.*

Nancy paused but did not look up. "Nervous prostration," she repeated like an underline. She continued.

*I am mostly over it, but perhaps it is better that
William and I stay apart. I am so much better now, and
my uncle John is working with a lawyer to get me released
to his custody. After all, I never hurt no one, and I was
always a good mother. I would appreciate your testimony in
this when the time comes, but meanwhile, if you could have
a word with my husband, perhaps it would soften his heart
to let them come to me.*

Nancy let out a big, shaky breath and read the last lines.

*Thank you for all you have done for Walker and
Avery and Isabel.*

I remain yours sincerely,

Martha King

*PS I am enclosing a letter for my older daughter, Molly. If
you could get this to her, I would be most grateful.*

I sat there with my hand hovering over my tablet, trying to get the 7 to go into the 66, but my mind was a blank
from the letter. To hear Nancy read Mama's words brought
so much confusion that my first response was to push it
away. After two years, I did not know if I wanted to see her.
She knew how Daddy was, how his temperament was so

severe; she must have known how I would have to suffer it once she was gone. Not to mention how the burdens of the household would fall my way, and me—still a child. Maybe my mama *was* half-crazy. *You have to forgive somebody if they are,* I kept telling myself.

Daddy sighed. "That is all well and good, Nancy. But I can*not* take time out from the field work to go traipsing off to Knoxville to the lunatic asylum. I don't think anyone is forgetting that she is the one who left these children, and now she wants to see them? And I do not know that it will be good for this girl to see such sights as may be there in that place."

I knew he wanted to keep me away from Mama, but he did not want to admit that to Nancy. He was going to act like a protective father and argue against it as best he could.

"William, all the things that have happened between you and Martha are beyond any conversation we ought to have," Nancy said. "But Isabel now—I will take her myself to Knoxville. If she is with me, she won't be in any danger. Pardon me for saying so, but I feel the girl has a right to see her own mother."

Nancy came and stood behind Queenie and wrapped her arms about her. A picture is worth a thousand words, and Nancy was clearly showing Daddy what my loss of a mother looked like. And she was also telling Daddy that she knew my mama's leaving came from somewhere, and he was in there somewhere.

There was a moment of stillness where I could hear the universe buzzing in my ears. Nancy was looking at me to see what I wanted to do.

"Walker and Avery can drive us in the wagon; they may want to go as well. If we start at daybreak, we can be there and back by nightfall." Nancy rocked up on her toes, trying to say the right thing, but Daddy kept a blank expression while he thought.

At long last, he turned to me, his eyes doubting but searching my face, seeing if he liked me well enough to do something nice.

"I want to go, Daddy," I said, looking down. I could hardly bear to see Queenie hanging on her mother's arms.

"And if you have any town errands, we can surely take care of them while we are at it," Nancy added, offering a practical purpose to help seal the plan.

Did I say I wanted to go just to get a trip away from the farm, from the work? Or was it to have a chance to spend a day with Nancy, who had been like a mother these past two years? Or was it to actually see my mama? Maybe it was all those reasons. Regardless, I stood up and went to Daddy, took him by his old hand—tough as a piece of shoe leather—and laid my cheek against his sleeve. He smelled of tobacco, sweat, and the mule.

Daddy sucked his cheeks and looked away out the window. He could not take affection, any kind of outward display, no matter how subtle.

"All right," he said. Queenie raised her eyebrows at me and softly clapped her hands. Daddy shook me loose.

Four

The Man at the Asylum

1913

*R*yan's Point Insane Asylum in Knoxville. It started out owned by an Irishman named Cornelius Ryan," Nancy said.

Ever the teacher, she filled our travel time with details about the flora and fauna we were passing. She knew the history too.

"Look," she said. "There's the Tennessee River. It runs by the institution, so we're getting close! It elevates the minds of the inmates and soothes their souls.

"The asylum is a very fine building. Before it was a hospital, it was a rich man's estate, and prior to that, the land was Cherokee hunting ground," Nancy went on. I sat in the middle of the wagon seat between her and Walker. Avery did not come. He preferred livestock to people, even his mama, and had stayed to help Daddy.

I enjoyed the view on our ride. The pine and poplar forests rolled away toward the Cumberland Mountains on the north and the French Broad River and the gray-blue steeps of North Carolina rose in the east. But there was no comfort in knowing that my mama had been sent back to a place that her ancestors had roamed and hunted. Such a free spot before, when it was just Indian people.

"Mr. Ryan ran a successful granite business but closed it up once the war started," Nancy continued her lesson. "During the fighting, the Yankees got hold of the place and used it as one of their headquarters. Then, after the surrender, the property became so corrupt and run down that the Ryans didn't want it anymore."

"I guess the family decided that once the Union Army had vacated the place, it was no longer fit for any sane Southerner," Walker said.

"Indeed! They sold off the property to the state of Tennessee to make a loony bin." Nancy laughed.

I pursed my mouth and she hushed.

"I'm sorry, honey. I'm sorry I said 'loony bin.' But I can joke about it because I do not think your mother is crazy."

"Tell what you think happened to her, then, Nancy. The Change cannot do it; else lots of other women would be there."

I had never asked her about it directly before. I cast my gaze out into the yellow field we were passing, an open pasture with a black horse and a white horse. A light breeze ruffled their manes, and I could hear their teeth tearing at the juicy grass. Walker kept his eyes straight ahead and flapped the reins a little to speed our own horse. I knew he followed Daddy in this regard; he would be deaf to any conversation about The Change.

"I think..." Nancy stretched her neck back and

sighed. "I think your mother has a particular kind of spirit that can't be boxed in. Not only that, but she needs happy people around her."

I was glad Nancy was being honest with me. "Yes, and I understand that being with Daddy can be like being with nobody. Well, not nobody, but somebody with a hard shell you can't get through. And all he does seem to want is for work to get done. He never talks about nothing else."

"That's right," Nancy said. "He and Martha were not—well, they are not—compatible in their dispositions, that's for sure." She tightened her chin, as if there was more to say, but she wasn't going to say it.

We made our way through the stone portals of the institution. The asylum sat on a beautiful piece of ground, up on a knoll, with stone entrances and a park of big oaks where the ill could sit and compose their thoughts or be escorted by their nurses. Granite knobs, bald and blank faced, topped the entrance posts. We rode through a grassy park up to the main building, with its wide porch and tall columns. I expected the place to be upsetting and dirty, like an orphanage in Charles Dickens, but it was peaceful, with only the sound of crickets chirping in the morning grass. In the distance, I could hear two other noises: the regular ring of a blacksmith's hammer on an anvil and the rush of a small waterfall. We stopped at the front, and Nancy climbed down from the wagon.

"Wait here while I find out where she is."

She hurried up the steps to the administration office. Walker tethered the horse to a rail and strolled out on the gravel to roll a cigarette. He was just fifteen. I knew he had been smoking for a year or so, but this was the first time he had been so open about it in front of me.

I watched him. I was nervous myself and wished I, too, had a habit that would calm me down. He took quick puffs and small talked, looking out over the green expanse.

"Wonder who keeps all this lawn cut. This is a lot of grass to tend." Walker rubbed the back of his neck as if he himself might be facing the task.

I started looking around, wondering if I might glimpse my mama. People were walking on the paths. They didn't look particularly crazy to me. It just struck me that they were unusually pale, and some of them were wearing dressing gowns or robes.

"Wish I had me a mirror," I muttered. I forgot to bring a comb, so I licked my fingers and drew them through my windblown hair, then picked at the corners of my eyes. Why did I care what Mama thought about how I looked? I didn't know why, but I did.

I stepped down to the ground. On the porch of the building was a line of white wicker rocking chairs. Most of the patients in those rockers were old women. They did not speak, and only one or two looked my way. One lady lifted her arm up above her head and kept picking at something in the air with her skinny claw fingers.

There was a girl among them, though, maybe eighteen, looking out of place, sitting forward in her rocker with her hands clasped tight in the folds of her skirt. She was pretty, with dark hair pulled back in a loose bun at the nape of her neck. Her head ticked just a little, like she was attached to a wire, and her eyes glittered, moving side to side. She darted her look in my direction, so I said, "Hello, it's a pretty day, isn't it? Are you having a nice day?" And she wound her mouth down and slowly shook her head, saying, "No." She kept doing it as I backed away.

Just then, Nancy came down the steps, holding her

skirts to keep from tripping. "Your mama's in the laundry," she said. "That's where she works." She pointed across the grounds to a four-story brick structure. "In there, then to the basement, and the grounds out back."

"Just a minute. I have to get that fruit I brought." Walker went round to the back of the wagon, lifted up a quilt, and took out a bushel basket of peaches. He and Avery had picked them off our own trees. Walker set the basket on his hip and began giving them out to patients who had suddenly tightened their promenade and materialized in a circle round him, each with a hand outstretched.

One man started jumping up and down, reaching for the basket. "My! Mine!" he insisted, pushing a lady aside.

"Hold on there, fella," Walker said, pulling back. "There's plenty to go around." He shook his head and looked to me, the crease deepening between his brows.

"What strangeness here, Isabel," he said. My mouth gaped open as I watched the scene.

"Mize well give them one too." Walker nodded up at the rockers. He took the basket up to the porch and gave one each to the elderly women, as well as to the girl who was there among them. She rolled it between her hands, caressing the fuzzy skin, and stared at Walker with her large brown eyes.

"Take a bite of it, honey. It's fresher than anything," Walker said. But she continued to hold it, so Walker set down the basket. He opened his pocketknife, took the girl's peach, and cut a section out of it. He peeled it, then offered her the piece. She opened her mouth and waited, so Walker fed it to her with a quick dart of two fingers, like she might bite. Her hands came up around his wrist and held his cuff, and she chewed the peach. Then her eyes welled with tears.

"My Lord," Walker said. "What kind of a place makes

people cry to eat peaches?" He pulled away from her as gently as he could.

The building we had been sent to was dreary after being in the sunny grounds, and there were blue flies buzzing loudly in the dim light. Down the hall, someone shouted over and over and over, "Come on and help me! Now, no, don't! Come on and help me! No, don't!"

It was so unsettling that I grabbed Nancy's hand.

I smelled bedpans. Looking in the doorways to the left and right, I noticed rows of white-painted iron beds, maybe five or six to a room. In one doorway, an old man with a scruffy beard and red eyes sat in a straight-back chair. As we passed, he stuttered and croaked, then scratched at the crotch of his union suit—that was all he wore. Walker stopped and gave him a peach.

In the next room, a bare-chested Negro in overalls sat on the side of a bed, picking out a tune on a banjo. He seemed very healthy and handsome. He was out of place here, like a flower on a winter tree. He had beautiful arms and long, agile fingers with nails like mother-of-pearl. His song was so jangly and sprite that I could not help but bob my shoulders. Nancy and Walker began to do the same. The Negro broke off.

"Howdy, folks," he said. "Nothing like a little music to lift the mood."

"Nice tune," Nancy said.

"'Preciate it." The banjo player gave us a full smile and saluted. "You visiting somebody, I guess?"

"My mama, name of Martha," I said.

He went quiet. "I see," he said. "I reckon she will enjoy that. I really do reckon she will."

"These are her children," Nancy said. "They have missed her." Walker and I nodded like a couple of puppets.

"Well, have a nice day," Nancy added and swept us ahead of her.

"Wonder what he's doing here," Walker murmured. "He can't possibly be an inmate, and it's hard to believe a janitor would be sitting around playing an instrument."

"A place like this has questions aplenty." Nancy moved ahead down the hall. "Like Pandora's box, you might say."

We descended a wide staircase. I trailed my hand along the banister, which was made of polished wood and smooth as glass to the touch. So many hands must have run along it. At the bottom was the laundry. It was a relief to smell soap and water instead of . . . what? How could I describe the odors of body and breath and despair that weighted the air of these hallways?

A woman with a stack of towels came out of a doorway and stood, staring at us as if mesmerized.

"Do you know where Martha King is?" asked Nancy. The woman had a long scar on her cheek. "Mar-tha," Nancy said again, like the people here were deaf and slow as well as mentally ill. The woman pointed through a door to a yard strung with clotheslines, where a woman was hanging sheets.

"How crazy can you be if you have the wits to do laundry?" Walker whispered to me.

"Martha," Nancy called to the woman at the clothes-line.

Mama turned around. The wind billowed the sheets and pushed her a little in our direction. She had three clothespins in her mouth and several more in her fist.

A feeling came over me like I was four years old again, and I nearly screamed to see her. I wanted to run and bury my head in her apron. At the same instant, she had hurt me, and I realized I was going to punish her by standing still. I

wanted to study her a little more, anyway. Mama's braid had
been cut off, and her black hair hung just below her ears. It
made her look disguised, as if she were wearing a wig.
Walker was beside me; he had stayed rooted too.

"She never would have agreed to have that braid cut.
It was done to her. And she's much thinner than I remember," he whispered.

For a moment, I saw her as a person, not just my
mama. I could feel my heart soften. Things had happened
to this woman. She put her fingers up to her face, and all
the clothespins fell around her on the ground.

I went to her and put my arms around her waist. She
cradled my head, and I could feel the moisture of her tears
in my hair.

"Look at you, look at you," she said, and then we didn't
say anything, we just hugged and looked and hugged again.
Mama let go of me with one arm and got hold of Walker.

"Hey, son. Hey, Nancy," she said and hugged her.
"Thank you. Thank you for coming."

"Less go sit down," Mama said and led us to some
benches under the trees.

"How do you feel?" Nancy asked.

"I'm okay," Mama said. "I feel good." She gazed at
Walker and me, running her hands over our faces and down
our shoulders and arms. "How's Avery? How's Molly and
Samuel and Dora?" she asked, naming Molly's husband and
their baby.

We stood twisting our cuffs in awkward silence for a
moment, seeing she was not going to ask about Anyone
Else.

"Molly and Samuel are fine," Nancy said. "We brought
you a letter from them and a photograph of Dora." She
winked sideways at me; there was a picture of me and

Walker and Avery too, but Nancy knew it was for me to show it. She continued, "You never saw such a head of hair as that Dora has. And we brought you all kinds of other things. Can you come with us to our wagon?"

"What time is it?" Mama asked. "If I get this laundry hung, I will have a little while to be with you."

"Almost noon." Walker looked at the pocket watch he had brought. Daddy had lent it to him for the trip. Mama widened her eyes at it, then looked away, up at the trees.

"We brought you a picnic." Nancy raised one finger in anticipation.

"All right," Mama said. "Just let me finish hanging these sheets. Maybe we can drive a little ways out on the grounds to eat. I hate to have something special and not share it." Mama looked past us to the doorway of the laundry. The woman with the scar on her face was standing there smiling, seeming like she wanted to join us.

"This is my family, honey," Mama called to her. "I'll be back in just a little bit, and I'll bring you a goody from our picnic."

She turned back to us. "That's Tilda," Mama said. "Her husband is the one that laid that mark on her cheek, but he claimed it was self-defense, and they put her in here."

"Is that the way the world works now?" Nancy clicked her tongue.

"She may never get out," Mama continued. "She don't have any children, and her own brother won't stand up for her." Mama sighed and smiled tight-lipped at us. "Well, I don't want to tell about unfortunate things. I want to talk about you all and hear the news. I'll join you as soon as these are pinned up."

I took a wet sheet out of the wicker basket beside the lines.

"I'll help you," I said and handed it to my mama.

Mama gave me a hopeful look, like maybe I wasn't going to hate her after all, and she pinned one corner.

When we were done, Walker drove us out into the park, and we set up under some oaks.

"I hope this is some of your favorites," Nancy said. She brought out fried trout—everyone knew how Mama loved fish—and a buttermilk pie. She set them down on the quilt we had spread under the trees.

"I thought we'd leave this with you," I said. I stroked the quilt, holding the sack with some of the gifts we had brought. The quilt was a wedding ring pattern Mama had made before I was born. It was blue and white, with just a little red, and one of the prettiest she'd ever done. Mama knelt beside me and ran her finger along some stitches.

"Oh my, I do remember making this." Her smile was sad. "I would love to keep this quilt, honey, but it would not be a good idea. It would just get stolen while I slept. I would rather you have it. What all else have you got there?" Mama changed the subject and raised her eyebrows at my sack. She moved close to me and put her arm around my shoulder. "I sure have missed you all," she said and kissed my forehead.

I was getting more confused by the minute. My mama did not seem the least bit insane. She seemed perfectly like her old self, only there was all that missing time and we were at Ryan's Point.

"It's got Molly's letter in it. And the pictures. And I made you a blouse," I mumbled. I cast my eyes down and handed over the sack.

"Oh my, would you look at how big Dora is!" Mama said, tilting the baby's portrait card in the dappled light.

"She is fat as the dickens," Walker said. He chuckled.

"Why, Walker," I said. "You surprise me. I never knew you had a soft spot for young 'uns."

My brother blushed.

"She has a temper, for a baby," I added. "She will stomp her foot if she doesn't get attention when she wants it."

"Tell her the other news." Nancy swatted at my hand and cut her eyes at Mama.

"Well, Molly's going to have another baby."

"Oh my," Mama said. She wiped at her eyes. "Looks like I am missing everything." She pulled out the picture of my brothers and me. It was mounted on heavy cardboard, and we had all signed it on the back. "I will treasure this." She touched her finger to Avery's face. "Is he all right?"

"He is," Walker said. "Quiet as ever. Manages the animals the way he was apparently born to do."

Mama nodded, then took out the blouse. It was black-and-white striped, with black buttons down the front. I had made it on her foot-treadle machine, but the buttonholes I had done by hand. They took me forever.

"And would you look at this pretty thing? What nice work on the buttonholes!" Mama pulled me to her again. "I can wear this on Sunday for church. Thank you, honey. Thank you so much."

She looked at all of us. "This is what you need to know—there is a hearing coming up in ninety days. I am going before a judge and some of the administrators here. My doctor is going to recommend that I be released. But he says if they do release me, I will need to go back to William. They all believe a wife belongs with her husband." She paused, looking especially at Nancy. "I have tried. You know I have tried."

Nancy nodded. Walker stood up and rolled another

cigarette. I guessed he felt bad for Daddy. Maybe he thought he was like Daddy himself, but he was not.

"Children," Mama went on. She spoke particularly in Walker's direction. "Your father is not really a bad man. But I cannot live with him anymore. It would kill my spirit."

"But what about us?" I asked. "Don't you want to be with us?"

"Of course I do," Mama said. "I will try to work something out with Molly and Samuel and stay with them. I will promise the judge and those others whatever I need to promise. They don't need to know I am with Molly instead of with William."

"Why did you run off like you did?" My tone was clipped, though I tried my best to keep my voice even and subdued. "Why didn't you go and live with Molly, then, instead of running away and having it turn out like this?"

"Isabel, there are things you don't know yet about married couples. Molly and Samuel had just gotten married. They did not need me barging in on their love nest." She looked away. "They don't need that now, but it can't be helped. There are things you just don't know about married couples," she repeated.

"Well, who is going to eat the rest of this fish?" Nancy asked. Her voice was very bright, and she bustled over to the picnic basket. "And the biscuits?"

There were some squirrels in a nearby tree, watching us and waiting for crumbs. One of them had a big length of his tail missing. I wondered if an inmate had chopped it off. He seemed like a happy squirrel, though. He just had his scar now, like Tilda. The clouds were lifting, and we all sat together in a patch of sun. It was a good couple of hours, and then afternoon started to fall into evening.

"It will be hard to travel after dark," Mama said. "I have been lucky to have this time with you. I will have to thank Tilda and the other girls for covering for me while we visited." We all stood up.

"Take them the rest of this food," Nancy said. She began to wrap the leftovers. I listened to the wind in the trees while I gathered courage for my final question.

"Can I see where you live before we go?" I bit my lip and waited.

"I supposed you can, but it is nothing but a room with a bed. Nothing I would . . . call home." She looked out into the distance before her gaze came back to me. She reached and took my hand. "Come on, then. I live in the same building as the laundry. You can help me try on my new blouse."

"We will meet you back there with the wagon," Nancy said. "Walker, will you hand that basket up to me?"

He did so, then took the quilt with both hands, flapped it up from the grass, and shook it.

When we got to the clotheslines, Mama led me inside and up the same stairs we had followed down to find her. As we were going up, the banjo player was going down. He had his instrument tucked under his arm. As he passed Mama, he lightly brushed her hip with his free hand. It was quick and so subtle, it could have been an accident, but I had seen the woman and the peddler in the woods and knew it was not.

"Ladies," he said. "Have a nice afternoon. Guess I got to do some work now. Gonna paint that stairwell a nice cream color, Martha, like we talked about."

"That will be so nice," Mama said, keeping her eyes down. I sensed her breathing quicken. We followed the hallway, and Mama stopped at the door where the banjo player had been when we met him. The rooms all looked alike, but I knew it was the same one, as I could see the depression on the cotton coverlet from where he had been sitting.

"Is that your bed?" I asked Mama.

"Yes," she said, then saw that I appeared stricken, staring at the place where she said she slept. We could hear the echoes of a woman screaming somewhere in the building. Gradually, the voice declined and was replaced by sobbing. I gripped the doorjamb and steadied myself.

"Don't be sad for me," Mama said, thinking I was relating the disturbance to what she lived through. But that was not the reason at all. "As much as I miss you, I do have some friends here." She pulled me to her. She did it just like she always used to, but inside myself, I had tightened, imagining who those new friends of hers might be, claiming her affections. She would not want to come home if that was how it was for her.

Mama continued, "Yes, it is bad here for some, but my situation is different. You can see I am not like that." She tossed her chin in the direction of the crying. "I will not be away from you much longer, I hope."

"I'm not sad." Our eyes met. "Well, not too much. Try on the blouse," I said.

Walker had brought the wagon around, and it was loaded up, and now we had to begin our goodbye hugs and kisses.

"Your outfit looks real nice," Walker said.

Mama spun in a circle and put her hand to her throat in a parody of fashion. We were all trying to keep the mood elevated.

"My dear," Nancy said, offering dainty fingers like a model from *Lady's Home Companion Magazine*. "That blouse fits you to a T. Isabel did a beautiful job."

"She really did. It is a wonderful thing to have it." Mama twisted a button and stroked the fabric of her sleeve.

"I hate that you have to leave, but I feel like we'll be together again soon," she said.

She walked after the wagon for several paces as Walker urged the horse forward.

"Be sure to give my love to Molly and her family," she called.

I watched her wipe her tears, the flats of her hands meeting across her face like the wings of a bird. I found I had a hurting in my rib, and I could not turn around and watch her as we drove away.

Five

Girl with an Emerald

1914

I dreaded the sight of somebody sitting at the kitchen table reading a letter. We were not a corresponding bunch, and a personal letter always meant something unusual had happened. First, there was the letter Nancy got, and now here one was again. Good or bad, a letter had to be gone over again and again until the paper was soft and the words could be digested, like an unfamiliar food.

We had just finished dinner, and the kitchen table was a mess of dirty dishes and coffee cups. Cornbread crumbs were all over. The postman had brought an important-looking letter earlier in the day. When I saw the return address of Ryan's Point, I put it in the cabinet under the bottom plate. Once Daddy took his last bite of the cobbler, I went and got it.

"It came this morning," I said, handing it over. It was only a few months after we had visited Mama. He gave me that look, the one that made me feel like I was some kind of mistake. He took up a bread knife and slit open the envelope. I watched the changes in his face as he sat reading the page and studying it. In a second, he put his forehead in his hand and threw the letter on the kitchen table beside the milk pitcher. It immediately got a molasses stain on it.

I grabbed the letter quick and went to wipe it clean. He couldn't read that well, but I could. I knew he'd probably go over it and over it. Below the seal for the Tennessee State Institute for the Insane, it said:

Dear Mr. King,

As you may have learned of the recent fire and tragedy at our facility in Knoxville, we regret to inform you of the death of Martha Franklin King and wish to extend our deepest sympathies on the loss of your loved one.

We had not heard of any such a thing—a fire! We did not subscribe to the *Knoxville Sentinel* and had no way of knowing.

"What does this mean?" I shrieked, my fingers whitening on the edge of the table.

Daddy put his cheek down against his shirtsleeve and raised it up again. I was astonished to see a tear in his eye, and he put his palms together like he might pray. But Daddy did not pray; he was a son of a bitch who found solace in plowing. He was not pious like that.

"Sweetheart, I think you know what it means." He spoke to me so kindly that I shrank back in horror. This loving tone was not his way.

Hysteria spilled out of me like there was a rip in my chest. "Tell me!" I pushed a plate across the table, scattering food. "It's not true!"

He did not answer me. His jaw was clamped tight, and

47

he got busy gathering cornbread crumbs into little piles with the side of his hand and wiping up the molasses.

Suddenly, I hated the sight of him.

"I'm going to Nancy and Queenie's!" I screamed. "You! You are the cause of this! She would not be dead but for *you!*"

He did not correct me or stop me when I stormed out. He just turned his head away.

No one will ever rescue you. Deep down you know it, but it's like you have two lives. There's the one where you work because you have to, and the one where you know who you really are inside your head. You say, "One of these days, I will." Will what? Will become what you are meant to be, what you can become? But of course, you just go on with one day connecting to the next.

I was twelve years old when I took my mama's place. Did you know—we never had any kind of a funeral service? Or even any kind of a grave? Walker pushed Daddy, so he did make a few inquiries. He was told that the wing Mama was in burned completely down. We were told it was an inmate, got hold of a match and set his own clothes on fire, and then ran through the halls, lighting curtains as he went.

The letter continued:

> *Due to the severity of the blaze, it was deemed neces-sary to raze the structure. The site has been declared for burials, and a memorial plaque commemorating those lost in this tragedy will be placed on the grounds.*

It was, we learned, hard to tell who was who.

Daddy never said, but I think he was relieved. He did

not want her to come home if she was not going to be in his household. And yet, if she had come back, he would have claimed to everyone that he had a deranged woman on his hands. He would have fought to keep her here and not at Molly's. He would have tried to keep her in line, like always.

Several weeks after the fire, the minister made the announcement in church, offering "condolences to the King family on the recent loss of their wife and mother, who was killed in a tragic accident while away in Knoxville."

Most people didn't even mention it, but you could tell they knew the story and didn't want to embarrass us by talking about it. There was only Nancy and Queenie and Queenie's daddy, Tate, coming up to talk about the weather with my daddy, and then Nancy saying, "You all are eating at our house tonight; I don't want to hear any excuses."

We went, and Nancy made Mama's apple stack cake for dessert. She gave me the recipe for it, in Mama's handwriting, before we left.

So that's how it was for me. The main result of my mama's death was that it ended my thinking that some miracle would allow her to come back and take care of me. She could not even rescue herself from her own life.

Once I was grown, I had compassion for the girl I used to be. I did not want to be the woman of the house; that is just the story of my childhood and my life. I just did what needed doing, waiting for the person who was really in charge to come in and rescue me.

From then on, wherever I lived, the work of the place fell to me. There was never a house I could call my own.

I had a tintype of Mama taken before she got married. In it, she looked pretty, with her long hair pulled back from her forehead and combed out around her shoulders. Her head was tilted, like she was listening to something. She was waiting, with no lines on her face. And I liked to think she went back to being that person, the one she was before it all got sidetracked.

I had aspirations for the girl in this picture, like she was a character in a novel I had just started to read and not my mama who went out and plowed when her husband told her to. I wanted her to have a happy ending.

After Mama died, Nancy gave me the book *Jane Eyre*. At first when you read it, you were afraid of the madwoman in the attic and even hated her a little. But later, when it all turned out fine for Jane and she had her Mr. Rochester, you just felt sorry for the wife who had been hidden away. It was unbelievable, of course, what Jane went through, and painful to witness the misunderstandings she had in her search for love. In the end, though, the only thing that mattered was that Jane kept a strong attitude and spirit. She had stayed strong, and she had prevailed. I decided to try to do the same.

The letter did not change much for my daddy and my brothers. They kept on growing corn and tobacco and raising hogs on our little farm. They got up before daylight and were out till after dark. I looked for signs of grief, but if they had it, it was barely discernible from Avery's usual quiet and Daddy's hard attention to business at hand. I did notice, several days after the letter, that our family good-luck charm, the three ears of corn that always hung by the doorway, had been ripped down.

"Did you do it?" I asked Walker.

"I did," he said, and his voice broke. We hung on each other and cried. But even Walker could not express much more about what the loss meant to him.

At twelve, I had barely got my woman's body, but I

was the closest thing to a housekeeper they had, and I was always strong. I had used a broom and toted water since I was little, even when Mama had been here, so the men did not consider it unusual for me to be running a household. Molly used to do it with me, but she had left and got married. She told us she was in love with Samuel, and I know she was, but maybe, too, she thought it would be easier to deal with housework if it was not under my daddy's eye.

Mend this. Clean and cook that. I was bossed a lot, but Daddy said, if I looked like I might complain, "There's always bosses, no matter how old you get, so best learn to mind."

He was right. Over the course of time, I learned it's better to work with life, rather than rage against it or anybody in it who might have power over you. Hateful feelings work against a person in the long run.

I did go to school off and on for a couple of years, as Daddy allowed. As I said, I loved books, and Nancy, always mindful of my motherless situation, found occasions to slip them into my hands. Clothes too, though Molly dropped by often enough with Dora and the new baby, Sallie, and she never came without food or hand-me-downs.

Gradually, with Queenie's help, I learned to read just about anything. Queenie herself stayed in school, and she graduated salutatorian of her eighth-grade class.

My daddy did not care too much for books himself. He could read the Bible. "This is the only book I need," he said time after time.

Once, only once, I neglected the washing for several days in favor of this story about a girl detective who was trying to find an emerald that was stolen from a museum. The emerald was big, nearly the size of a plum, and cut and polished so it practically shone in the dark.

I was in the middle of the most exciting part. The heroine was so brave and beautiful, and she was so close to recovering the treasure. Just then, my daddy came out of his bedroom in his long johns and threw a pair of muddy denims at me.

"I ain't got nothing else to wear but these overhalls, and I been patient, Isabel, waiting for a clean pair to show up. Now, I want you off your high horse with that reading. You get the washpot boiling, and I want clean clothes *today*."

Well, I was so mad. I got up from there and was hot enough to light the stove with a scratch of my finger. I got the water going, and then I turned on my heel and flicked my dress up behind at the empty doorway where my daddy had just been looming. That was my opinion of the whole laundry business.

I sat right back down to the book, where the heroine was hanging off the top of a train trying to keep the emerald away from the thieves. (She had found it when one of the thieves, disguised as a fine gentleman, had carelessly left it unattended under his napkin in the dining car while he flirted with a lady passenger.)

Meanwhile, the wash water boiled up, and I didn't know a thing about it until I heard it running over and sizzling on the stove top. Well, Daddy heard it before me, and he came striding into the kitchen in his underwear and boots.

My daddy was six feet five. It took him three steps and one sweep of his long arm to reach over and rip the story right out of my hand.

I stood up and said, "Daddy, that's Queenie's book from the *library!*"

He didn't even turn around. He said, "I'm going to Wheat soon, and I will give the damn liberry back their property. Now, let's see some washing and renching going on in here."

I got up slow. Dark blotches came up in front of my eyes. I wanted to scream at him so bad, but backtalking led to a whipping. My voice was stuffed back in my throat like a swallowed sock. I went over to the pot on the stove top and put one hand on each handle. The hot steam laid itself over my face like a thin, wet cloth. And before I knew it, in my anger, I *jerked* the pot hard, and the scalding water came lifting toward me in tongues, then fell and hit my legs.

The skin ran just like melting wax and sagged to a stop at the edge of my high-top shoes. And then I screamed, oh yes.

It felt so good to scream. Avery ran for Granny. Everyone called her that; she never had any children, but she could draw out fire.

"Lord, child," she said when she saw my legs. The skin had bloomed up from the bone, and the blisters were already full of water. "Lie down there and let me blow out the heat. If we don't, the fire will go down to the bone and you'll have pain like you've never known."

She leaned over me and sucked in her breath, like she was pulling smoke in her lungs. I didn't believe anything would happen, but what difference did it make? Then she went into the kitchen, somewhere we couldn't see her, and she said a secret Bible verse.

Let her try. Somebody please, just take care of me, I thought. *It doesn't make a bit of difference what they do, just take me out of my own hands.*

She came back two or three times. I never went to a

doctor. It took about three weeks for the burns to go down. Finally, the bubbles broke and scabbed. Granny gave herself credit. That was fine. I've had these long white scars on my legs ever since.

But I learned. Don't let the anger and the pain out, it will circle round and damage you. You learn to keep disappointment in control or else you wreck yourself.

Later, I went and looked for that book so I could finish it. I never did find it. I sort of had a suspicion that Daddy did something with it instead of taking it back. Queenie and Nancy never brought it up, what with my legs.

In a way, I was glad it happened. After that, the housework made me feel close to my mama, who had also learned about burning. Nancy kept telling me things about her, how she made the best apple butter, what a beautiful singing voice she had in church. That was Nancy's way: making sure I kept a good opinion of Mama. For years, people gossiped behind their hands. *Part Cherokee; what did you expect?*

I look at my scars, the water tracks mapped permanent down my shins. After I remember my mama, I think of the girl on the train in the book I didn't finish. I wanted things to turn out triumphant, so I finished her story in my mind. There she was, standing right up on top of the boxcar, panting a little. She was starting to resemble my mama in her early tintype, but saucier, with a brunette curl tumbling over one eye. The thieves had fallen off down a ravine miles back, and in her fist, she was clutching the emerald. The train went on around the bend, into the dark tunnel, smoke pouring out of the smokestack, but oh Lord, it is all right. She had got it, the great prize. It was hers, and she wouldn't let it go.

Six

Nancy and Queenie

1914

Queenie was at school a lot of the time, so I saw her mostly at church on Sunday.

"Show me what you're studying," I would beg after the services. I missed learning most terribly and could never have enough of her occasional tutoring. I felt jealous of other children whose families found a way to get farming and household chores done so they could go. Some boys and girls did all they could to get out of it; I never understood that. I loved to brighten my mind with new information and new words. Geography and history were favorites of mine, and poetry. I found out what a *simile* was, and suddenly, the days were going by like fast train cars and my heart was as shattered as a rose with most of its petals gone.

When the weather got warm, everyone stayed and had dinner on the grounds. I spent nearly all my Saturdays getting our food ready to take and felt excited about being around people. My brothers and daddy did not count.

Sometimes, after the final amen, there was a ball game, a cleanup in the cemetery, or a baptism. I remember my own baptism right before Mama left. The preacher and I waded out waist deep into Step Creek. I held my nose, and he tilted me back. I came up gasping, my white linen dress stuck to my body. Mama had brought a quilt with her, and she wrapped me up in it when I staggered out. I didn't feel anything had changed, except the crowd was now singing "The beautiful, the beautiful river." But the tears on Mama's face and the kiss she gave my forehead—now, that felt holy.

Sitting in the pews, I could barely wait through the formalities of religion to get to the benediction; that is, to the start of the fun. The sermon lasted an hour and a half, and I was not the only one distracted by the sun playing through the windows and the calling of a mockingbird.

At last, the afternoon opened up for socializing. Walker and Avery stood in a little huddle of teenage boys. They kept their fingers hooked in their pants while they stole glances at the girls, then went off to play baseball while Daddy talked to other men about crops.

Queenie and me and a couple of other girls made a place under a tree and played school. Queenie knew it was not entirely a game, as far as I was concerned.

"All right, children," she'd say. "Now we are going to learn about the states and their capitals. Isabel, would you please draw the map for us?"

I took a stick and drew the edges of the United States in the dirt—the curve of California, then Texas, Florida, and Maine reaching out. I wanted to talk about Arizona, which had just become the forty-eighth state. After the Ryan's Point fire that killed my mama, and us never knowing about it until we got a letter, Walker and I badgered Daddy to subscribe to the Knoxville paper. Which he reluctantly did, so that is how I learned about Arizona. I was fascinated by the desert and the Indian tribes found there. The cactus, and the temperatures over 110—an egg would fry on a rock for the cowboys on the range.

"That's enough, now, about tepees and such. It's time for mathematics," Queenie said finally in her prim schoolmarm voice. She took her foot and erased the ground.

The others got tired of playing school after a while. Eventually, we'd play jump rope or count one-potato, two-potato to get "it" for hide-and-seek. Or it would be time to eat, much to my disappointment—as I never got enough geography or spelling to satisfy me.

One Sunday, Queenie said to me, "Come here— Mama's got a new book she wants you to see." Nancy's books, some from before she married, were often old, but regardless of their tattered condition or what subject they were, I was eager to explore their pages.

But a brand-new one?

"It's anatomy," Queenie said, and she framed her mouth in a big O and looked up at me with a wink. We were thirteen. Queenie had reached her full adult height of five feet two, while I was five six and still getting taller. I opened the book at random, and there was a diagram of the milk ducts of the female breast. I shut the book with a clap.

"I can't," I told Queenie. "What do you think my daddy is going to say if he sees me setting around with a book, 'specially one like this?"

"A young lady needs certain knowledge," Nancy said, coming up beside us. Queenie grinned. Apparently, she had already obtained this knowledge. We both knew that if her mother had decided I needed to get it too, the matter was settled. Nancy took my hand and led me near where the men were talking.

"Here, Isabel." She flourished the volume in the air with a large gesture so that my daddy could see it as she handed it over. "I am lending you this book." She emphasized *lending*. "I know you will not neglect any of your chores, and you may find time to read of an evening after work is done. You were always such a promising student when you went to school," she said. She held the side of her dress and lifted one shoulder as she swept past the men. Daddy would not take away any book Nancy herself had put into my hand—that was for certain.

Daddy stood with Queenie's father. Daddy respected Tate and sold some corn to him every year; he wouldn't want to do anything to upset that relationship. Tate caught Nancy's glance, and he knew what he was supposed to do. They were a good pair.

"A lot of female fluttering, you ask me." Tate leaned toward Daddy behind his hand. "Harmless."

Daddy stuck his tongue out on his bottom lip, spat a fleck of tobacco, but kept quiet, and I took the book home. Later that year, I got my monthlies. Thank goodness for the book; the things Molly had tried to tell me here and there finally made sense.

There was no pattern to the reading material I got hold of. Everything was fodder for my haphazard education. One volume was called *The Child's Book of Health*. It was endorsed by the Department of Scientific Instruction of the Women's Christian Temperance Union in Boston. In my reading, I had a way of pulling out important bits and skimming impatiently through the rest. In *The Child's Book of Health*, it was immediately clear that the point was to steer young readers away from the evils of alcohol:

How necessary it is to have the water we drink be

pure and wholesome! Should you not think people would be satisfied with pure cold water to drink? Are they not? Not at all. More than this, is it not strange that people should want drinks which are certain to do them a great deal of harm?

Liquor was the topic on every other page. But that was not what I was after. I wanted to know about blood, the lungs, the skin, and other facts, such as how the heart worked, so I skipped a lot. In later years with John L., I often wished I had paid closer attention to that little book, which warned of bad company and the dangers of drink.

By this age, I could read anything I wanted. Queenie showed me how to use a dictionary and had given me one the size of my palm for Christmas. I kept it in my apron pocket and liked to feel it banging around while I cooked and swept.

I have ever been amazed how a single thing, like a word, can be two ways or more at once. All my life, I have had a large vocabulary, but what was in my mind was not always what was in my mouth. Many a word I saw, I knew the definition of, but I never said it out loud. Sometimes, when I would try a word in good company, I would mispronounce it and be embarrassed. Once, I said, "It's certainly for-two-wishes to meet you here today," instead of "for-to-it-us" for the word *fortuitous*.

I can switch from writing and speaking the King's English to the accents and poor grammar of all the folks who lived in the countryside. It's like I know two languages: one for the world and one for paper. If a thing *exists*, how can it be different from the one way it is? It can't really, but perceptions are infinite, I am sure you know. I amuse myself with these little philosophies.

Another book Nancy brought me was *Mrs. Browning's Poems*, and I was thrilled to see a piece called "Isabel's Child!" But I was so sad when the baby died. For days, I read and reread the tale of Aurora Leigh, who had lost her mother at the age of four. Aurora was a beautiful seamstress who got led astray, and I thought how that could happen to a woman without a mother to advise her. Thank God I had Nancy keeping an eye out for me. I will not tell you more about the poem, as you may want to read it yourself sometime.

But I felt like Aurora Leigh many times. Days are when I wonder why. Why have I bothered to learn anything at all? I am not important to the universe—there seems to be no great purpose for me, and all my little tragedies have no rhyme nor reason. Often I feel flawed and slow, not able to figure things out, like a bird who won't fly out an open door. But a part of me keeps believing that there's a reason I am here, despite pain, despite death and cruelty.

The truth that has crept up to me, as I have absorbed the books that passed my way, seems to be this: We have our choices about happiness. We can accept our lot and try to be grateful, or we can always be dissatisfied, like spoiled and wealthy children who want the next new and better thing.

I am driven to seek, to know the why of myself.

Finally, I believe this: Truth can appear if you are patient and wait for it. There are objects you sense in darkness. Unsure in the close quarters of your own mind, things you questioned can be resolved. Morning does come.

Seven

Gallatin

1916

When I was fourteen, I discovered I could love more than books, love more than learning facts about China or the names of my teeth. Love more even than what my daddy called "useless" stories that captured my blood.

I had been engrossed in the novelist Mrs. Behn, enjoying her tale of the dark prince Oroonoko. The book came from Nancy's attic—she gave me free rein to read anything in her house. But this was from an old and forgotten assortment, and I doubted she was aware of what the box contained. Surely, if she knew the exotic and near-lurid nature of the story, she might have held it back for fear my daddy would glance through it.

There was coupling, there was violence, there was all manner of evil and intrigue in that volume. Oroonoko was tortured and kept apart from his lover, Imoinda. She herself was forced to submit to all kinds of indignities and injustices, despite her beauty and character.

About that time, I met Gallatin Greene, the mysterious, handsome boy who had six fingers on each hand.

I'd heard dramatic reports of him; he was a legend of sorts, and, truth be known, I started feeling for him before I ever knew him. I shaped him into a romantic figure beginning with the beautiful word that was his name. Gallatin—like *galaxy, Galahad, Galilee.*

Nowadays, a family would simply take the child to a doctor and say, "Please do a little amputation here so this boy can get on with his life." But his folks were ashamed, you see. The story had grown so that Gallatin had not just four thumbs but a cleft palate, a club foot, and a hump. He was talked about like something that would be put in a jar of alcohol for display at the sideshow.

Because of his deformity, Gallatin, a year older than me, had not been allowed to come to school or church. The minister kept trying to convince the family he needed to come to church, at least, for the salvation of his soul.

The love I had for him was partly feeling that here was "another one"—one like me who had been held back and hidden away.

His whole family was full of characters; it amused me they didn't see this and considered Gallatin to be the only odd one. His little sister Katy was a tall, wiry girl with big ears. They stuck through her lank brown hair like pale lily pads. I had heard it was possible to cut the cords behind a person's ears so they'd lay flat against the head. Snip, snip; now there's an operation that might have helped. Would have improved her personality, if not her appearance. She was always fighting over Gallatin. A boy would say, "Yer brother is a monster," and Katy would jump on him.

"Take it back! Take it back!" she'd warn and then grab his arm and wrench it so he either flipped over backward or else dislocated his shoulder. Katy would never deny, though, that her brother was a monster. Instead, she would point out, "With his hands in his pockets, he looks like everybody else."

His other sister, Mary, was fragile, with sharp black eyes and bowl-cut black hair. Cruel children used to scare her into thinking she might be like her brother by grabbing her wrist and saying, "Mary! There's a fingernail growing out of your hand!" And they would pull out the mica chip they had slid from their palm to hers.

"Leave me alone! Leave him alone!" Mary shouted, wiping her tears.

Most girls used Gallatin's name to mean everything they were afraid of about boys. When a high school girl was found bruised and unconscious by the creek crossing, she wasn't able to tell who did it. Somebody made a suggestion, a reference flimsy as fog on a ridge, and that was all it took. The next thing you knew, they were investigating at the Greenes. Nothing ever came of it, but it started a line of thought, a tendency to say, "Don't go walking on a full-moon night; Gallatin might be lurking out there."

My temper rose to think he was so misunderstood. Everything about him—what I knew, what I didn't know—made him desirable. Even if it turned out he was ugly, he would still have sweetness and appeal, I thought, same as Quasimodo in *The Hunchback of Notre-Dame*. In my heart, he began as beautiful. He was my shadow prince, and I longed to stand up for him. But not like a sister. Imoinda! Oroonoko! If only they could be united!

We met up by accident one afternoon. I was berry picking and had found a line of bushes that ran straight up Black Oak Ridge. I was in that lazy, mindless rhythm you get—eat a few, drop a few, move on a few paces. A storm was starting; still I walked higher and higher. As long as there's room in your bucket, you don't quit. And I was just so happy to be away from the kitchen.

While I was dawdling along, the wind started whipping. I picked a little faster. The underbrush stirred back and forth, and a briar drew a long red line down my forearm. I should have known to turn back—once the clouds start to roil and you feel the swoop of a downdraft, the lightning and the rain are just a minute behind. I could tell I was almost to the top of the mountain; I could feel the wide-open air becoming a backdrop to the trees. Three more steps up and I had that giddy, weightless sense of the ground dropping off.

The raindrops were falling now, fat and heavy like melted nickels, and lightning struck a tree so near to me, I was blinded. The energy of it vibrated the living roots inches beneath my feet.

I was looking for a safe place to hide when Gallatin appeared in the clearing, drenched to the skin and with lightning bolts behind him. He was wearing a loose white shirt that blew half-open. I knew him immediately by his hand, bigger than anyone's—and it was beckoning me.

"Come follow," he yelled through the wind. Which I did, since the only alternative was to lie flat in the open or crowd into the thorny brush. He led us to an outcropping of rock that cupped over a little sheltering cave.

We hurried in through a gray sheet of rain clattering through the trees. I sat wet and tense, feeling his shirtsleeve a whisper away from my shoulder. He put his hands under his armpits, and he turned his head toward me just a bit and said, "It'll let up in a minute or two."

I glanced back and thought Katy was right: he would blend in anywhere—middling tall and ordinary dark-brown hair. But handsome featured and slim through his chest and hips. I nearly swooned.

So I offered him some berries. Forgot what I'd heard and marveled how, with four thumbs, he could take up twice as many as anyone else.

He reached right into my bucket, looking in my face all the while to see whether I would shrink back at his freakish aspect.

"They are sweet," he said, popping several in his mouth.

"Yes, they are. Help yourself," I said, staring straight back at him. That's how we started.

He had a way of holding his face when he looked at things. Sort of questioning, with his mouth drawn in. Some people would have thought "up to something," but he wasn't. He was just always thinking—being mostly alone had made him a philosopher is what it was.

Finally, the rain stopped. We came out into the wet purple light, and there was something between us. We both felt it, but we didn't speak its name. I began to make excuses to take a walk sometimes. I got Queenie to go with me so my family didn't suspect. I waited for him by the Greenes' barn, and Queenie would occupy his sisters, Mary and Katy.

You will not believe that nothing was going on except walking and talking and getting to know each other, but that's all it was. A couple of times we were lucky and nobody was home at his house, so we sat and drank lemonade.

I did start making myself a special dress during this time. A yellow dress. As I sewed it, I kept thinking about Gallatin seeing me in it, the way his eyes would approve, his big hands against the fabric and me inside it.

Gallatin was a juggler. I found everything fascinating about him, but this talent especially so. He had a little collection of red rubber balls, and he would take six of them and circle them in a blur. Or he would take three lightweight twig chairs off the porch and toss them in the air one after another, and they would fly round and round like a tornado had hit.

My favorite trick was what he used to call "the dinner table." He'd take knives, forks, and spoons and put a handful under one arm and a handful under the other and then pull them out so fast you'd barely know he'd done it. Only there was this silver curve in the air with little glints of light on it. You didn't even notice his extra fingers—everything went like a flash.

But then suddenly, he'd just stop. Hold out both hands like a blessing. And all the silver would hail down into his palms.

We would laugh, and he would look at me, and I would look at him. I would be all eyes and shallow breathing from the sight of him, until I felt the two of us going round and round like we were the whole world. It was magic the way nothing had happened between us, and yet everything had. Like I said, there was nothing wrong with him at all except his thumbs, but the Greenes didn't have much in the way of money or property, and my daddy would think that I— that is, our family—could do better.

"My parents have saved up enough to send me to Knoxville for the operation," Gallatin told me one day. We were walking in the fields and could see his house in the distance.

"Are you ready for that?" My heart started beating in fear for him.

"I don't want to do it, Isabel. I've had 'em too long to give 'em up now. I have learned to use my hands the way they are. They are a problem for others, but not for me."

"I hope you don't count me as 'others,'" I said quickly. He shook his head and smiled at me. "I don't. But you know I am not accepted, and there is no other way to cope with this except to leave."

I thought I would die if he left.

"Don't," I said. "What will I do without you?" It was the first time I had said out loud how much I thought of him.

"This is how I'm made," he said. "I think this is how I'll stay. I guess I'll join the circus." He put his hand against my face. "You're a little crazy yourself. Want to come too?"

We were back at his house. He picked up a saucer from the porch and shook off a couple of drops of milk the cat had left.

He threw it in the air, bounced it off his shoe, then caught it, and waited.

I felt something come apart in me. I had loved my mama and I loved him, but I was not a runaway person.

I felt my face start to crumple with tears. Slowly, I went to him and crept my arms around his waist. It was the beginning of goodbye.

I loved the smell of his shirt.

"Show me how to do it, how to juggle?"

He pulled away and smoothed my hair, then leaped up to his door and disappeared inside. When he came back, he was holding three hard-boiled eggs.

"Here," he said. "We'll use these."

He tried and tried, and I tried and tried, but I couldn't catch on. I had two hands and I could hold two eggs, but the extra one seemed to be something I could not think about at the same time. I seemed to know better than to try and control things I could not touch, things that were over my head.

I dropped the eggs again and again, until they were mapped with cracks and the shells were hanging on by the membrane. Finally, we finished removing the shells and washed the eggs in the pump. We sat on the steps and ate them. He tried again to explain.

"You got to see each thing separate," he tried again. "You got to see that one thing and how it moves out of your hand and back in again. And then"—he took another bite of egg—"this is the hard part: you have to see all the things together at once, and that's one thing moving too." He looked at me. "In motion, everything together is one thing."

I sighed. I knew he was freakish in a sense, like the Albino Boy or the Bearded Girl, but I didn't care at all. Gallatin Greene existed more than other people did, somehow. His hands reminded me that a human being was a thing that could be made. Created in its own way, like a leaf or a dog. With him, you felt you were closer to God than you'd been before.

"I understand," I told him to please him, though then I didn't understand at all. He leaned over and kissed me. It was the strangest first kiss anyone ever had, since we were both flecked with bits of yolk and egg white.

"I'll leave you a sign," he said. He kissed me again, slower this time. How I did like slow! And soon after, he was gone, fixing his legend once and for all.

I didn't find his sign until the next year, when the berries came round again. Queenie was with me, and I took her to visit the rain-sheltering cave.

"There it is, over there," I pointed, and we walked toward it over the gnarled roots of huge rhododendrons.

"Oh my, Isabel, would you looky." Queenie had run ahead of me and put her hand on the rock beside the entrance. Solemnly, she took her palm away, revealing the print he had left there. He had dipped his hand in white-wash and pressed it against the rock. Six fingers.

"Different is normal for some people," I mused. All kinds of emotions crackled through me. "He will make something of himself. I feel sure of it, Queenie."

"Gallatin, stay alive," I whispered into the cave. And faintly the echo came back to me: "*Alive.*"

Eight

The Spanish Influenza

1918

I spent as much time as I could at Nancy's or at Molly's. Queenie was living in Knoxville, sent to a high school for talented girls. Walker had enlisted and become a doughboy. Daddy didn't like it, as it shorted him a farmhand, but he couldn't very well deny the military his son. The neighbors would have thought ill of him if he kept his boy from his patriotic duty.

Avery got a deferment, partly because of the farm and partly because the recruiters had met him and knew he was not soldier material. Walker was sent to France, and we got letters from him, written in pencil on fragile paper. The envelopes were dirty, and we figured it was because of the time it took for the mail to arrive. Then again, maybe he was writing from some muddy trench. The paper smelled like cigarette smoke and bacon grease, but I loved my brother's handwriting.

I am thinking about you, Isabel, and the farm. I see you

*with your hair in two braids and growing taller and not
smiling. And then I think of you and make you smile in
my mind. And I see the peach trees in the spring and how
the snow dusts the fallow fields in the winter like confec-
tionery sugar . . . I have got trained as a medic. There is a
flu here that is killing us faster than warfare. It goes to
pneumonia and takes boys down in a day or two. Doctoring
people is not so much different from taking care of animals.
It is hard to see creatures in pain.*

The house was bleak with Walker gone. Anytime I
could get it, I moved to my room and read—anything to
escape Daddy's dictate to "get it done, get it done." There
was always something to labor over from the moment your
feet hit the floor to the moment your head hit the pillow.
He drove Avery and me and never gave us thanks or much
in the way of love or joy.

I learned to pace myself, to not be affected by Daddy's
intensity. I watched Avery. He had learned, or maybe it was
just inborn. Nothing seemed to faze him. He floated
through his work like an angel, hardly speaking.

"Get more hay!" Daddy would shout at him. "Mend
that harness, would you?" he'd add, and it had to be done
that morning. Avery would not react, except to slowly begin
the job.

More and more, I understood the worry they had day
to day: about crops and animals, about food, about fire-
wood and taxes. Work was a stress but also a tonic. They
did not know or want any other kind of happiness, and they
did not resent their labor. In my own case, though, anxiety
from Daddy's demands clawed at me constantly.

With Nancy and my sister, Molly, I found some respite:
a cool drink, a funny story, an invitation to sit. Those

moments of ease, precious few, shored me up upon my return home.

In the fall of 1918, one out of every three people in Knoxville and the surrounding counties got the grippe, the Spanish influenza that Walker had written about. In Wheat and the other little Anderson County towns, there were no public gatherings, and schools got canceled. To tell the truth, our family was considered sort of lucky because no one died of the sickness outright. I myself had it—nearly everybody in our church under the age of thirty had it. Gallatin's sister Katy caught it and was gone within two days. They said her face turned pale blue and blood ran from her nose. I was glad Gallatin was not here to know about it.

Mine was on me hard for a week: The coughing kept on and on, until I thought my ribs would break. I could not get up, and I had strange dreams about my mama, about Gallatin, where they stood at a distance down some road and motioned for me to come to them. My arms and legs felt paralyzed, so I could not move, and I woke in tears. When my flu finally subsided, I was left blank headed, limp, and ten pounds lighter than I was—and I was already thin. Near the end of my illness, Walker returned to us. He had had the sickness in Europe, caught it on the ship that took him from England to Normandy, so he was spared a second bout.

"I am sorry, brother, but you are going to have to be me until I can sit up again." I was still in bed, and it took all the energy I could muster just to say a sentence.

I listened close for his reply, but hearing nothing, I fluttered my eyes. It was a great effort to peer beyond the bars of my lashes. Walker was staring off into the distance out the window. He had done this since he'd been back, just let his mind wander out. We'd see nobody home behind his eyes, and then suddenly, he would blink and slip back inside his body.

He smoked steadily all the time now, and I could see and smell the steel-gray tobacco haze that surrounded him. Sometimes, it worried me because he did it in the barn. The air was full of hay dust, and the tiniest dropped spark could burst into fingers of orange in an instant. But he had stood in the light of exploding shells and lived.

"Leave me alone. I know how to be careful," he snapped at me when I commented on the cig forever at his lips.

He had changed. There were things he did not talk about, but I also noticed that he stood up to Daddy more than he ever had. He used some of his mustering-out money to buy us an old Model A car and a used John Deere tractor. Daddy, old-fashioned and stubborn as he was, had had to accept those gifts to the family and the farm. And what do you know, he grudgingly learned to appreciate the advancements.

I wasn't the nicest when I was ill. I forced myself up on one elbow and reached for my bedside cup, my lips parched and cracking.

"Don't like them apples, Walker, do you? Women's work, I mean."

"Not much. I didn't like it the first time in France, neither. But I was a medic, so that helped. I knew sanitation, I understood what was happening to me too, so I wasn't scared of it. I fought the sickness. They say it's a germ, a virus you can't do nothing about. But I know different. If you want to live and make up your mind to, it does help the healing. But it don't pay to get well first. You have to nursey-maid the rest of 'em." Walker sounded grim, but then he was beside me, kneeling and firmly holding my head. "It'll take quite a sickness to impair you, Isabel. What a big mess this is."

"Sure," I whispered. "I'll be up in no time and criticizing your cooking."

"No need to do that," said Walker. "Daddy's letting me know plenty about my skills, in the kitchen and everywhere else. He can't wait until you recover and we can get out of quarantine. Nancy left us a pie and a casserole by the mailbox, that has tided us over the past few days."

"In that case, maybe I'll feign sick a while longer."

Actually, despite his sourness, Daddy had been pulling his share of the burden. Avery was hit harder even than I was and lay in the next room. That meant Daddy was left doing the work of three men. He had been sleeping in the barn and doing all the outside labor and tending the animals single-handedly. He was prostrate from exhaustion, but he did not fall ill. The grippe seemed to hit younger folks the worst.

"Wash the towels now," I said in a fuzzy voice to Walker. "We will stay sick if we don't stay clean." I had such pain behind my eyes, I could not look at the light, and my ears ached from the insides out. I told Walker how to make an onion poultice for Avery—he had not stood up from the bed for days, and I could hear his wretched, ragged breathing through the wall. I would have laughed to see Walker shedding tears over cut onions and then working a frying pan, only I was worried Avery would die.

"My heart, my heart hurts," Avery said, and I knew it was the flu in his lungs. I cried to hear him in his pitiful state. We always clung to anything he uttered, as he spoke so little, but this time, his words could have meant so many other things as well.

"Molly and Samuel has both got it too," Walker reported when I was in the middle of my own struggle. "And Sallie, pore little thing."

"Oh Lord, no." I tried again to sit up. Molly was seven months pregnant with her third child. But much as I wanted to go to them, it was impossible. I could barely sip the cup of chicken broth Walker brought me or squat beside the bed and use a chamber pot.

It was a month before I was fully on my feet, and by then, Molly was mere weeks from delivery. I wanted to be with her. Avery was sitting up in his bed; he was not ready to do anything yet, but he would be all right, thank God.

My daddy stood in my bedroom doorway, watching me fold a few clothes into a suitcase. I was behind in the housework, but I had at least been able to do the cooking the past week, to the men's relief.

"Daddy, I am sorry, but I am going over to help."

And he had the nerve to object.

"Don't you think you are needed here? You are finally up and about, and so Walker is finally free to come back to farm chores, and you tell me your older sister is not able to handle her own household? What about this?" He flourished his hand at the jumble of dishes, the unswept floor, the whole domestic disaster. Walker had managed it all, but not specially well.

"Look at me, Daddy. Do you see how weak I am still? Molly is like this too, and she needs all the rest she can get before this baby comes. You all will not starve! Her two girls are a handful, and if you were not so selfish, you would see I am more needed there."

I turned to Walker. "Drive me, would you?"

To my daddy, I added, "And I better not hear that you had Avery out in the fields until next week at least." I went

in to kiss my brother, then pointed my finger first at the one
with the car key in his hand, and then at the one with his
head still on a pillow.

"Avery is *not* to go in the field. Do you *hear* me?" My
brothers both nodded a slow yes, though leery of Daddy's
disapproval.

When I got there, my brother-in-law, Samuel, opened
the door with Sallie in his arms. "How is Molly?" I asked
him.

"Aunt Isabel!" said Sallie before her father could speak,
and she reached for me. I took her up.

"Hello, sweet thing," I said. "How are you?"

"I'm not sick anymore," she said. "I got hungry again."

"Well, if you are hungry, I am going to fix us maple
pancakes first thing tomorrow." I kissed her cheek, which
was not as fat as it had been.

"I told Molly to go on and lie down. She's some better,
but by this time of day, she's kindly wore down," Samuel
said. He was pale, and his face was as sharp as I'd ever seen
it.

Then I noticed little Dora, standing deeper in the room
with her arms folded across her chest.

"What are you doing here?" she asked. It was a mystery
why my niece disliked me, but then, she was a peculiar child,
and I took it with a grain of salt.

"Is that a way to talk?" Samuel said. "Aunt Isabel is going to help us out until your mama is stronger and the new
baby is born." He looked at me in a desperate way. He had
pale-blue eyes, and for a moment, they seemed to go one
shade lighter. "Dora is the only one of us who didn't get
sick. She is a strong 'un. But of course, she's just five, so she
couldn't really do much, maybe fetch something if we
needed it. I am so thankful you're here."

Molly and Samuel got married when they were both sixteen, just before Mama left. At first, they lived in a little house on Samuel's daddy's property. They helped his daddy farm for a couple of years, but after Molly started having children, Samuel took a job at the sawmill in Devonia, and they moved over there.

Molly looked like Mama and had her same single thick braid and her outgoing way. She had brown skin, which looked warm, and it was warm when you touched her hands. "Come in here. I just made oatmeal cookies. I had a feeling you'd be by," she'd say and put her arm around your shoulder. She wanted everyone to have just what he or she needed. She would do anything for a person. She seemed a lot older than she was, the way she organized their lives.

I say she managed everything, but she could not do a lot with Dora. No one could, to tell the truth. Not at all like Sallie, blonde and dimpled, everybody's darling.

Samuel, calm as still water, called Dora their "dark child" because of her black curls, but the label seemed to apply to her personality as well. They could not figure out her bossiness, her way of demanding that she be given this doll or that pair of shoes she had seen in the store. Since she was so tiny and sturdy, it seemed cute, and she had a vocabulary that made people exchange glances and drop their jaws.

"What a gorgeous waning moon," she'd comment, looking out of her bedroom window at night. "I love filigree lace," she'd say, touching a visitor's cuff.

Molly said, "The nearest I can figure, Dora is a cross between Daddy and that uppity aunt of Samuel's who married money. You know, the one who went off to Asheville with her fine husband and a little pug dog named Alexander."

When I went to Molly's, I shared Dora and Sallie's room. They had me a cot set up. Sallie was sweet as pie, always climbed in bed with me to cuddle, but not Dora. She made it very clear I was an outsider and stayed away.

We were all around the dinner table one night when Dora suddenly pinned her gaze on me. Molly was still so frail; it was all she could do to sit up and eat with us. She felt so bad, she had not braided her hair all day, and it fell in lank ropes past her shoulders. I served the food, then got the extra chair from the desk in the parlor for myself, the way I had been doing.

Dora followed me with her eyes as I carried it over. "When the new baby gets here, you will be going home," she said flatly. "There won't be any room for you."

Samuel wrinkled his brow. "Dora, apologize." He turned to Molly with his mouth open.

"Dora, that is very impolite." In her illness, Molly's voice was mild; her chastisement carried the weight of a feather. "Aunt Isabel is here to help us."

"Aunt Isabel can sit in my chair wif me," said Sallie.

"Thank you, honey." I squeezed her plump little arm across the table. "But Dora is right. I will be going back to Grampa's house soon after the new baby gets here."

"I think that will be best," Dora said. She stuck her fork in a piece of meat. I didn't know why she didn't like me; maybe it was just that I wasn't intimidated by her, the brat. I saw through her from day one. I would have taken her down a peg or two early on, but at the time, it was not my place. I just looked at Samuel and Molly.

"Certainly wouldn't want to overstay my welcome," I said.

They both stared down at their plates.

"This is very good chicken," Samuel said.

"Thank you."

Molly pushed her own plate away, put one hand to the side of her belly, and considered.

"Ooh, that was a big one, that kick," she said. She looked at me. "Let me take a few bites, then I'll help with the dishes before I lie down again."

"No, don't. I've got everything. It's not much."

Dora swallowed a bite, studying us all the while. She was by far the healthiest person in the room.

Now tell me this: Who gets chills down their spine from a five-year-old?

Nine

Molly's Family

1918–1920

*I*t did not happen the way that Dora had hoped it would. It did not happen the way anyone thought. In the end, I was very much needed, and they made room for me.

The baby was a big one, Granny Wilburn declared. She had arrived when Molly's pains started.

"It's coming feet first. I'm going to try to turn it. But Avery, fetch me an axe. I want to put it under the bed to cut the pain."

My brother had come to help Samuel with some light chores, so he was there when Molly's labor started. He was back in an instant, his face white.

"This is nonsense," he said, as he handed the tool over to Granny. "I'm going for the damn doctor." He headed to saddle a horse.

By the time they returned, Molly had been in labor for more than six hours. The doctor felt the situation with both hands, looked at my sister going in and out of consciousness, and then put a chloroform rag over Molly's nose.

I had stood with her through most of the labor. She nearly broke the bones of my hand squeezing, but once the anesthesia hit her, her grip went limp.

"Leave the room, Isabel," the doctor said. "Granny's going to help me." I saw him unroll a felt package of scalpels and knives.

I tried to drink a cup of tea while they did it. The procedure didn't take long. The doctor brought a baby boy out and put him in my arms, his weight like a small sack of damp sand.

"He was definitely in the britches position," the doctor said. "Really almost sideways. She never could have done it, weak as she is." He went right back. Through the open door I could smell the birth. Blood odor hung thick as butchery in the air. The doctor sewed Molly back up, but it was no use.

"The baby's all right?" were her first difficult words when she woke up again.

"Yes, darling, it's a beautiful boy. A son. Thank you." Samuel leaned over her, limp with emotion and worry. "Honey, what shall we name him?"

She said in a whisper, "Dip in the Bible." He went and got the family book, opened it at random, and pointed at random.

"It's the book of Jeremiah," said Samuel.

"That's perfect," Molly breathed. "Jeremiah is a fine name."

We got him a wet nurse and he was healthy, but Molly only lasted three days. The doctor said it was childbed fever, and she was too exhausted to fight it. Spanish influenza plus a hard labor that ended in a cesarean section was just too much.

We didn't know it at that moment, but the fact was, I had come to stay at Molly's for good. After the funeral, Sam spoke to Daddy.

"Mr. King, if you could see your way clear to letting Isabel be with us for a while, it would sure be a blessing." His eyes were bleary and red, and it was hard for him to speak. The family stood in a little cluster by a cross of white carnations on a wire stand. We all waited while the last dirt was shoveled in. It was a bone-chilling day with a light drizzle, not good for any of us, but I set my jaw and narrowed my eyes. I thought to God, *Go ahead with your weather; raw is exactly how I feel anyway.* I did not cry, not then.

Sam had picked up Dora, and she clung to him, her face buried in his neck. He pulled out his handkerchief and blew his nose. The wet nurse Granny Wilburn had brought in stood nearby with the infant, Jeremiah, bundled in her arms, while I held Sallie close against me and shushed her weeping. Anyone could see how things were falling apart, but my daddy, selfish as he was, hesitated.

I spoke up, my pain and the cold wind in my soul helping me. "Daddy," I said, "Sam and those children need me more than three grown men do. Now, if you want to hire a woman to take care of your grandchildren so I can stay with you, that will be just fine, but until you do, you better learn how to scramble eggs and wash shirts." I did not care how I spoke to him. I felt myself nearly a woman, and if I was to be told that keeping house was my job, Daddy better not be surprised that I was damn well going to claim ownership of that domain.

Thoughts of Gallatin came into my head. I imagined he would be proud of me for the way I had just spoken.

"If you're not going to leave," he might say, "at least stay on your own terms. Don't let people push you around."

"For God sakes, Daddy, Molly's dead!" In the silence, Avery spoke, and there was a deep groove between his brows. He lifted one foot and stepped forward toward our daddy. It was a small move, and he was still weak from his own ordeal with influenza, but it was the most intense thing we ever saw or heard.

Daddy paled as if he had received a threat from Lazarus himself.

"You. Let. Isabel. Go." Avery's words were precise as the mark of a knife, and I saw my daddy flinch slightly behind his eyes.

"We'll make do," Walker affirmed, looking at Avery in surprise. Simultaneously, Sam and I gave my brothers a nod of gratitude. My daddy slapped his hat against his leg, outnumbered.

"Go on, then," he said to me and stalked away.

It started out I was just Aunt Isabel helping out with the little girls while Samuel worked. Jeremiah came back to us when he was eight months old and was weaned onto a bottle of cow's milk. Despite missing Molly, I was strangely happy, for a change. I had never been to many places except church, or once to visit Queenie in Knoxville before she graduated. She was now going to a teacher's college in North Carolina.

I left Daddy and the boys to a bachelor life, with no regrets. I showed them where I kept the flour and wrote out directions for making and baking cornbread. For a year after I moved, Daddy made Walker bring me their shirts to boil and starch. And of course, I did it. Resentment encouraged the chatter in my head, one voice saying, "Do your Christian duty for your family," and the other saying, "You know who you really are, Isabel. You are not a laundress." The angel and the devil sitting each on a shoulder, like in the funny papers.

For a good while, Samuel and the children and I moved through our sorrow over Molly. She was so young and with so much life left to have, it was like a blow to the back of the neck. In all kinds of simple situations, we'd see her everywhere we looked. A shirt she was making for Samuel with only one sleeve set in. All the summer beans and tomatoes canned up in the cellar with writing on the labels in her fancy, swirling style.

A letter from an old childhood friend came for her about a month after she died. That tore me up. Where was she? I should put that envelope in her hand.

"It's for your mama," I said to Dora, who had found me holding it, my hands shaking. How I missed my sister.

"So it's not for you," she said. "Give it here." Her little mouth pursed into a knot. She snatched it and gave it to Sam. He went and sat in the rocking chair and read it, rubbing the paper slowly between his fingers. The raspy noise got me so agitated, I had to leave the room. It was like he was thinking about an old lover, and of course, he was.

My own sister. My own sister's husband. Such an odd mixture of sorrow and jealousy it brought out in me. That was the first time I recognized I had feelings for him, but I pushed them down. For a while, I pushed them down.

And the children—Sallie would stare at the stove fire and twist her hair around her finger. It reminded me of Molly, as that had been a habit of hers. The sweet girl cried easily, and I cuddled her, distracted her with little games and toys, with cookies. And Jeremiah, the baby, looked just like his mother around the eyes when he laughed. He was a tonic for all of us.

Dora was a bitter pill, but I admitted she had a right to be. I didn't blame her that much—the cold wind was blowing through her little soul. I knew from my own loss of a mother how hard it was not to scapegoat my pain. But she could have been a little nicer, even for a child, I thought. I had welcomed anyone who was soft with me after my mama died.

All of us would have tears start up unexpected. Samuel and me passed in the hallway with our eyes down; he barely said thank you for his meals.

For the longest time, I didn't really fit in. I was just a pair of busy hands rattling around in the empty space left by Molly's passing. Each of us in our own way lived out that long first winter of grief. We forced ourselves through the routines. We kept the life machine going. Food, laundry, the wood to the stove, Samuel leaving for his job at the mill every day.

I did motherly things, but I wasn't a mother. I smacked my nieces' bottoms, hugged them, and listened to their prayers. And our gray hearts beat stiff and slow till time came around and we saw we could be happy again.

Ten

Flowers

1920

It was April, and Jeremiah came toddling in from the yard with a couple of Queen Anne's lace he had found. He had on a little white dress like all babies wore, and he wrapped himself around my leg. His snotty upper lip was smeared with dirt.

"Pity fowers," he said and gave them to me.

Samuel was at the table eating a leftover ham biscuit, and he spoke up like his feelings were hurt. His cheek was full of food.

"Well, why didn't you bring me any? Don't you think Daddy would like some pretty flowers too?" He looked at me with the joke in his eye.

And Jeremiah, all serious, looked back and forth between us and shrugged his little arms. "Don't got," he said. "Fowers all gone."

He took me by the hand and led me over to Samuel so I could give him a Queen Anne's lace. Sam took it and smelled it like it was good, though of course Queen Anne's lace doesn't smell like anything except the grass. But it was pleasing the baby. My eyes met Samuel's.

"Isabel." He smiled at me. "What are we going to do about this?"

I said, "I guess I will get a glass of water for the flower."

"That's not what I mean, and you know it." He reached for my hand, and I felt desire rise and fall in me so hard, I could barely stand up straight.

"Should we make it formal?" he said. He circled his thumb round and round on the back of my hand. It moved me so much, I sat there dumbstruck, wanting him to move his touch farther up my arm. I had begun to feel Molly's ghost lift up and spread peaceful away. The rooms of the house had opened up, and I didn't have to try and fit into her space anymore.

"Yes, let's do," I replied. I turned his hand over and pressed my lips to the palm. And without more words or gestures than that, we knew we would marry.

Samuel and I were real good friends. Everything was ready for me—from the kitchen table with spots worn smooth from people's elbows, to the three children, to the bed.

I did not take that bed, believe me, until the time came. Two and a half years later, I married my brother-in-law. Just like in the Bible, where a woman dies and the man accepts the next sister as his wife. But I don't think it was just for practicality's sake. We loved each other.

The preacher met us at the church one Saturday afternoon. Walker was to be best man for Sam, and Queenie, back from college for the occasion, stood up for me. Jeremiah would not quit running around, so I picked him up and bounced him in my arms.

"I do," I said and smiled at my new husband. I was half-distracted by a toddler pulling off my earbobs. It was rare that I wore jewelry, and the sparkle of the garnets attracted the little ones.

To tell the truth, they hurt my ears. I removed them and gave them to Queenie to entertain Sallie as soon as the preacher said, "I now pronounce you man and wife."

After the ceremony, we all ate the red velvet cake Nancy had brought, and then Sam and I had a portrait made. Nancy and her husband, Tate, had a new camera, so Tate took us out under the trees and set us up in straight-back chairs like dolls. Two people never looked so ridiculous. Sam wore a tall, stiff collar that choked him and made his eyes bulge out. He said it was more he was in shock, not believing he had entered matrimony again. He never could smile for a photographer anyway, he added, because his teeth were so bad. I begged to differ—he had nice teeth; they were just a little crooked was all.

I had agonized about my own appearance, meanwhile. "No need to look so scared," said Queenie. "You act like you just asked somebody to save your life and are hanging on for the answer."

"Stop laughing at me!" I tried to compose my face.

"And what happened to your hair?" Queenie continued. "It's a standing-up mess. It wasn't like that when I fixed it before the ceremony. It's lying down right on one side and curling up wrong on the other."

"Thanks a lot," I said. "It's this wind out here. And maybe, just maybe, I have a couple of other things on my mind!"

My dress was nice, though. It showed my neck and had an extra-wide piece of lace falling past my shoulders. Right as Tate, looking down into the camera eye, said, "Look happy now; you just got married," Dora came over and lolled on Sam's lap.

"Come on, honey; let's stand over here and watch," said Queenie. She took Dora's hand. The child gave me a temperamental look.

"That's my daddy," she said and stepped on my foot as she was led away. There was a devil in that child.

When we finally came home, Samuel said, "It's all yours," spreading his arm out to show the kitchen and the parlor and the porch and the bedroom and the privy like it was a palace. He reached to lift me over the threshold.

"No, you don't!" Suddenly, I resisted and stood there in my marriage clothes. I looked at him. "What do you think?" I asked. "Is this a new place, something I haven't seen before?"

For a second, it seemed Molly's ghost came forward from the wall and stood there. I saw her like she was made of water. Her high forehead and thick braid. All her features like white shadows painted on fog. And through her, I could see Sam's new-shaved chin, some flakes of starch on his collar. I could smell her, I swear. But then she smiled and melted back, leaving Sam standing with his wrists hanging out of his sleeves.

"Oh, all *right*," I said and let him. I let him pick me up and carry me in. The house was quiet with the children gone, and there was a bouquet of red clover, daisies, and black-eyed Susans in a vase by the bed that Queenie left for us, along with a heart-shaped tin of chocolates. She had taken all the kids to Nancy's for the weekend. So we sat down on the coverlet, fed each other candies, and did many simple and pleasant things that were just for the two of us to know about. And so, we had our little honeymoon.

Eleven

Janeyre

1924

The three children were certainly enough for us, but expecting things to happen the way they do, we were prepared for more babies to come along. But I did not have my daughter until we had been married a while.

I had a couple of miscarriages. I got my hopes up both times and was depressed after the losses. So the third time, I stayed very calm and did not dare to look at any baby clothes or dust off the cradle and make plans.

When she finally came, I named her Janeyre after my favorite heroine. Many things in Charlotte Brontë's story had echoes I recognized: a second wife, a poor girl struggling to find her place, helpful teachers. But mostly the narrative had brought me confirmation that, though many things might go wrong in life, there is happiness in the end, and so it had proved to be for us with our daughter's birth.

Sam did not know the book. I wrote the name on a piece of paper and handed it to him, and he pronounced it

"Jane E-ray, Janey Ray," which endeared him to me all the more.

The thing that surprised Sam and me the most was how the other kids took to the baby once she arrived. Sallie and Dora were absolute little mothers—they loved to carry Janey around, dress her up, talk to her, and make her their living doll.

Even Jeremiah kept an eye on her. "I think she's ready to be fed. Get her to stop that caterwauling," he'd complain. But then he'd stand at her crib and smile down. He let the baby hold his finger, and she would get quiet and clutch his finger. Jeremiah started to believe they had a connection, and once she began to laugh for him, he was lovestruck.

It wasn't long, though, before I saw that Dora was going to claim Janey for her own. It was midsummer. Sam was working at the sawmill like always, and the kids did not go back to school until late August. Janey was about six months old then. I saw Sallie sitting on the porch swing, holding an old doll by one arm and smacking it up and down in a rhythm with her thoughts. It had been around since before I came to live with them; the pink painted skin was scabbed off in places, and a chunk of the fingers on one hand was gone. Still, it was the only doll they had, and I did not know why Sallie was being so mean to it.

"Why, honey, you are getting the dolly all tore up and dirty. Let's take her and—" I looked around. "Where's Dora got to with Janey?"

Sallie twisted her hair and threw the doll against the porch floor. It was not like her to be petulant. "Dora hogs the baby. She barely lets me pet her, much less have my turn to keep her. I'm almost eleven years old—too big for this old thing! I want to take care of a real baby. How come she gets to rock her to sleep every time?"

"Well, you can do it next time," I said. I didn't know where they had got to, but Dora had proven to be an attentive babysitter. I could see she loved Janey, and I trusted her to watch her. I had so much work to do, I was actually glad to have her.

I put my arm around Sallie; she was such a tender heart, really, and we were always close. "I remember when you wasn't much more than a baby yourself. And now you are so big and can be helpful in so many ways, not just watching Janey. Anybody can hold a baby. Strong as you are, how about you helping me lift the rugs out to the porch rail so we can beat 'em? Then we'll set awhile and have milk and oatmeal cookies." I pulled her into my side and kissed her on her temple.

We finished our snack and brought the rugs back in. While we moved the furniture back on top, I started to think about Samuel coming home from the mill and Jeremiah coming home from fishing. I'd have to get dinner ready soon. As we paused, I felt the tingle of my milk letting down, and now I really did want to know—where were Dora and Janey?

"Sallie, honey, please chop this corn off the cobs for me. Set right here at the table and wait. First, we'll put this newspaper underneath. I am going to find your sisters. Now, be real careful with that paring knife." I had waited rather long to feed Janey. Now that I had turned my mind to finding Dora and the baby, I could think of little else.

I went down the back steps and called, "Dora? Dora! Come back in now, honey!" Some birds twittered and a dog barked down at a neighbor's, but that is all I heard. My heart started to race, and wet circles appeared quick as magic on the front of my dress.

Dora was nowhere in sight—not out by the gate where

they often sat; the baby carriage stood empty in the yard. I walked down the lane a bit toward town and met Jeremiah coming up with a pole and his wicker creel. He opened the lid. "Looky, Aunt Isabel, I caught four fish. Pretty good size. What are you doing out here?" He noticed the rings on my clothing; he knew what they were.

"Jeremiah, have you seen Dora? She's been gone awhile, and she's got Janey with her."

I saw his head tick a little and his mouth clamp down. He was only seven years old and did not know how to lie to me yet. I knelt down and took him by his shoulders. "I need to know, honey. Dora should not have taken the baby away this long and without telling me. I need to feed her now."

"Well, I didn't see 'em, but Dora has a little place she made down in the shady grove. I'm not supposed to tell anybody. She's gonna kill me."

"You just take me there, now, and we'll see who is going to kill who. Now, mind me, let's go."

He turned and ran down the road, his pole marking a line in the dust as he went. I ran too, holding up my heavy, leaking breasts with the backs of my fists. He dropped his fishing gear at the edge of a ditch and jumped over into our neighbor's field. There was a little string of woods that sat on the property line, and I saw a faint trail beaten into the grass. I followed the boy as he ducked into the trees and then cut aside, deeper into the foliage. Through the branches, I saw the back of Dora's head. She was sitting in a little bower of rhododendrons in a ragged ladder-back chair she had scavenged from somewhere.

I caught up to Jeremiah. "Honey, all right." I was breathing hard and was crazy to feed Janey; it hurt now. "Thank you for bringing me here. You go on home now and tell Sallie we'll be there in a few minutes."

I gave him a hug. He smelled of fish and dirt and sunshine. "Go on, now. It's okay."

I didn't want to scare Dora, so I made a big rustle with my feet. She heard me and turned, dropping something she had in her lap. I saw it was an old Sears catalog.

"I was just fixin' to come back," she said, rubbing her face. She stuffed the catalog in a hollow at the base of a tree.

"What in the world, Dora, are you doing out here? You scared me to death, going off with Janey like that!" I saw the baby lying on a blanket at Dora's feet; she was asleep. I got down on my knees, unbuttoning my dress.

"Sweetheart, here I am," I whispered and lifted her to me. She jerked awake, recognized me, and began a heart-breaking wail, as if I had suddenly appeared after a long desertion, which I guess I had. I put her in the crook of my arm, and she latched on desperately, closed her eyes back, and sighed deeply.

Dora leaned to pick up the blanket and shake it out, and I saw a trickle of blood run down her leg. There was a stain on the back of her dress.

"Why, Dora, your time has come round. Are you all right? We need to get both of you home. You ought not to have taken Janey so far from the house."

Janey was taking my milk in great gulping drafts. I switched her to the other side and looked around the little clearing. Besides the chair and the Sears catalog, I saw that a stump had been rolled in and covered with a piece of lace curtain. An old canning jar with honeysuckle in it sat on top.

"Dora, what is this place?"

"It's just my place, my pretty place." She looked at Janey nursing. "Janey is such a pretty baby, and she is so good, I thought it would be nice to bring her here with me."

"Well, you better not do this again. I didn't know where you were, and I was worried to death."

"Okay, fine. I won't." She clenched the muscle in her jaw. "I thought I could have some place of my own, where I could make things the way I wanted, but of course you would ruin it; it's all ruined now. Don't you think I know how pitiful this is?" She flung her arms up to indicate her bower. "I can't wait until I can have something real, something better than this. This shadow of a room." She spun toward the path. "I'm going home."

"Dora, wait. I don't want you to think I'm angry. And I don't want you to think I don't trust you with Janey. I appreciate how much you help me with her." I stopped. Blood was still running down Dora's leg. "Honey, get that catalog and tear out a page; wipe up if you can."

She grabbed it and ripped out a couple of pages and stuffed them down the front of her bloomers. She rustled when she took a step; you could not help but notice it came from her crotch.

I stood up. "You know, you will be a really good mother, when the time comes. I wish you had known your own mother more, but we are all doing the best we can."

"I won't. I won't be a mother. Don't ask me how I know. I don't even know why, why *this* happens to me!" Dora put her hands against her lower abdomen and then flicked them wide, a gesture of dismissal. "Janey is probably the only baby I'll ever have."

"That's not true," I tried to say, but Dora headed out to the open field and the road. There was a car coming down in a rumble of gravel and dust, and I saw it was Sam and the other men on their way home from the mill.

"Dora, wait . . ." I wanted to urge her to stay back, as

blood spots were visible on her clothes, and I knew pictures out of the catalog wouldn't stanch her flow for long. But Dora hallooed and ran forward to greet them. They slowed, so she tripped alongside for a few steps, waving. The car stopped, and I saw Sam's hand come out the window to touch Dora. And from within the vehicle, other voices.

"Why, Sam, your girl's all growed up. Now, ain't you getting pretty?"

And Dora, dark and brooding just moments before, stood smiling and basking in the praise as if it were her natural right. I hefted Janey and struggled after, buttoning my dress together. None of them, not even Sam, noticed me as I crossed the ditch.

Twelve

Samuel

1928

The first I suspected something was wrong with Sam was when I found he had not gone in to work and had hidden the fact from me. I did know that he was feeling under the weather, as he had begun to have a rasp in his chest and had been trying to lay off cigarettes to keep from coughing. The work he did at the Clinch Forest Millworks was the main cause of it, of course.

He had started working there after he married Molly, at first part-time while he was still in the fields with his father. But as time went on, the mill boss saw he was reliable and good at learning any new thing, so they asked him to come on full-time. And it was worth it: steady pay—compared to farming, which kept you in food well enough but got you cash only a few times a year. Of course, raising crops was hit-and-miss.

Over time, Sam did every mill job there was. Some-times, he was in the woods as a donkey puncher. It sounds coarse, but a donkey is a machine with a winch; it's basically a log hauler that pulls cut trees out of the woods, like a horse team used to do. A puncher is the man who operates the machine. Other times, he was in the mill itself, running one of the big saws or overseeing parts of the floor operation.

As Sam came from farming people, he liked being outside, but running the steam donkey kept him out in all sorts of weather. And the hours got long. Sometimes, Sam would be way over in Morristown, as the donkey was also used to power the cherry picker, which picked up the logs and put them on a rail car. Clinch Forest was a small company—they sent a good bit of lumber north to a paper plant in Berlin, New Hampshire, for processing. But they did everything that could be done to a log. They sold framing timbers and floor planks and did special treatments for a fine-furniture company over in Johnson City.

Sam was about six feet two and strong but of a slight, rather lanky build. He was stubborn too, and if he got a bad cold, he would not stay home. Off he would go, and he would be assigned to work inside. They thought they were doing him a favor, keeping him from the elements. However, inside the mill, every breath was sawdust and heat, and he stayed to get overtime pay, so it just made things worse. The noise from the machines was already causing his hearing to go bad, but we did not give that much thought—as long as he was in a good frame of mind and able to get up and go to work, we thought all was well.

He had had a couple of winters with bad lungs. He always recovered, but along about the time Janey was six, he started sitting on the porch weekends, carving small toys and figurines out of leftover bits of wood he brought home in his pockets. At first, it was just a little bird to amuse Sallie or a slingshot frame for Jeremiah. I was pleased to see him occupied in this way. I thought it was a quieter task that allowed him to sit resting and was glad he was saving his energy for the mill.

We collaborated once on a doll for Janey—it was his idea. He carved arms and legs and a head and shoulders. I painted on hair and a face, then made a cloth body and put the thing together and dressed it. But I finally realized he was making toys, one after another, like his life depended on it. He was spending all his spare time on them, and he had so many different wooden animals lining the window-sills, I said, "Sam, what in the world do you think the kids are going to do, start a zoo?"

And he had started doing figures of people by then too.

"Well, I thought I would sell some of them. The cook out at the logging camp has been talking of going over to Asheville to see can he get on at the Grove Park Inn. He is tired of the rough life in the field and wants to apply to serve his best green bean casserole to the uppity-ups in their nice, warm dining room. We thought we'd thumb a ride over there together. There is a shop there that sells all this kind of carving and other handiwork, so I thought I would take a bunch and see what they thought of them." He shaved a bit on a black bear that was emerging out his wood block, then held it at arm's length and looked at it.

"Of course, I had to tell a white lie, as my boss would never see his way clear to letting me off a day, not to go showin' off some play pretties I'd made. So, don't let on to anyone where we've gone. I told him I had to attend a funeral."

I made an extra-big lunch and waved him down the road a couple of days later.

When he came back, I asked him, "Well, what did they think? Your work is good; I know that."

He could not look me in the eye, and I thought it was because he was embarrassed that he had not sold anything.

"Well, to tell the truth, it was quite a funeral," he joked, alluding to his little lie. "They liked 'em well enough, but they told me they already had a couple of fellers who did carvings for 'em regular and they didn't need any more. So I just put 'em in a corner out in the shed for now. I'll figure out what to do with 'em later."

"I'm sorry," I said and went behind him and leaned over the chair where he sat. I put my arms around his neck.

That night, as he prepared for bed, he went into a big coughing fit and put his hand over his chest as he tried to breathe.

"Here," I said. I brought him a clean handkerchief and wet a washrag to wipe his face and neck, like he was a little boy.

"Must be all that dust from the trip," he said.

"Probably. You lie down, and I'll bring you some water."

Later, as we lay in bed, he struggled to be still and quiet. "Sawing logs even at home, ain't I?" he quipped.

"I'll make some honey drops tomorrow," I said. "That will soothe that cough. Now, why don't you turn on your side and cuddle me up." I spooned back into him and held his hand as he wrapped me.

"Isabel," he whispered.

"What is it?"

"Don't never feel like you were, or are, second best. Please don't."

I widened my eyes. All the familiar objects—the bureau, the chair, the window ledge—were cloaked shapes, like rocks in the darkness. The idea had never occurred to me that I was no more than a substitute for Molly, but now that he said it, it seemed like something that should have crossed my mind. I kept the silence for another moment, then squeezed his hand. There was a clamping pain across my heart, but it was all right.

I said, "I won't. I don't."

"Good," he breathed and released to sleep.

He worked on at the mill for another year before he got too sick to go. His dying took about three months. He was only forty-two years old, but he had worked in sawdust for twenty years by then. His chest got thinner and thinner, and his cheeks fell in. I made him big pots of soup with chicken broth and potatoes.

Sometimes, Dora or Sallie would go in and sit up with him and feed him two or three bites with the big silver spoon. Then he would shake his head: *No, no more.* Sallie, when she stayed with him, would eat the remainder of the bowl and tell him about her day. Dora never would. She would climb up on the bed and lie by him, stroking his arm.

"Breathe like this, Daddy," she'd say. Like she wanted to teach him proper lung mechanics, like she was trying to regulate the in and out for him. Sometimes, she would read to him from the society page of the Knoxville paper or a section of the Bible.

One night close to the end, he caught my hand and said, "There's a lawyer in town." He gave me his name and told me to go to him as soon as things were over.

"Clinch Forest won't pay you a thing," he whispered.

"Now, don't go worrying yourself," I told him. "You just stop that kind of talk." Though the truth was, I was very worried.

"Just go, like I told you," he insisted. And that is how I found out about the insurance policy. It was dated about the time he had made his trip to sell his carvings, which were not in the shed and not anywhere I looked. I saw that Sam must have sold all his little figures to buy the insurance, then forced himself to work that last year so the policy would take effect. It was for $10,000, and I was the beneficiary.

I put it all in a savings account, and because of it, we were able to live comfortably for a few years after he died.

Thirteen

John L.

1934

*Y*ou might be thinking, *It's hard to keep the names and times straight of all her deaths.* You might think, *Nobody can have all this tragedy.* Well, lots of people do. Though I admit, it's a trick to harden yourself enough to stay together yet keep soft enough to feel the press of love that remains. A heart can be eaten up so fast if you let it.

It only takes a minute to read a gravestone, and I didn't let myself think below the ground. I wanted to keep to the grass and trees and sky above. Let dirt do its work. Like when you plant: The main thing is, remember, something will grow out of the barren, out of the black. Seedlings are in there; they will show after a blind and cold time. They come up green and thin, looking for all the world like somebody reaching with fragile, curling arms.

In his books, Charles Dickens would say something about the intervening years, how Pip or Oliver or David lived quite happily.

So I will tell you, my intervening years before Sam died were good ones. Not without challenges, not without sorrow, but the things that happened did not seem too different from what was occurring in the lives of my friends and neighbors.

After a while, I got comfortable at Molly's. I already knew the physical premises down to a nail, but it wasn't my house. To make things more my own, I rearranged the cupboards and got new sheets, but there never was a stick of furniture or a dish in that house I picked out myself. Finally, I decided that I just wasn't going to mind about it. This was where I was; I was living here, so what difference did it make that it wasn't originally mine?

And the children. The only one I gave birth to was Jane, but I valued and claimed them all. But then we lost Samuel. Everything level slowly slid to one side and then off the map.

Sallie ran off with some boy none of us knew. She turned sixteen, and it was like ripe fruit dropping off the tree. It hurt me some, as we got along so well, but maybe I was a little jealous too. I sure couldn't up and go somewhere. I think he was a drummer passing through, and she got infatuated.

She came to our family reunion years later, divorced and saying she had two kids and worked in Akron at the company cafeteria of Goodyear Tires. She had converted to a Catholic too. I had read that Catholics don't divorce, but I didn't want to get into that. After all, we were happy to see her. She was as sweet as ever and seemed happy to see us. After that one visit, though, she never came back. We wrote, but she had moved and the letters got returned. Finally, it was like she died too, but we didn't have a grave.

At the time, her leaving was a relief, in a way. One less

mouth to worry about feeding, and you tell yourself, *Well, it is time for her to have a life of her own; there is not much future here.* It sounds callous, but when you are as used to death as I was, the disappearance of a teenage girl is not so much. And she had done it on her own; nobody made her.

Soon after Sallie's departure, Dora moved to Knoxville and clerked at a store to put herself through secretarial school. She got close to her boss, J.C. He divorced his wife and married Dora. They went to a justice of the peace; none of the family was invited to attend.

We heard J.C.'s ex-wife went off to Chattanooga to live with her and J.C.'s son. Everybody pretended that J.C.'s first wife had gotten sick and died in a sanatorium and that Dora had come along and helped the man out of his grief.

It was strange how Dora's story and mine (that is, my story of how I came to marry Samuel) were parallel in people's minds; only, my story was true and hers wasn't. But now, even Dora and J.C. half believed it, the way people do with a lie that gets started and no one objects to.

Dora was pretty—her hair framed her face in soft ringlets she renewed nightly with bobby-pin curls. She had chocolate eyes and honey skin. She rubbed just a touch of rouge on her cheeks. She was large chested—a head turner, but not a hussy or a vamp, the sort of woman who stole men away from other women. Poor little mousy J.C. He probably had been hoping she *was* a hussy, as it was the kind of thing he might have always dreamed about. However, hussiness requires effort; there is personal upkeep and performance required, and that was not Dora's game. She was just your basic conniver; she wanted to make sure she would always have money and would never have to turn her hand to the drudgery of farm life. A house with sidewalks and nice rugs and no children is what she wanted. J.C. took care of the first two things, and Dora took care of the last thing. It was no surprise that, once Dora got the man, she turned from a country girl into the most proper lady you could ever imagine. Walker and Avery and I looked askance about these developments at the time, but I will have to say, Dora pulled herself up in the world and has done the best of any of us.

Meanwhile, I budgeted hard on the money from the insurance policy and managed to keep the house for a few more years. It was family property, paid off by Samuel's father, and it had been deeded to Sam, so I didn't pay rent. But Tennessee decided to put through a new highway, and they told me I had to sell it whether I wanted to or not, so Jeremiah and Janey and I moved to Knoxville to a little rent place with only half our furniture.

It was strange; even though it was rented, I felt like the house was mine. I felt that and then laughed at the way I deluded myself. I never met the landlord, but as long as we paid his collector on time, we didn't hear from or see him.

Daddy and the boys did not help us much. I am sure Walker and Avery wanted to, but Daddy did not allow it. Walker came to see us a couple of times; he brought us two chickens once and built a coop in the backyard. You can't starve if you have eggs.

It was all right, but it was not enough. I remember thinking, *Too bad turnabout's not fair play.* When Mama left, and when Molly died, I stepped in both times. When a man needs a new woman, a new wife, he looks right away for a replacement. But it can't work the other way around, with women doing the asking.

I started working in a laundry. It was the beginning of the Depression and the worst possible time to be a single mother looking for a job. The laundry was not my first choice. I had tried to get a job in the library, but I had no diploma, not even for eighth grade. It did not matter that I could read as well as anyone or discuss literature with a college professor. This was something I came to understand later in life, with a good deal of bitterness: the importance of documents that provide an entitlement or a so-called proof of something. Truth is not as important as pieces of paper sometimes.

Anyway, at the library, they let me fill out an application, which I did, sitting at the reference table wearing stockings and my best hat. When I went to the counter to turn in the paper, I knew, just looking at the woman's face, I did not have a snowball's chance in hell of getting the job.

"We have had many applicants," she said, looking across the room and rapping her pencil at two young boys talking behind some shelves. "I see you have not completed junior high? You can imagine that we need someone with a certain education level here."

"I can read anything you put before me," I said. "I am a very reliable worker, and I do know the Dewey Decimal System." I gave her a couple of sentences about my homeschooling and how I had stepped into my mama's role while still a child.

I suppose I said too much. She started shifting around the stapler and the book stamp on the counter. She picked up a magnifying glass and twirled it before putting it in a container of pencils. She glanced down at my application, folded it in half, and held it.

"We will call you if you need to come in for an additional interview." She adjusted her rimless glasses.

"We do not have a phone," I said. "I can check back with you."

The woman pursed her mouth, and it was like I could

hear her thinking, *Well, of course a type of person like you wouldn't have a phone.* But instead, she said, "That will be fine. Thank you for coming in."

The library was sort of tainted for me after that. I told myself, "You know who you are; don't let 'a type of person like her' convince you otherwise," and then I went and applied for a job at a clothing store.

This time, I did not even have to fill out an application; they just took one look at my outfit: my suit jacket, brushed clean but going soft in the elbows; my brown shoes, polished but worn on the sides; my little hat, a couple of years out of style and needing a new feather.

The manager of the store was a man, and the two other employees were young women just out of high school. They slid their eyes at each other and folded their arms under their cute little bosoms. I figured I could learn to fit in anywhere, but again, people have to let you fit in.

The manager kept looking at my hands, and so I looked at my hands, which were wrinkled and reddened, with plain, unpolished nails.

Maybe if I had come in wearing gloves, the outcome would have been different, but the work I had done in life was stamped on me. I wrote to Queenie. She was married to a lawyer in Asheville; I knew they were well off.

"If you can find a way to move here, I know we can get you work," she replied. "I have lots of friends who would take a good housekeeper like you."

The distance now between Queenie's life and mine desolated me almost more than anything, but I thought about taking her offer. When you need money and you have a chance to make some, you think about it. Really, though, I did not want to take Jeremiah and Jane out of school again. They had been going to the little school in Devonia and had made the transition to Knoxville City Schools, and their education was progressing. They had friends. Dora and J.C. were nearby, and Wheat, where Walker and Avery lived, was not that far.

So I clung on and took the job at the laundry. All the women employed there were just like me, only they hadn't any learning to speak of. My few years of formal school hardly set me apart from them. To the outside world, this is where I fit, but I felt my mind shrink like a drop of water on a hot skillet in this society. Movie stars and neighborhood gossip is what the other women wanted to talk about. I was reading *The Good Earth* by Pearl S. Buck and the poems of Emily Dickinson. I discussed these with no one.

It was always hot where I worked, even in winter. On the one hand, it was desirable, because a body wants to be warm. At home, it was cold as a slab of granite, unless I burned the stove, which I did for a while at night to cook our dinner or if we wanted to heat water to bathe. The laundry kept me thin; you never want to eat when you sweat like that. It would be December. I'd come out from the shop into the icy night, and the sweat would freeze on my face so I couldn't smile. My breath in the air reminded me of a cloud of starch. Sometimes, I thought, *This is a woman's sawmill, only I eat white dust while the men inhale yellow, the ground powder of the hearts of trees.* My heart broke if I thought too much about Samuel.

I used to take Janey to school, then go to work. J.C. or Dora picked her up from school, kept her at the store, then put her on the cross-town trolley at five thirty. By then, I would be home, or Jeremiah would be. He had started working for J.C., stocking the store and doing deliveries. It was helpful; he would bring us small necessities, like soap or oatmeal, and sometimes luxuries, like a box of Jell-O or a package of Clove gum. But I knew it would not be long until Jeremiah, too, would get an itchy foot and want to leave.

The constant standing at the laundry got old. My legs and feet hurt. The floor was poured concrete, and I hadn't heard of insoles or support stockings. But you keep on. I did good work, managed the little touchy stuff like the sleeve press and the collar machine. Sometimes, I did specialty stuff, like fluted cuffs and ruffles down the front of a shirt.

One day, Nell, this woman who worked there, said, "You know, you are too cute to stay single long. There's a right good-looking fellow I'd like you to meet." This gal was having a little supper at her house after church and asked me to come.

"Come on; it might be fun. He's a widower. I'd say it's been a while since you had any fun."

Which was right. But alarm bells should have gone off at that word *widower*. But I was tired, and I was lonely. Despite having been married, with my shyness, I knew as much about men as horses know about cows. Same field, whole different animal. I just thought, *Well, it's people from her church.*

John L. Keller wasn't churchy; I should have seen that. He was too handsome and still too young to need God for much. He had this blue-black shock of hair he kept flipping back from his forehead. He was one of those men with pretty skin. You're amazed and jealous how flawless it is. Very little beard, and cheeks that flamed like a child's. But there's something strange in such beauty for a man. It's dangerous. I say that now.

I said he was young, but he was about forty. He had two daughters, fifteen and sixteen. They were pretty as him, with black eyes glittering like onyx. Hard, when they thought no one was looking. They could change out expressions like stereopticon slides: here's sweetness; here's surprise; and their favorite—this coy, flirty look. I forgave them. I thought it was because they had to grow up fast with no mother. But Thelma and Amy were mean, and prissy with their clothes. To myself, I called them "the stepsisters," after the pair in Cinderella.

What John L. needed church for, it turned out, was to find a woman. Plotted Sunday mornings, same as Dora had done Monday through Friday, ready to latch onto J.C. She was thinking behind the store counter all that time how to do it. And John L.'s girls were cut from the same cloth; they scanned a congregation, looking for good haircuts and expensive suits like bird dogs searching for quail. No farmers; they were scouting strictly for upper class. It was Amy and Thelma who urged John L. to try church as a good place to get a wife.

John L. drank. Let's get that out. I didn't think to wonder about his habits until after we married. I guess I thought all men drank when the mood struck—on the sly, at least. Walker and Avery surely enjoyed their little moonshine behind the barn from time to time.

The first time I saw him, he was standing up singing "Blessed Assurance" with his girls, one at each shoulder. He wore an orange tie that ran like a flame up the center of his body. You could see he was performing, the way he made each word so clear and kept his eyes rolling side to side. I knew it, yet I couldn't stop my own fascination with the way his jaw moved, his mouth shaping the letter O on "O, what a foretaste of glory divine."

All the hymns we sang began to take on overtones. "I will arise and go to Jesus, He will embrace me in His arms . . ." Handsome, caring Savior. He had my future laid out. He wanted me to put everything in His hands.

At the supper party, I was keeping myself busy serving punch, just standing behind a table covered with paper lace and nodding at folks while I ladled up cup after cup of red fruit juice. I was hoping people would stay thirsty, because I didn't want to have to go socialize. But then I saw Nell pointing me out to John L., and he came right over.

"Hello. I don't believe we've been introduced."

"No, we haven't. I did see you in church. But our mutual friend was determined our paths should cross socially."

"Yes, indeed. So nice to finally meet you, Isabel. Nell has been telling me about you, and now I see for myself how sweet you are. Working and serving, letting others enjoy themselves."

"Well," I said, "parties are not my forte." I handed him a cup of punch and then stood there, stirring the bowl with the ladle like an idiot.

John L. walked around the table and took my arm. He swiveled me around and took the ladle out of my hand.

"This young lady has another engagement, so if you would be so kind," he said to a stout matron passing by. He handed her the ladle and led me to a seat, then leaned over to hand me a cup. Before he gave it to me, he reached in the breast pocket of his jacket and took out a little flask. He looked left and right, then put a finger to his lips. "Shh. A little enhancement does wonders; don't tell." He unscrewed the flask and poured something into the punch cup.

He said, "Thou shalt not do dishes nor yet feed the swine."

"What is it? What are you talking about?" I looked at him, puzzled. I meant, what was the liquor, and what was the rhyme for? He laughed and touched my hair. It was too familiar, too soon, but at the moment, I just felt flustered.

"You know," he said, "like in the nursery poem. 'Curly Locks, Curly Locks, wilt thou be mine? Thou shalt not wash dishes nor yet feed the swine.'"

I fell for it. In my whole life, I had never been courted or made to blush. He was doing both to me in about five minutes flat. It was like I was going on sixteen again. I'd never had a beau, unless you counted Gallatin. (Samuel was my husband, but he'd been Molly's beau.) It might have been Mother Goose to most people, but it was high poetry to me.

Fourteen

Wing Key's

1936

I still had looks left, I guess. I never thought so at the time, working in the laundry like I was.

I curled my hair with a hot iron and rubbed lipstick on my cheeks for rouge. He took me on a "date."

We went to a Mandarin restaurant in a part of town I never knew existed.

I could count on my hands the number of times in my life I had ever been in any restaurant, much less a Chinese one. Wing Key China Cuisine was just a little hole in the wall with a giant winking eye on a swinging board over the door ("Winky—get it?" John L. said, squinting his own eye in a roguish way). It had cloudy windows and rickety tables, each with its own bottle of soy sauce. My naivete and the exotic nature of the whole enterprise disguised any negatives. My old love of geography and all things foreign flooded back to me. I smelled overheated cooking oil and noticed how fat, pock-marked Wing Kee himself and John

L. already seemed to know each other. But the red paper lanterns and chopsticks seemed romantic. I was fascinated to learn about the vegetables that came with the chicken. Did snow peas and bean sprouts grow in Tennessee?

"There is a little farm outside of town," John L. said, flicking his cigarette. "They grow all manner of exotic vegetables there." He seemed to know a little about a lot of subjects.

The owner/waiter hovered around and gave John L. special service. These courtesies apparently extended to his friends.

"Howdy-do, little lady," Wing Kee said, bowing deeply in my direction. I lifted my chin as he flicked the seat of my chair clean with his pudgy fingers, then handed me a menu thick as a library tome, with a tassel hanging from it.

I didn't notice anything unusual about my companion's behavior, the excessive chivalry in pulling out my chair, the snapping of fingers to order my tea in a tiny porcelain cup. (He insisted it needed just a little something extra, though, and fortunately, he had brought along his flask.) I thought, *This just must be what happens in such situations, on "dates."*

I wasn't used to liquor, either, and halfway through the meal, my hearing went dim, and everything John L. said struck me as brilliant and hilarious. He worked at a furniture store, he said, and told a story about a customer who was a midget. The man had bought an expensive table, then got John L. to cut six inches off the legs. Wasn't that fascinating? We laughed when I managed to carry a tiny clot of rice halfway to my mouth with chopsticks and then dropped it in my lap.

After the meal, he took my hand and held it while he smoked a cigarette, then ran his fingers up to my elbow, drawing a line of chill bumps and a thunderbolt that went straight to my core.

"There's a back room," he said, and my jaw dropped, mistaking his meaning at first, but then he added, "where I play cards sometimes. Want to watch?"

In my half-drunk stupor and out of politeness, I nodded. I stared while he threw five dollars on the table. It was a reckless amount. I could have fed my family for a week on it, but I followed him through the narrow kitchen, where a tiny Chinese woman in a dirty white apron screamed in pidgin English. Over and over, she hit one of the cooks on the back of his head with a wooden spoon. I could hear jazz music coming from somewhere.

"Come in, Mister John." Wing Kee appeared suddenly out of the dining room and opened the wall at the end of the corridor for John L.

We were now in a room with a dozen tables, and every one had a bottle on it. A piano in the corner was bouncing up and down on the floor, or so it seemed from how hard the man was playing it. Two red-lipped girls in sleeveless, sequined shifts and spangled hairbands came over to greet John L. One on each side.

"Hello, Daddy," they said and kissed his cheeks.

I barely recognized Thelma and Amy in their costumes. They smiled at me.

"Hey, Miz Dixon," they said. Thelma handed John L. a mug of beer, and Amy gave him a shot glass; I guessed it was full of whiskey. The shot made a clink in the beer as he dropped it in, and then he took a drink.

I was just watching, like I was twelve.

"It's not illegal now," John L. said, noticing me so wide eyed. "Oh, it was, but Wink just never took down the wall between the front and back, even after Prohibition ended."

John L. took a step away from the girls and put an arm around my waist. "We won't stay long," he said, pulling me with him. "I'll just play a couple of hands." He got me a chair.

I sat back from the action like a dog waiting for its owner and breathed. I tried to keep my mind clear. Somewhere along the line, I had been given a glass of what I thought was water, but my neck twirled in a little circle as I realized it was not. I told myself firmly that people acted drunk when they didn't have to, that if they only tried a little harder, they could straighten up and pull their wits together. It was like when Walker said he had ordered himself to get better from the flu. In comparison to the people around me, I should have been the soberest one, anyway.

Meanwhile, I watched the game table. I didn't know how to play any card games except Fish and Solitaire. Still, I was able to tell that John L. was an experienced poker player. He showed a lot of confidence, his thumb fanning out his cards with expert precision.

"Hey, hey!" he said and rubbed his palms together, delighted when a king or queen he played topped the round. He bluffed his way to a win and collected an astonishing stack of ten- and twenty-dollar bills. He called to me, "Say hello to President Jackson!" He held his hands in the air, and the money seemed to nod at me like an array of leaves.

Wing Kee was standing just off my shoulder, monitoring the room. I realized it was in case something got out of hand, but he was also shaking his head with satisfaction. He leaned in to speak to me, smelling heavily of soy sauce and garlic.

"You fella the best, little lady," he said. "You betta stick with that one."

John L. stood up from the game, and one of the other

players grabbed his arm. "Johnny, hey, you can't leave yet, buddy. Gimme a chance to win something back. That was a week's wages."

John L. pointed to me. "Got to take baby home," he said. "Too much excitement for one day already." He put up his hands in mock helplessness as there was general protest and booing. Thelma and Amy put down their trays for a moment and gave me a shrug of their shoulders and a teensy bye-bye with their fingers. The evening was young, really, and they had liquor to serve. Our host unlocked the wall and stood aside as we passed back into the kitchen. "Here you go, Wink," John L. said, and he palmed him one of the bills he had won. "See you next time."

"Okay, boss," Wing said, and the paper went up his sleeve.

The air outside in the street revived me, and I was ready to ask a few questions as he drove me home.

"Why did he call you 'boss?'" I wanted to know.

"Oh, that's just an expression. He calls every white man who goes in there 'boss.'"

"So, you're not the owner or anything like that?"

He laughed and pushed down on the accelerator. "Certainly not."

"Well, and I hope you don't mind me asking, but why do you let your daughters work in a place like that? Aren't you worried something might happen?"

I could see the silhouette of his profile tighten. "Thelma and Amy know how to take care of themselves. They—we—have been on our own since their mother left when they were eight and nine years old. You know how hard it is to get any job. They won't work there forever. The money they make in a month is more than they'd see in a year doing—well, doing the kind of thing you are doing, for instance. They are careful. As long as I am known there, no one will lay a hand on them."

I was silent. I didn't want to ask right then why his wife had left. So, he wasn't a "widower" after all. I didn't want to criticize the choices they had made. It was the Depression, and we were all in survival mode.

He walked me to my door and put both arms around my back, then pulled me into his chest like he knew I wanted him to. He knew it before I knew it.

"When can I take you out again?" he asked.

"I don't know." I tried to put some space between us. We were standing by the window, which was open. The lamp was still on, which meant Jeremiah was up, and I didn't want him to hear us.

"You are a pretty woman, Isabel." He put his hand to my face. "And I am moved by your ways. How did you stay so sweet and innocent?"

I just stood there listening to these words about myself and letting him touch me. Was I? Was I pretty? Was it good to be innocent?

"I don't spend all my time at card tables, you know." John L. kept his voice confidential. "I do have a job. Would you like to go to Fanning Furniture on Gay Street? I will take you there and show you around. It's very upstanding."

He kissed my neck. I closed my eyes and said yes.

Fifteen

Jeremiah

1936

*V*ery soon after our first dinner date, he did indeed take
me to the Fanning Furniture Store on Gay Street. He
had a key, and we went in by the alleyway, after hours.

"It's so I can really show you around, let you see how
respectable I am. It will be fun, without other customers
there." His lower lip pointed like the tip of a fishhook when
he smiled. He turned on a couple of side lights, just enough
to create a golden glow that threw our shadows together
over the rows of sofas and tables.

The building had four floors. He escorted me into an
elevator like it was a ride at an amusement park. He drew
closed an iron gate that unfolded into rows of Xs. Then
there was another iron gate, fancier, with the scrolled letters
FF in the center. I felt I was trapped in an elegant birdcage,
and I liked it quite a lot.

Once the elevator began to ascend, he came to me and
put his hand under the hem of my dress and pulled me

120

against him. Overhead, the cable whirred as it slowly raised us up. We kissed and kissed again while the elevator did its delicate shaking. Of its own volition, my left leg came off the ground and wrapped around his thigh like a twining vine. He inched two fingers up deeper, past another layer of my clothing. I gasped as I had never known I could do. He caressed my bare thigh just above my stocking tops.

My mouth lolled, and I did not pull away, but just then, the elevator stopped and the outer door opened. He had to let go of me to open the inner gates and turn on a light, and I saw that this was the floor with all the beds. I got hold of myself in the nick of time and would not leave the elevator.

"You just push that button," I said to him, panting and laughing, "and take me right back down to the ground floor." He tugged on my hand, but I held on to the inner rail, so he relented.

I had not thought any of this through. He seemed to think so highly of me, and I wanted him desperately. I would not have to work at the laundry anymore, he had said, arguing for us to marry. I asked if it wasn't too soon, and he said he adored me so I should let him put a ring on my finger. It had got to where John L. and I could not keep our minds off sleeping together. Well, anyway, I couldn't. Me, as old as I was, and here I had been worrying about "falling" like a teenage virgin.

After going out for four months, I met him at a justice of the peace. We were married for two weeks before I had the nerve to tell my children.

Nights I had been alone, I would hear his voice in my head. How it swept through me to think I was adored! He added that I would make it possible for Amy and Thelma to have a real home with a good female influence, and I could always be there for Jane and Jeremiah.

So that's when we made our plan. I was the one who wanted it to be secret at first. I needed to give the landlord notice, I said. I needed time to prepare Janey and Jeremiah and myself to move in with him. I think I needed to give myself time to get used to what I had done.

"Jeremiah, I have something important to tell you." I had hidden my ring in the flour canister, but it was time to start putting things in boxes and moving our furniture. Jane still didn't know. She was in school, but (I'm ashamed to admit this) I told Jeremiah so he could help move some of the heavier items.

"I have been seeing someone . . . for quite a while. And we have gotten married. He has asked me—asked us—to come and live with him. And I said yes."

Jeremiah looked at me as if I were an alien creature, his mouth agog. "What? When? Who is it?"

I told him.

Jeremiah immediately took up a kitchen chair in his clenched hands and aimed it at me, then stopped himself and threw it at the wall instead. It shattered one leg and made a hole in the plaster.

"You broke it! What *have* you done that for?"

"What have *I* done? What have *you* done? You do *not* know the disaster you have stepped in! That man, of all people! How could you have done this without consulting us?"

He hammered on the kitchen table until I thought it would break too, and then he put his palms to his head. He started to tell me things about John L.: the women he saw, the reputation he had, the illegal dealings.

I immediately began to defend and deny.

"But, Jeremiah, you knew I had gone out with him!

Why didn't you say something then if you didn't like him, if you thought there was anything disreputable about him?"

"I have always loved you. Called you Aunt Is, but in my heart, you were Mother." He closed his eyes, but a tear leaked out. "I thought you would see the truth for yourself, that you needed to get it out of your system. Didn't he take you to that Chinese gambling club? Didn't you see it with your own eyes? He allows his daughters to work there! I never, ever, in a million years thought you would marry him!"

"Need *what*? Get *what* out of my system?" I was shrieking at him. "Who do you think I am?" I felt guilty because I knew his meaning and saw my own weakness. We stopped our exchange then. I did not want to discuss with Jeremiah—or with anyone—the things I needed beyond food and shelter. I barely admitted those things even to myself.

I began to babble about the furniture store, heard myself say it was "a clean, decent job," and vowed that I cared for John L., as well as for Jeremiah himself and Jane, and how things were going to be different and a step up now that we had started this new life.

He turned his head away as if he didn't know me, and he clipped his words.

"I will not go and live in his house," he said. "Believe what you want to believe about him. I have warned you." He was nearly spitting. I think Jeremiah hated me for a time, but I did not know how to reconcile the situation.

My mistake was, I expected him to accept it, like a boy would have to. But he was seventeen, almost out of school, and had been working and taking on responsibility to help support us for three or four years. He was not a boy, but he had let me treat him like one. All the while, he had been shielding me from the hard realities of the things he had come to know about street life. He knew about the ways some men got money, how they assessed women, and how they spent their time.

Jeremiah did not move with us; he enlisted in the navy. I never thought he would be thrilled about my revelation, but I thought he would see the bright side and even come to like it after a time. I thought he would be happy for me and see how our life was improved.

I felt so guilty when he left, but I rationalized that in a way, I had forced him to follow his own dreams. There was not yet the danger that was to come in four years. I knew he would have adventures and be putting money in his pocket.

He might have grown up faster than I realized, but there was still an adolescent in him, a boy playing soldier, thinking about airplanes and submarines and grenades. Like a lot of young fellows, he dreamed of being a man's man, of putting on a uniform and being transformed, as if navy whites or army greens were a Charles Atlas course. He had been too long in a domestic world, that was all. He would have done this eventually anyway, is what I told myself.

I didn't even miss Jeremiah for about a year. When he came home on his first leave, he stayed with Dora and J.C., but he did come by to see me. He was smoking openly, and I realized this was only one of the many things he had hidden from me. It was only one of the minor deceits that had gone on to keep me untainted, uncorrupted, and in the dark. He had been to Wing Key's himself, had let go of his cash there. Had probably stolen money from my purse to gamble with. I remember when it went missing, and at the time, I blamed myself for losing it, never thinking there might be another reason.

He admitted he had started to smoke behind our backs when he was about ten. It's a wonder he got as tall as he did. *The Child's Book of Health* warned that tobacco stunts your growth. Jeremiah was skinny as a beanpole but always looked older in the face. He was making his career in the navy as a cook, and he gave me his recipe for chipped beef on toast. Already, he had awful tattoos on his arms: anchors, hearts, and leopards.

I asked him, "Jeremiah, what do all those decorations have to do with each other?" I guess I expected some sort of theme. He just looked at me and smiled and took another drag on his Lucky Strike.

"Well, I'm not sure," he said. "But I can tell you where I was when I got each one of 'em, and that's more than some guys can say."

I thought then of how women collect whatnots, and it made heartbreaking sense. Nothing on the shelf seems to tie into anything else, but what it all is, is somebody longing for beauty but not able to create it at all. That's how it was in my marriage with John L: a set of imperfect things, imperfect events, reaching for something, for some meaning.

I was happy just to stand in the doorway of the bathroom and watch John L. shave. He would take his shirt off and stand in front of the medicine cabinet and soap his beard. Then he'd look in the mirror at me behind him and wiggle his eyebrows and run his tongue over his upper lip. I would smile a little and make a fanning gesture to my face. It was all I could do to keep from pressing myself against his back and wrapping him up with my arms.

I hated for him to leave me and go off to work. He did pretty well selling furniture for the Fannings, before he fell off the wagon in a big way. I would pack him a lunch and dangle it at the end of my arm, so sad that he was going away for the day. He would take it from me and quote one of the baby rhymes that trademarked our interactions: "Here's Sulky Sue, what shall we do? Turn her face to the wall till she comes to." And I would make a child's face with a petulant lip, and we would both laugh.

His smile promised, "I am for you, and you alone." He seemed like a miracle, and I felt special and powerful to have his touch upon me, and upon my life.

Things I know now and can't cast off. The things he did to my body, and the reactions I had. Togetherness with Sam had been sweet, but I did not crave it like I did when John L. slid under the covers and began to kiss me. And there were other things he taught me, other ways to get what we were after. We worked on it often in the middle of the night, in the pitch dark. It seemed timeless, done in a hidden space where nothing was controlled, and in the morning, we did not speak of it.

He told me he was born out west, in Washington state. That interested me, as most of the people I knew had never lived anywhere but that state of Tennessee. Or maybe they left and went to California and were never heard from again, except for a postcard with an image of lemon trees in the desert.

We were sitting up in bed once, after loving, and he told me the story.

"My father worked at a copper mine, and he was killed in an underground explosion," he said. John L. always liked a slim cigarillo in bed, and there was an ashtray nestled in the sheets, along with a dish of grapes I had fetched us to quench our thirst.

"My mother started working for the mine after that," he said. "She did laundry to bring in money." He picked up my hand. "I guess that is one thing that occurred to me when I met you—to rescue a pretty woman from a laundry."

I told him about my mama too, about the insane asylum, about how the last time I saw her, she was hanging sheets on a line.

"It's some of the easiest work in the world," I said, "because you don't need any education at all. But it's some of the hardest, the most backbreaking, the most numbing labor for the mind. I'm sure you saw your mother wore down from it. And the strangeness of it being about making things clean and good, but always dealing with dirt, and stains, and sometimes . . ." I paused, because I had seen things that gave me insight into people's lives, their thoughts and secrets, and I had to pretend it didn't matter, or that I hadn't really seen.

"What is it, sugar?" John L. could be extremely gentle with me at times, so concerned. But maybe it was just him thinking about his own childhood, because he continued, "My mother, she did things, other things, to make ends meet. Eventually, she sent me back here to Knoxville, to her cousin and his wife. He owned a company that made American flags. He never liked me much, but he sure used me! All he did was put me to work on the assembly line when I was fourteen. I went out on my own as soon as I could."

"I am so sorry," I said.

John L. was not bad, not really, but life had puzzled him out in a certain way, and I did not put the pieces together until later. When things fell apart, I did not want to remember what had been possible between us; I did not want to want it anymore. It was all dirty, something filled with damage and pain. But then again, I did want it, wanted it with a sorrow beyond all reckoning. I see now that I squandered love on someone who never intended to be sacred. But there is no going back. I have heard the expression "I could read him like a book."

I thought John L. was the answer to my prayers.

Surfaces don't always predict what lies inside, like an apple all pretty and red but rotten and mushy when you bite in. That handsome face and the confidence of an orange tie. Read him like a book? No. I was a fool and an illiterate where it mattered most.

Sixteen

Thelma and Amy

John L. was happy to have me taking care of his house, giving everyone good meals. But his daughters wore me thin.

I did a lot of sewing for Amy and Thelma. It was something I knew well how to do, and it was a blessing to not have to stand up all day working a laundry press and sweating. The girls were always telling me about some dress pattern they had seen in such-and-such a style and how such-and-such a boy would go crazy to see them in puffy little sleeves and a dozen set-in gores swirling about their knees. Janey got their hand-me-downs, and she didn't complain, since it was better than anything she had been used to. She got on all right with John L. She had lost her father, and I was glad for her to have someone taking an interest. He would pat his knee and she would sit on his lap. Then he would put his arm around her and ask about her day. Only later did it strike me as wrong.

John L. kept on going to the establishment behind

Wing Key's. His girls too. They didn't work at home, and they didn't have marriage prospects.

In fact, it was dawning on me that it was just a series of fellas. One young man showed up with his stringy Adam's apple and sticking-out ears, his hair pasted flat to his head.

I said, "So. You been seeing Amy over a month now. Seems like you two are getting a little bit serious!" And a red flush walked from his tie knot to his widow's peak.

He tucked his chin down and said, "Well, actually, ma'am, it's Thelma I have a date with today." That confused me for the longest time, that the boys would see either one.

And then one day, John L. slapped my face for not having fixed the ham he said he wanted for supper. (I was saving it for Sunday.) The smack seemed to come out of nowhere, and immediately I thought, *I won't have that*. But I made up a reason, which was that I had not listened well and made him lose his temper. But I began to be on guard.

I paid more attention to how I was a lady's maid for the stepdaughters, who had who-knew-what kind of morals, and a housekeeper for them all. Curly Locks might wash dishes, sit on a cushion, and sew a fine seam, even feed the swine. But she wouldn't be hit, and the litany of Jeremiah's cautions came back to mind. All I knew (but had not admitted to myself that I did) began to sound in my head.

That's when the first idea of leaving him began to surface. I began to dream again about Gallatin or my mama, like I did when I had the flu. But I was afraid. I had changed my life to be here, so I pushed the possibility of failure away. In my dream, Gallatin would take my hand and put an egg in it.

"Take it, honey; this is a magic egg," he would say, his face close to mine, but I would shake my head and give it back. In the daylight, I hoped everything around John L. would stay calm, that any arguments would go away, were really something out of the ordinary, and so forth. And so on.

They did happen again, of course, always unexpectedly. But before I could debate further with myself about John L., or forgive and forget, which I tried to do each time, there came the straw that broke the camel's back.

What Janey told me happened was this: she had come home from school and found no one there but John L. with his bottle. It was true he had been going on more drinking sprees. Usually, he was quiet about it; he would just lay there on the couch, drinking and listening to the radio. Every now and then, he'd get up for the outhouse and stumble by the cupboard, causing a saucer to shiver loose and break.

He would actually say he was sorry. I would stack the china sections one on top of another and then sweep up the tiny shards with the side of my hand.

"It's just a *thing*," I'd say and not look at it. And at the time, I'd send thanks to my lucky stars that Jeremiah was out on his own and not here to say he told me so or to see John L. rage, like he would sometimes if he felt his "rest" was disturbed. Jeremiah would have tried to fight him, and Jeremiah would not have won.

And then came the day when I got home and found Jane in the tree. I saw her blue dress up above me and thought it was a piece of the sky.

I told her to start putting things in the suitcase, and I swallowed my pride. I went to the kitchen and picked up the phone to call Dora. My plan came to me clear-cut as a story I knew I had to tell. I would go back home, home to my brothers' farm, and I would leave Janey with Dora. She would be safe with her and J.C.—that was the main thing.

Keep on going to school and have everything she needed. It did not matter at all what anyone said about me. I would have to deal with myself later, with the fact that if I had not been so stupid as to attach myself to this man, none of it would have happened.

"Please give me Sycamore 3147." I gave the telephone operator Dora's number. I could feel myself hesitating to leave, like a bird in a cage with an open door. But this was for Jane.

"Do it," I whispered under my breath. My eyes closed.

I waited for the connection. I had never had a telephone until I married John L. It was still a miracle to me how the communication took place, like motes of light on a string, carrying my words through the dark.

"Hang up. I said, *hang up*," John L. said. He had come to a little and was giving me a weak order. But he was still too intoxicated to get up and make me do it. The room had an air of unreality. I felt like I was in a play. Just then, Amy and Thelma came home from wherever they had been.

"I'm just here to change clothes," Amy said, and she sat her purse on the kitchen table.

"Yes, we're meeting our fellows at the movies," Thelma said, and she pulled her lips into a bow. Both of them were oblivious to what was going on.

"Well, I would change my plans if I were you." I put my hand over the receiver for an instant. "I'm leaving your father, and Jane is going with me. So, you're going to have a bit more work than usual, and you might as well start now."

I didn't try to have any privacy or keep my voice down. I was not about to give graphic details, but neither was I going to shield Amy and Thelma from this information about their father. I knew where these girls worked; they had seen plenty and were not innocents.

"How can you do this to us?" Amy asked. She set her fists on her hips in anger. "How can you be so awful?"

"And who is going to help me with my clothes?" Thelma asked. She always was the ruder of the two.

"You'll have to find a new maid," I told her. Just then I heard Dora.

"Hello, hello, I'm here, who is this?"

"Dora," I said, with no introduction whatsoever, after the connection went through. This was no time for empty pleasantries. "I am sorry to bother you, but something has happened. I am leaving John L. and taking me and Janey out of here. I need to bring her to you; could I do that please?"

There was a surprised silence. I could almost see Dora's eyes lighting up at my failure. But then she composed herself and said, "I see. Well, of course you know Jane is always welcome with me and J.C. Do you need to come straightaway? Surely not tonight; I need to get a room ready for her at least." I stayed quiet and allowed the severity of the situation to dawn on Dora. "Isabel, what is it?" she said finally, with a degree of alarm.

"I cannot keep Jane in this house. It's not a tolerable situation. I can explain when we get there." I appreciated that she didn't ask a lot of questions about why this had become necessary. But neither did she ask what I myself expected to do or offer for me to stay at her house with Jane.

"Well then, of course, bring her on to us. Of course," Dora said.

I knew Dora always did think John L. was no good. Jeremiah had helped that case along before he left, and I'm sure it was a great satisfaction to her to be proved right.

I said, "It's true, Dora, we can't stay here. But I will stay with her in a motel tonight, and we will be there first thing in the morning. Thank you, Dora. Jane's going to be in high school soon. She is used to it here in Knoxville and has made friends. I guess I will go back to Wheat and help your uncles run the farm. I could take her with me, but . . ." My voice trailed. "Dora, I will make it clear tomorrow, if you will just trust me."

"All right, Isabel. Are you sure you don't need J.C. to drive over now and get Jane?" As easy as this plan sounded, I could not do it, could not allow myself to hand her over so quickly.

"Yes, I'm sure. I just want to stay with her tonight. See you tomorrow." I hung up.

I stood there for a moment, eyes closed, one arm around Jane. I didn't say anything, just let my forehead and one arm rest against the wallpaper.

I heard John L. trying to sit up. "Feel a little sick," he said. I ignored him, but finally, I had to open my eyes because Amy and Thelma would not shut up.

Amy nudged Thelma. "What is she talking about? *What* is going on?" Amy was standing by the stove with a curling iron, single-mindedly carrying on with preparations for her evening outing. She had rolled a pompadour on top of her head. It looked like a carved scroll of wood that bobbled when she spoke. Thelma was sitting at the kitchen table, wearing a purple satin dress I had made her. It had a fitted bodice, three-quarter length sleeves, covered buttons, and a full skirt. I had thought it was a work of art when I completed it, but somehow, on her, it looked cheap. She was using a jar of Vaseline to paste curls around her face.

"Janey, what is going on?" Thelma hooked her finger

in the jar and brought out a yellowish glob as she passed the question down the line, but Janey didn't answer.

She just backed up against me and whispered, "Mother, what now?"

For the first time, I saw a look pass over Thelma's face. She turned to her sister, and I saw fear come up in Amy's eyes as well. As one, they turned to me, beseeching now, all arrogance gone.

"Isabel?" Thelma asked. Her voice was tiny.

"You better not move," I said to John L., without turning around. "There are butcher knives in this drawer here, and I am thinking about which one is my favorite."

"You're leaving?" Amy asked. "How can you just leave? Daddy?" She turned to the body on the sofa. "Daddy, she said they are leaving! Get up and do something!" She shook a wrinkled slip with flounces on it. I whirled to confront her and jerked it from her hand. I took it to the sink and wet it and mixed up some new starch. I put the iron on the stove top. Everyone just watched like maybe I was going to perform an operation.

"Maybe not a butcher knife," I said. "A hot iron will work just as well for the damage I want to do."

No one spoke.

"I'll fix your slip before I go, Amy," I said. Thelma sat drooping in her chair, her mouth down. Out of the corner of my eye, I could see all around the room that it never got to be mine; it was still someone else's, only with my pictures and dish towels mixed in. Funny I never noticed the nicks on the stove that had been there when I came. Wonder who made those? An image of another woman came into my head: my predecessor. A silhouette throwing a pot and chipping the enamel. Now that I saw it, it was like she had just stepped outside. A runaway urge rose in me, but I could see it from the outside. The situation felt so familiar, only this time, I was my mama and Janey was me. Through my anger and anguish, there was one thing I was sure of: I was not going to leave Janey.

I set my lips and turned to my daughter. "Don't dawdle. Finish the packing, honey." I went in the bedroom and got another suitcase off the top of the wardrobe and tossed it to her. It was only cardboard, covered with paper to look like leather. Flimsy, like so many things in my life, I thought bitterly. "Fill it up," I warned her. "We won't be back."

I put my hands on my hips and yelled in John L.'s direction, "I'm fixing some supper now!" As if I was speaking to the deaf, or the dead. He had fallen back asleep, holding a half-laced boot in his hands. His bottle was still on the coffee table with an inch of liquor in it. I snatched it up and poured it into the sink. I pointed Thelma to a saucepan and gave her a can of tomato soup. She stood there, sullen, as if I had given her a rock. "See that he gets some of that down. Spoon-feed him, if you have to. I'll put the cornbread in, but I want you to watch it. Amy, set the table."

By the time the cornbread was ready, I had the door propped open with two suitcases and the Singer sewing machine John L. gave me for a wedding present. It was electric, and I had been thrilled when I got it, but it hadn't taken me long to figure out why he gave it to me. I took my daddy's Bible, my earrings and watch, some clothes—nothing else.

I ate fast, standing up. I barely tasted it, but I knew I would have to have strength. "Eat, honey," I urged Jane, but she couldn't. Janey sat stirring, looking down at the red soup with orange foam on top.

She shook her head. "I don't want it." Finally, I nodded

at her, then walked to the phone one more time and called a taxi. Jane dropped the spoon, then picked up her suitcase and went outside to wait.

I went to John L.'s bureau and took all the money he had there. It was $34.23. I looked at myself in the mirror. My eyes were mechanical, my skin pale. My hair fell loose from the pins. I saw my hand put the money in my purse. The woman in the mirror turned away and walked to the front door.

The taxi came and we drove away. And it was that simple. Through my pain, I swore I was through with marriage, through with men. I would have to spend the rest of my life making amends for what I had done.

There were a few things I had cared about, some furniture that had come from Sam and Molly's. Some special plates with edges of *24 karat gold*, as the maker noted on the undersides. At the time we left, I had in mind to return in a few days with boxes, but ultimately, I didn't have the stomach to see John L.

I never saw my few housewares, tables, and chairs again. I never saw Thelma or Amy again, either. I wish I had had more love for them, but the truth is that I did not. I left them there. I left those girls there with that man. The poor, lost souls, prettiness their only hope, and that would never last. "I'm sorry," I wanted to say to them. "I wish I had not had to make that decision, but I could not save you; I could not carry you." It makes my heart twist with regret that I did not try harder, find a way to drag them out.

I never went back—wary, I suppose, that if John L. was cleaned up and sober and charming, I would not be able to trust myself. He would convince me to stay, and then I would have been lost as well. Every now and then, I do think about that dress I made for Thelma, though. I did a wonderful job, if I do say so. It was elegant, not the sort of thing anyone would want to cast aside. I spent a lot of energy on it, and I was proud of it at the time. I wonder if it still exists, somewhere in the world.

Seventeen

The Man in Folsom's Woods

M y family, all the people I had known as a child in Wheat, there near Black Oak Ridge—they lived by a rule of silence. It is contrary to the way people do things now, which is to gossip about a person or an event. They dwell on it, keep looking at some evil or disgrace with glee. Eventually, it loses its scandal and is rubbed down to a simple fact. Once you do that, you can deal with it like a nondescript ball you keep bouncing in the palm of your hand.

Life back home was hard, but some things were too dark to talk about at all. The point was to keep on going and do your best, in spite of what happened. You can't change the past. What doesn't kill you makes you stronger. All that.

And one reason I felt Janey would be all right is that I was all right when something similar happened to me. I was older, maybe fifteen. I had kept it put away in my mind. I did not allow myself to openly recollect it, but now it came forward.

There used to be church services now and then at Folsom's Woods, which was a shady grove near the Clinch

River. They would have revivals there in the summer and set up a brush arbor for prayer and preaching.

It would last all day on a Sunday, with services morning and night. In between, we would walk and explore in the forest—there were trails there and about. Lots of boys and girls courted there. It was very pleasant in the cool of the leaves, and places to hide and steal a kiss were behind every tree.

It was after Gallatin left, but before I married Sam. There was a community dance the last day of a revival. Queenie and several of our friends decided to go. I was feeling about as pretty as I would ever feel in my life. I had a brand-new yellow dress, which I had started making when I met Gallatin. The material came from the Sears catalog. I was sad Gallatin would never see it, but eventually, I decided to finish it. It had puffed sleeves and a lace collar. The fabric was sprigged with tiny white flowers. I also had new black patent-leather shoes.

When we got there, Queenie took the hand of Alton, a tall boy with red hair, and they disappeared like smoke, both smiling. I was by myself but sitting up, optimistic and pert, in one of the chairs along the side of the wall. Finally, Queenie and Alton reappeared and began dancing. I couldn't help but notice they had both recombed their hair. His was all slicked back, and she was laughing at him a little to see his white forehead sprouting a crooked part.

As he spun her away, she waved at me. I watched them go around the room. There was someone on the opposite wall, and she waved to him too, spoke a word, and pointed. I knew she was telling him to ask me to dance. I don't know why this always happened to me. I couldn't seem to accomplish a relationship on my own. I knew I was good-looking in my own way, but I did not look like other young girls.

Because of working too hard at a young age, perhaps, innocence and freedom did not show in my face.

I sighed. The dance floor was so crowded, I couldn't quite see who he was. The people square-danced up to and back from each other and twined in and out like a Maypole in a picture book. When that ended, the fiddler started up "Put Your Little Foot." This is a dance where the man stands behind the lady, holds one of her hands, and puts his other arm around her waist. I was whirled out of my seat—standing suddenly and then moving like a gust of wind had nudged me. I realized I was dancing with someone.

Because of the way you do the dance, I couldn't see his face, but I could tell my partner was muscular, and I could see his hand, which felt warm.

"Hello there," his voice said off my shoulder. I could see his navy-blue coat sleeve and the white cuff of his shirt. His breath was behind me, a little tinged with whiskey, and one part of me thought, *The nerve of you.*

I was amazed and a little frightened at being taken up by a stranger. The other part of me was about to faint with delight. I was too shy to jerk away and make a scene. It was just so nice to dance.

We went around the room. He was guiding me real smooth.

"You're a good dancer," he said. I doubted that; I was more like a boat paddled by an expert. We came near Queenie and Alton.

"Hey, you finally met!' Queenie squealed, as if she had orchestrated a great project. They nodded and grinned as if watching us row by from a picnic on the shore. Then we circled by Walker and an acquaintance he was dancing with. My girlfriends materialized over by the pie table with some local boys. Everyone seemed to know my handler, and they all smiled and said, "Hey there!" They looked at me as if this was perfectly natural, as if they were pleased with who I was with and that I was having so much fun.

Of course, I later learned who he was, and we took our own walk in Folsom's Woods. I can tell you that I walked willingly out of the music and down the path into the night, but I did not agree to all that happened after that.

In the years that followed, my experience became the stuff of a recurring dream. I never told anyone, not even Queenie. The dream is a little different, different times. I will turn at the end of the dance to the man at my back and see a pleasant, dark-haired stranger—like a young Abe Lincoln, reassuring and rather handsome. Other times, I know it's Gallatin, and he leads me outside to the porch by a wall of honeysuckle, and we kiss and kiss, nothing more than that. I'm loving kissing Gallatin. We go on and on, like we never got to do in real life.

But other times, I break away because I see the hand holding mine has six fingers, only they have long, sharpened fingernails. They look evil and scare me, so I pull away and run to a back room where there's a piece of cloudy mirror. I look in the mirror at my startled face and see a black-headed somebody coming into the room behind me.

I say, "No!" and jerk awake, panting.

For most women, when you have children, the first thing that's on your mind is to make sure they are safe, body and soul. I was almost nothing to myself for the longest time, on account of the family to take care of. You just do what you got to do. You try, you try not to fail, but sometimes, you do.

Eighteen

Dora's House

1936–1940

*W*e stayed in a motel, Janey and me, for the first time ever. I could have taken her straight to Dora's, but we needed an interim, a tiny moment for just the two of us to catch our breath and realize that things were about to change. If circumstances had been different, we could have had fun, noting the matching towels stacked so neat and the paper strip across the toilet and the tiny, wrapped soaps. Under other circumstances, I would have enjoyed it. But Janey was too worried about how we would explain everything, and also worried that John L. would come after us.

"He won't," I assured her. "He doesn't know where we're going, for starters. And if he does find out, well, J.C. is an important and respected person in the business community and has friends in law enforcement. All he has to do is say the word, and it will be known that John L. is on the blacklist. With the associates he has anyway, he won't want to bring more attention down on himself."

I was trying hard not to cry. I wanted with all my heart for this not to have happened. But also, I wanted Jane to see that I was—that we both were—all right.

"I really think he is a coward. And I am not important enough for him to straighten up and seek me out again."

We talked more, and from what my daughter told me, I was able to determine that with John L. as drunk as he had been, he had not been able to do anything physical. Though he made an attempt as they struggled in the hedge.

She said, "I don't want us—well, at least, I don't want you to have to leave on account of me. Maybe we should go back. Now that I know what he's capable of, I will be watchful and know how to handle him next time."

I was pacing and shaking my head as she spoke, but she continued. "I won't let him be in the house alone with me. Not anymore. It was really the liquor's fault and not his fault, anyway."

"No." I was emphatic. "We are not going to excuse him anymore or give him another chance."

"What about you, then, Mother? Aren't you going to stay at Dora's too?"

"I don't think that would be a good idea, Jane. Dora's household is Dora's household, and it would not be wise for me to intrude on it. I need to go back to work. I will be fine back with Uncle Walker and Uncle Avery and Grandaddy. They will be happy for me to come and cook and clean for them again."

"How are we going to explain this to Dora?" Jane threw herself down on the bed and clutched a pillow to her stomach.

"I will tell Dora," I said. "We will not have to say much. She is so excited to have you come and stay with her. And later on, when you are ready, you can tell her as much about it as you care to."

I tried to cheer us both up. "You're going to live in *The Palace* now." That's what we always called Dora and J.C.'s house. "I guess we can finally let Dora buy you all those clothes she's been wanting to get you. When high school starts in September, you won't be wearing anybody's hand-me-downs. It will work out fine."

We talked about it some more the next morning as we rode in the taxi, about how much she loved Dora and her husband, J.C., and how I would write to her all the time and call and wouldn't be too far away since I would be on the farm with Walker and Avery. The calmer Jane got, the better I liked it, but the worse I felt.

The taxi stopped at The Palace Gate, which ran across the bottom of Dora's driveway.

"Don't leave," I told the man. "I am not staying." I handed him a five-dollar bill out of my purse and leaned over to inch out some of the old, soft singles I had stuffed into my sock. "I'll be right back," I said, waving them in his direction. Outside of what I took from John L., I had saved up a little here and there and sewed it in my coat.

Dora came to the door wearing house slippers. She hugged Jane into the cavern between her breasts and looked at me, her eyes full of questions and disdain.

"Honey," she said to Jane, "I've got cantaloupe and eggs and bacon waiting. Go on in the kitchen. J.C. and I are so glad to have you."

She let go of Janey with one hand and took her suitcase and moved it inside the doorway. Dora looked at the taxi waiting at the bottom of the driveway and then at me and asked, already knowing the answer, "Can you stay, Isabel, and have a bite?"

"Thanks, no," I said. "I'm going to try to get to the farm before dark." I reached back into my purse and took out the roll of money I had cut from the lining of my coat and handed it to Dora. "I will send more if I can."

"We should be all right," Dora said. She glanced at the bills. I could tell they didn't amount to a hill of beans in her estimation, but she tucked the dollars in her bosom anyway. "She's only as big as a minute and doesn't eat much. "Do you, honey?" She turned to Janey.

"Come here," I said and held my daughter.

She fell against me, then hugged me and kissed me. "Mama."

Her tears began to stream, but I said, "No need for that now. I'll write to you just as soon as I get back to Wheat. Go on, now; go see J.C. and get some bacon before he eats it all. You just let Dora take care of you, and don't worry about me. I know how to take care of myself." I gave her a little push.

When she was out of the room, I said, "Dora, I am so sorry to have to do this. But John L. is not the man I thought he was, and Jane will not be safe as long as we stay in his house. We have had a very close call, and I don't want to expose her to any more of his . . . advances." It was as much as I could bear to say.

Dora's eyes bored into me, her mouth in a line. She looked side to side, nodding her head as if there was something she knew all along. "How could you, Isabel? How could you be so . . . so stupid?"

"Dora, you don't have to say that to me. That is a question I will keep asking myself for years to come." I did not bother to remind her that she had done the same thing I had: married someone, in part, because of the life they seemed to offer. Only, Dora had gotten lucky and I had not.

In her case, it was J.C. who had suffered by the match, because he loved Dora and she had used that. She might have cared for J.C. in her way, but she did not love him as much as she loved the material goods he provided.

"You know what Jane means to me, that I would do anything for her," Dora said. And that was true; I could never have left my daughter there if I had not believed that Dora would cherish her. Dora still had one hand on the edge of her door. But she did finally ask, "What will you do, Isabel? Surely you will not go back to that man?"

"Most certainly not. I will be fine, staying at the farm indefinitely."

Dora nodded. I could see how the farm looked to her, the pitiful house compared to here. She did not look me in the eyes.

I said, "We will work it out, I hope. I appreciate this, and maybe it won't have to be for long."

I reached then for Dora. She was my niece and my stepdaughter, after all, and she put her chin over my shoulder, patted little pats on my back, and waited for me to stop clutching her.

Jane was there for much longer than any of us knew she would be. I know she was only twelve, but still, it hurt a little to see how easy she let go. I believe that a door shut in her mind when she moved to The Palace.

Walking back to the taxi in my shabby coat, I could see myself from Janey and Dora's point of view. I was what they'd come from. The Palace was their true home. It was what they deserved and where they belonged.

Janey had been there many, many times. It was already her second residence, as she used to stay there or at the store when I was working for the laundry. She always admired the size of the staircase and the pictures hanging by their wires from the crown molding. The portraits of Pinkie and Blue Boy were in the guest room where she would stay. I knew she would come to despise the Indian princess on the feed-and-grain calendar in her room at John L.'s, though all the way here, she'd been wishing she'd brought it.

There was so much in Dora's house to admire. It would keep Janey busy for weeks, rediscovering it all. The little cedar closet in the bathroom, for example, or that large basement room which was filled with boxes of old *National Geographics* and an antique phonograph.

By the time the bus pulled up to the store that served as a Greyhound station near where I'd lived for the first seventeen years of my life, I had already left John L. His daughters were in a little corner of my brain where I could find them if I wanted to.

But of course, I couldn't go long without thinking about Janey and Jeremiah. Over the years I lived back in Wheat, I wrote them both letters, asking a series of questions and then answering them as if they had asked.

To Janey, I wrote:

> *Do you need anything well I guess they have everything at the Palace are you doing OK in your schoolwork? I know you are Hows Dora and J.C? Is the wether weather there nice? Silly of me to ask you are only 20 miles away it must be the same as here Your uncles get to town regular and bring me all the sewing notions I ask for, I don't need a thing The housework is going along about as usual I beat the parlor rug yesterday I dont think it has been took out for ten years or more Both Walker and Avery are doing fine tho Walker has bad artharitis in his finger he broke years ago its a wonder Avery doesnt get sore too he always looked to Walker to know how to be The weather here has*

been a mite cold I wish we lived where the Johnsons do lower down the valley and dont get near the wind we do Miss you very much, Love.

I imagined her reading my letter sitting in Dora's huge living room. You can feel the quiet of the house there, and the space of the ten-foot ceilings. From the couch on one wall to the couch on the opposite wall seems like a big distance. You think of landscaping, and not interior decoration, when you go into that room. Despite all she had, Dora would remind me later that the furniture left at John L. Keller's had originally belonged to "her mother, Molly." She never forgave me for losing her mother's sofa and rocker and those dishes with the twenty-four-carat trim. I kept telling her they were only grocery-store giveaways, but the way she talked, you would have thought it was Haviland.

Parallel to her living room was an entry hall—the doorbell that rang there had eight notes of the Westminster chimes, not just a buzzer. Through an arch far away on the other side of the living room, you could see into the dining room, with its china cabinet and sideboard. The dining table was fitted with ten chairs, and all around the edges of the room, you could see real oil paintings and silver services, which included many things no one ever used. There was a thing Dora told me was a samovar from Russia, and there was a candy tray with tiers that got smaller and smaller toward the top, like the Tower of Babel. The room had an antique Persian carpet. It was the color of dried blood and thin, but you just knew it would never wear out its paisleys.

The floor of the guest bedroom, which was now Jane's room, was parquet. When Janey first got there, she wrote, "a service is going to come in and redo the room." I did not understand, but it turned out the service meant the floor service, which stripped the wax and relaid it smooth and shiny as still water.

Dora ran her house as efficient as a school. There was a certain cycle of cleaning she adhered to. It was interesting that as much money as she had now, she didn't have a housekeeper. If she had not married the way she did, Dora might have made an elegant janitor. I see her dressed fit to kill but turning up chairs and getting out the push broom at precisely 3:15 when the school day was over.

Janey wrote me:

Dear Mother,

I miss you. But I am fine here. Dora has given me the guest bedroom all to myself. I can hardly believe now that I slept on the screen porch at our old house, or on that single bed in the room next to Thelma and Amy. My bedroom now has its own bath, two walk-in closets, a window seat, and German lace curtains.

I also cannot believe I ever used a privy. I guess I shouldn't say that. I know you have one at the farm!

After school, I don't come home. I go to J.C.'s store just like I used to when I was in elementary school. Dora is there keeping the books, and there are two sales ladies and one man in the men's department. J.C. gives me money, and I can run to the drugstore for an ice cream. Everything would be perfect if you were here.

Love,

Janey

I was happy for Janey to be in such a pretty, modern place and to be safe and secure from all alarms, as the hymn said. I saw her reading my letter. She sat on the sofa with her knees up in front of her. When she wiggled her bare feet, her toenails zip-zipped over the slubs in the rose satin fabric. As she read, I was like a shadow in the room. *Everything would be perfect if you were here,* she said, so I will be.

But I wanted her to be proud of me. I'd have liked her to see me wearing not my old brown cloth coat, but something really nice, with a lace collar and cuffs, and maybe a cameo at the neck. Maybe a delicate shell cameo edged in gold with a carving of a profile on it.

Just the sort of quality jewelry that was way beyond anything I had ever really owned.

Nineteen

The Prophet of Black Oak Ridge

1942

*W*hen I was little, we had a collie named Brownie. When Daddy wanted Brownie to get off the porch or out of the barn, he would point a finger down at the animal and repeat, "I said *git*." Brownie would sulk off—head down, tail between his legs, hating to leave whatever warm spot he had found. The creature's own wishes mattered not at all.

That is pretty much the way I felt when I went back to the farm where I grew up and took up housekeeping again with Walker and Avery. I would have done practically anything to avoid it, but at the time, I could not think of any option that would have ensured my own survival. I felt that the most important thing had been done: I had gotten Janey to a safe place, away from her stepfather. What happened to me was not nearly so important as that.

My daddy had gentled and seemed grateful to have me around. His body was broken down by a life of physical labor, but physical labor was all he knew. So when arthritis hobbled him and he was not doing much but sitting on the porch and mending a harness, he got restless. I hadn't been there long before he went out to chop a little kindling and had a heart attack.

Walker stood at the kitchen door, his angular body taking up the frame while the cold air rushed inside.

"It's Daddy," he said. It was a January day, bright blue and iced in the cracks of the ground. "He's dead, and I can't get the axe out of his hand." His face crumpled. He had not shed tears for so long, the crying noise he made sounded like a goose honking.

Avery took the lead, as he had ever been known to do when we least expected it. He got our brother by the arm and pulled him by the coat sleeve back out of doors.

"The two of us can lift him; come on now," he said. They brought Daddy in and laid him on the bed with his arm still crooked and his hand curled for the axe handle. When his body thawed, I washed him and dressed him in a suit fifty years old, the only one he'd ever had, and crossed his hands across his chest. We buried him next to Molly and Sam.

For three more years, I did what I knew how to do, which was to cook, clean, wash, iron, mend, milk cows, gather eggs, plant a garden, can beans and tomatoes, cut hair, make mustard plasters, cure warts—every domestic thing you can think of.

With Daddy gone, I did these things in my own way. In my spare time, I wrote letters to Janey and Queenie. I read library books and the Bible, went to Sunday school and church, bought groceries, made my dresses, pieced quilts, and watched babies for neighbors.

In 1941, Pearl Harbor had happened. Jeremiah was in the military, but in a supporting role. He had started as a ship's cook, but now managed food supplies and had not seen combat, I was relieved to know. I collected scrap metal and helped other women make care packages for their own men in the service.

This was about the whole of my life. It was not so bad, these things, but something restless had been growing. Finally, I was aware I needed to make a good plan. My future was like a shadow following me around, but I was busy most of the time and couldn't see anything but an empty spot where the idea ought to be. I did not know what to do with myself, except the things I had always done.

My brothers were bachelors. It happens with farmers, I think, if they miss a crucial window in their youth. They are often loners anyway; for sure, Avery was. If he spoke occasionally, it was about a hog, a cow, a chicken, a dog, a row of corn or tobacco, the weather, or the dirt itself. Some men just got too caught up with their crops and their animals. For fun, they would just as soon roll a cigarette or take a secret nip of moonshine behind the feed-and-grain store with other farmers as exhaust their time and energy on a woman. Especially since they had gas-powered equipment now, and me around to do the housework. As for the other aspects, I suppose they had their methods and ways of getting their needs met.

They were not unattractive men. Walker, I knew, had had a romance in Europe. (I found a picture and some letters, with writing in French, in his dresser drawer when I was putting away clothes.) He also squired around with a widow lady when he was about thirty, but I doubt she liked the prospect of life at our place on Wheat Road. He had given up trying after that one woman. (She eventually married a car mechanic.)

Walker's experience had been enough to show Avery

that the whole business was just too exhausting to be worth the benefits, which, while enticing, could be sure to result in anxiety over a bunch of extra mouths to feed. They had learned to get along without a mother from the time they were teenagers, and could do the basics for themselves. To be sure, my presence notched up the quality of the household meals again and filled the rooms with what they liked to call "a woman's touch." But I guess all three of us always felt I was optional. To a certain extent, they felt obligated to look after me (as they referred to it), being as I had a failed marriage and was their baby sister and all.

I was touched, I have to say, by their offer to go down to Knoxville and confront John L. and punish him for what he had done to Jane.

"We'll make him do right by you, Isabel," said Walker, and Avery nodded yes, but I declined. Even if I could have stood to go back, I could not stand the thought of what such a confrontation would look like. The results would have been disastrous for my brothers. I had no doubts about how it would go if two farm boys went up against my husband and the gambling, bootlegging ne'er-do-wells he might call to back up his fight.

Upon my return, I looked at our homestead in a different light. I had a sort of resignation about it, but also a sort of gratitude that I had never had before. It was small, about two hundred acres. The house was set high on a bank with stone steps running from the road up to the front yard. The property fronted on the Clinch River, and from the porch, we could see the footbridge strung shore to shore. Through the woods on the other side was Nancy and Tate's house. I still called it that, though Nancy and Tate had both died and new people owned it now.

Our grandfather had started this place as a one-room

cabin, but it had been added on to over the years and had a front parlor, two bedrooms, and a kitchen with our big wood stove and a sink with a hand pump. Electric lights had been added about eight years ago, so all in all, the boys felt the place was to-date. Out back were the springhouse, the chicken coop, the privy, my vegetable garden, a tool shed, and a woodpile with a roof over it. The barn was set in the pasture a little to the north. We had two mules, a few cows, and a horse, and we raised hogs for market and our own ham and bacon. To the south of the house was the bulk of the land where the tobacco and beans grew, along with several acres of apple and peach trees. Those were the cash crops.

For this time and this place, our abode wasn't unusual or outstanding, but it was, as they say, home and had been in the family for over a century and a half. My brothers knew how to live here: they knew how to account for runoff on the slope of a field when they planted, and they knew the way the sun would fall on a given patch of ground at every season of the year. All that takes time to learn, and you get the feel for your land by working it year in and year out.

Then came a day in December 1942. Walker came into the kitchen at two o'clock in the afternoon and slapped a piece of paper on the table.

"Found this posted on the tree by the front steps." He looked grim.

The notice said:

UNITED STATES OF AMERICA
vs.
56,200 Acres of land, more or less, situate in Roane and Anderson Counties . . .

Notice as to Declaration of Taking . . .

You are hereby commanded to notify J.D. Davis (whoever the hell he was) *or his tenants and/or agents . . .*

And so forth, and so on. At the bottom, it said we were to "forthwith vacate said premises IMMEDIATELY" because "they" were going to build a demolition range.

I read through it and handed it back to Walker. My hand shook a little, and I said, "I don't know if anything can be done. The whole tone of this is like the voice of God Almighty, which you know the United States government very nearly is. In the Bible, if God has a use for a bush, He can very well come and burn it and talk to people out of it for whatever purpose He pleases. So if Washington wants this place and comes and tears it all to nothing so a bunch of soldiers can practice throwing grenades, I don't see how you or anyone can prevent it."

"I just plowed under that acreage by Flat Creek," Walker said, as if the government should change its mind on account of that.

"Does Avery know?" I asked.

"He's gone to see the Irwins and the McGills. I talked to old Mr. Range just an hour ago. There's going to be a meeting at Step Creek Church tomorrow night, and a G-man is going to tell us as much details as we can expect. He's also going to let us know how much Uncle Sam would offer to pay us."

Walker stood up and walked to the icebox to pour himself some buttermilk. He swirled it around in his glass and didn't drink it. "There ain't no price they can offer that I would take," he said. "This was Daddy's land, and his daddy's before him. I can't see no good reason why they want these little old farms for a demolition range. There's too many trees. The land ain't even very flat."

"Trees can get chopped might quick. And bulldozers can take out a hill in a day's time." I was folding sheets, and I kept on doing it, only faster. "Walker, I don't think you understand. You don't have a choice. They are going to do what they want, and you will get however much they want to give you. Whose land was it before our family?" I went on.

Walker wrinkled his brow and squinted at me. To him, I had asked a question that had nothing to do with the situation.

"I don't remember," he replied. "I think a man name of Taylor. We've got the deed somewhere."

"And where did Mr. Taylor get it?" I persisted.

"Well, the king of England, I reckon," Walker said. He slapped his side in exasperation. "What does that have to do with anything? Me and Avery own it now, and we ain't givin' it up without a fight."

I couldn't do anything except squeeze his shoulder. "Sit down. I just made a apple pie, and I'm giving you the first piece." There was no use to remind him of all the arrowheads we had found on the property, or of the fact that we had a good dose of Cherokee blood in our veins. King of England, my foot. What goes around comes around, and what went around had now come and fallen here.

I was thinking, though, *Lord, what will become of us?* This surprised me, how I felt so hurt. When I came back here so reluctantly—well, it was perfect I was sitting on the River Clinch. That word described me to a T, the way I was all tightened up inside, resenting my lot. After a time, I had to let myself love the place again; otherwise, I would have been one eternal knot. Nobody can live long like that. I should have known, though. I always lost things I let myself love.

I looked again at the declaration of taking. It was nearly inconceivable to think that life as we had known it would end in thirty days' time.

"I'm going over to the Irwins'," Walker said. He washed his hands and wiped his face and neck with a wet cloth. "I'll get Avery, and we'll go and talk to the others, see if we can all get our minds around this thing—see is there any way to get out of it."

"I'll wait supper till you get back," I said. I went to the desk and got out some paper and an envelope and wrote to our cousin. His place was in Virginia, about seventy-five miles away, and he did the same thing we did, though he had more corn than soybeans and bred hunting dogs. I hoped he might have some advice. He was the type to put every extra dollar he made into land, so maybe he could tell of some property where the boys could take up where they left off.

I knew for sure Walker and Avery would never do anything but farm.

I thought all this was comparable to what we were told about the church; that is, about the body of believers: Christ is the bridegroom, and the church is His bride. The church is talked about like it's a woman, a woman who is being given. Her future is arranged; it is not her decision.

It felt the same to me now. The government was Uncle Sam; it was a man. And like it or not, us girls would go along with the plan or suffer the consequences. We would have to ride out of here like virgins, just trusting, and with our little white souls in the palms of our hands. We were going to have to tell ourselves it was good to be chosen.

That night, the little meeting house at Step Creek was packed. People from about sixty families came, plus the government man. We had heard that about a thousand families were being asked to leave their homes in the valley below Black Oak Ridge. That included Robertsville and Scarboro, as well as the Wheat community. For all the effort folks made to speak quietly, the room still jangled with anxiety. It could have been a funeral for a murder victim, and no killer to finger. People here more or less did what they wanted, and they did that slow. This new project was a racehorse, and it had thrown everyone into turmoil.

"We know it's a hardship to you," said J.D. Davis, the government man of declaration fame. He was the only one present wearing a suit and tie. "And I wish I could tell you more about the project that will be put in place here. But national security is involved, and even I do not know the details. All I can say is, everyone in America is being called on right now to make sacrifices to win the war against Germany and Japan. No doubt, some of you in this room have sons serving in Europe and the Pacific, so you know how crucial it is that we do everything possible to end this conflict as soon as possible."

I was sitting with Mary Greene McGill, Gallatin's little sister, and her baby girl. Chelsie was a big, energetic thing with dimpled legs and lots of yellow hair, just the opposite of her bony mother. Mary's looks had not improved as she matured; she was always fragile, and life had not handled her delicately. She was as faded as her dress.

"There isn't nothing that's going to help," Mary said. "Walt is tired all the time as it is, out in the field sunup to sundown, and now he's heartsick, to boot, over being done this way. We are going to take our money and go to Akron. Katy's husband went there, you know, after she died from the flu. He works at the tire factory there and says he can get Walt a job." She looked at the pulpit where J.D. was still talking, and kicked up her chin in his direction. "I bet he knows what is really goin' on! To him and his bosses, we are just country people. They think they can walk all over us and we won't be able to do a thing about it, and they would be right. It's just another cross we have to bear, the biggest one yet, and the most we can do is believe it's all to the good of the war. It's not that I ain't behind the war. Of course, we all are. But sacrificing up your home . . . at least I just have little 'uns and don't have to give 'em big boys for the fighting," she added.

"Thank the Lord for that," I said, and I patted her hand. I thought of Jeremiah, possibly in harm's way out in the middle of the ocean, but I let my mind stay neutral. I had had plenty of death to tally and did not need to ponder more. Being here with Mary, I thought, too, of Gallatin and his leaving all those years ago. I would always have a tender spot for him, but until now, I had never ventured to ask his sisters what became of him. Asking questions would have given them license to start questioning me. We were a blank community when it came to family secrets. No one ever knew anything. I'm sure it was whispered about behind hands that I had a second husband. Most people had heard that I had married again after Samuel died and that it hadn't worked out. I had never given the whole story to anyone but Queenie and Walker and Avery.

"Nice that you might be able to go to Akron and start over," I said and plunged on. "Anybody else in the family you could call on?" I looked Mary straight in the face, and she recognized my question for what I really wanted.

"Hadn't heard from my brother for years, but, well, you know Gallatin," she said, as if she understood we were sweet on each other and I had seen him just yesterday. She studied the crowd of neighbors in our little sanctuary. "We heard tell he went to Sarasota, Florida, to a Ringling Brothers camp there. He sent us a picture postcard a couple of years after he left, just that one time. He was wearing pointy shoes with a pair of A-rab pants and a fancy little vest and holding some juggling pins." Her face folded and her eyes glittered. "I wish it had been different, Isabel, I really do."

"I thank you for that." I smiled to think of him all suited up like Aladdin. *Gallatin. Galladin the Great,* I thought, and smiled even more.

Mary sniffled and jiggled Chelsie. "What are you all going to do when you leave?"

I motioned across the church aisle in my brothers' direction. "The boys are resisting what's got to happen. Avery was standing out in the cemetery right before he came in here and just stood looking at Daddy's stone, as if he could get some advice from beyond the grave. It's going to be hard to convince them they can raise hogs and tobacco just as good on another piece of land. We have some cousins up over the Virginia line that may be able to help us. They have a big property and may be willing to sell a little of it or know somebody who's got a farm they want out of."

I paused. The boys' future in farming was like a plot in a boring novel I was telling about. It struck me that I did not particularly consider myself to be a character in their tale. I saw no reason for my own course to be bound up with Avery and Walker's. *Isabel the Great, what are you going to do now?* I thought. It was like I saw the title page of my own life, with a woman emoting dramatically, her hand flung up over her forehead, and a curly-edged Declaration of Taking in giant Victorian letters on the desk before her.

"Looky there," Mary said. She ticked her tongue. "It's Mr. Range. He's sixty years old if he's a day. He's too old to start over."

Mr. Range, wiry as a teenage boy but with white hair, stood up. He was wearing the overalls he had worked in that day. I could see the place where his wife had sewed one strap back on, and there was a red bandanna hanging out of his back pocket. I'd known Stewart Range all my life. If ever the phrase "salt of the earth" applied to a person, it was him. He stood there rotating his felt hat in his tree-root hands as he began to clear his throat.

"The house we are in, my grandfather built it hisself. It means everything to me." He halted and looked back at Range Jr., his son, sitting beside him. Mr. Davis lifted his eyebrows.

"I understand," he said, not even trying to pretend like he did. He twiddled his pen between two fingers. Everyone waited.

I closed my eyes and tried to breathe. All you had to do was look from Mr. Range to Mr. Davis to see it was over. No sentiment or pleading words or argument would keep the government from appropriating our land. Mr. Davis let several other men stand up and make weak arguments and emote. The air was full of patriotism and pain.

When we left the church, the men were talking in low, depressed voices about salvaging as much as they could. Tobacco was still curing in their barns; not all the corn shocks were gathered. They were going to sell off livestock, but who did they know who wanted thirty cows at one time? The women were mournful and clinging to each other, but also looking to sell or even give away beds and stoves and iceboxes to neighbors whose property wouldn't be taken.

We were devastated, but still, we were all workers first and foremost—we did the next thing that needed doing.

On the way out, I heard a name being bandied about in a side conversation. I asked Mary, "Did *you* ever hear tell of John Hendrix, who owned the farm off Bethel Road?" She nodded, looking at me with knowing eyes.

"Yes," she whispered. "I've heard many a one mention him these past two days. I remember when his little girl died after a bad fever. She was only eight years old. His wife blamed him for it because he'd spanked her just before she got sick. John went out and lay down in the middle of his fallow field and cried. They always called him the Prophet of Black Oak Ridge, but now they say it without mocking," she said.

"Yes." I nodded. "They thought he'd gone a little crazy out of sorrow."

The story was, John came home and told everyone he'd had a vision of things coming to the valley. It was a premonition of construction, of railroad tracks, engines, and factories. He said our lives henceforward would be forever changed. At the time, people had just listened, surprised and suspicious. Now the man was our Elijah.

People like us, you see, we didn't put much stock in things that were "foretold."

Twenty

A Vision of the Apocalypse

1942

At the time, of course, we all wanted to support the war effort, but I was sad, sad especially for my brothers and for the spirit of my daddy. God rest his goddamned soul. They had put so much work into those fields, and they didn't know how to do anything but till soil in spring and reap in fall. Moving hogs to another pen was one thing, but wiping out our pretty orchards was another. And to lose the house . . . for it to be torn down, no matter how insignificant it looked on its little plot, was painful. Still, as I had tried to say to Walker, the land belonged to the Cherokees before us if it belonged to anybody at all, and we took it, so it wasn't exactly unfair. Lost to a stronger bunch. We got some of what we gave.

The government told us giving up our homes and our land was a noble cause, and that we were helping in an important way. They would take our rock and soil and make it the foundation for something that would help America fight, that would help us win. (You are supposed to hear "The Star-Spangled Banner" playing as I say this.)

I am no prophet. I am just a little person, and my dream was only about me and my family, the way most dreams are.

In the dream, this house, my childhood home, was there. It was on an empty rock ground, abandoned, all its window eyes staring blank and lonely.

There was a cane-bottomed chair beside the house, and I came and sat in it and folded my hands on my lap. It was like there was going to be a stage play, and I was the sole character in it. Out to the side, behind a curtain, a hand moved in the dark to pull a switch and start things moving.

And then the ground rumbled and shook, a blinding light came up, and a great wind rose and swept me and the house away like a broom moving over crumbs. My hair blew back and came off my head in one piece like a wig. My clothes and skin went to tatters, and the house beside me became a powder of wood dust and glass sand flying all around me. A hot breath lifted me up, and I began to move fast through the darkness. Bodiless, I streamed through the black. I was carried, flying on. I seemed to still have my mind, so I prayed, *O God, please, let there be someplace where I will wake and be whole.*

Twenty-One

Gallatin's Ghost

1943

Queenie, honey, I can't thank you enough. You know I will
land on my feet. I promise not to take up your space too
long. . . . Yes, I know you do. Thanks, honey. See you
soon."

I hung up the Johnsons' telephone. It was a relief to
have made the call I just had. Queenie had said for me to
come to her in Asheville, and so I said I would and make a
plan from there.

The Johnsons lived further down Wheat Road than we
did, and it had been easy for Ma Bell to string a line to their
house. I had had a phone when I lived with John L. Keller,
so moving home four years ago and not having communication was like going back in time.

Like I mentioned, Walker and Avery had electricity,
barely. The wiring for the lights was stapled straight onto
the walls and ran up to a bulb in the center of each room,
but we did not have a telephone. The Johnsons, on the

other hand, had the phone but no electricity. Orval Johnson farmed tobacco, and all his money went into a new tractor and repairs on his Ford truck. He liked me, though, and didn't seem to mind lending me the use of his phone in exchange for pleasant words and an occasional pie.

Orval's mother was snapping beans, sitting on the front porch on a plush sofa with all the stuffing coming out on one side. It made me think of Dora. She would have said the sofa had good structure; she would have talked it away from old Mrs. Johnson, had it recovered in red velvet, and then put it in her bedroom and bragged about how she got an antique mahogany fainting couch for nothing. I sat down and reached into Mrs. Johnson's bowl and grabbed up a handful of beans.

"You are lucky your property is outside the boundary of the declaration of taking," I told the old woman. I snapped a few pods and looked on the bright side. "Avery and Walker will farm some acreage in Virginia belonging to a cousin of ours. It is like to kill us, getting everything moved up there. But once things are squared away, I am looking forward to visiting my friend in Asheville. You remember Queenie, don't you? That's who I was talking to."

Mrs. Johnson was eighty-two years old. She said, "Isn't she the one that had that out-of-wedlock baby? Such a shame. I hope her life turns out better than mine has. I wouldn't wish the life I've had on nobody. I broke my leg when I was sixteen while I was pregnant with Orval, and I hadden been the same since. I'm just living because I got no choice. As long as my heart keeps on beating, I have to keep on looking out from inside my head. Seems like I cain't move for life, but I cain't move for death neither."

"Queenie did not have an out-of-wedlock baby," I started, but there was no stopping her. I was used to it.

She said, "I got this numbness? Hit's right here in that leg. I keep a safety pin stuck here in this sofa, and sometimes, I poke it into my leg, just to make sure there's feeling in there somewhere."

I saw Mrs. Johnson reach for her pin, so I grabbed it and gave her some beans I'd done instead. Her voice ran on like water.

"You see that ole mountain over there? That ole mountain is just sitting and waiting, same as me. Sometimes, I think there's a giant up there, standing with his arms raised, and any moment, he'll pounce down and smother me. You know how kids see pictures in the clouds—a white dog, a man with a long, flowing beard? Well, that mountain has more shapes than the sky. The dirt and the forest seem to hang on the rock like a heavy quilt hiding that giant. One day, the quilt will drop and there he'll be, and I'll be setting here and cain't move to get away."

I threw my last handful of beans in the bowl. Listening to his mother always drained my energy, but it was another way of thanking Orval for the use of his phone.

"Miz Johnson, I better get on home now. We have a lot to do to pack up the house." I called through the screen, "I'm going, Orval. Thanks again."

Orval came to the door. He was getting older and living with his ancient mother. He had a port-wine birthmark on his face and smelled like hay and onions. "You're welcome, Isabel," he said and then cleared his throat. "I been meaning to ask—could I see you to church again this Sunday? Might be the last chanst we'll have, unless a miracle hap-pens."

Orval was a nice person, but I had no interest in him and never had. He had asked me about three times now and I had gone, but I didn't like it one bit, him trying to court me this way. Especially not now, with everything that was going on. Everybody knew I was about to be homeless, so his timing was bad—or good, depending on a person's perspective of my situation.

His mother would be dead soon, and I could see what was happening plain as day. I thought, *Am I that bad looking? Do I look like a man's answer to a need for a broom, a mended shirt, and a hot meal? Is that all they see when they look at me?* Looking at Orval, it was painful to consider.

I lifted my head. "Orval, I can't. Now listen." I put my hand on his for the first time ever, and his eyes got very wide. "I am going to tell you plain. I 'preciate what you are thinking and all, but the only man I plan to love from here on out is Jesus." It was a lie, but I knew he could accept that kind of competition.

Orval stared at me, digesting, and I remembered a line from a song we sang in church: "He will take me in His arms." More and more, I saw why religion appealed to women. I did not need a man to complete me anymore. Everybody always turned things over to me eventually, and I was tired of it. If you dedicate your future to Jesus, He is there to help, always young and virile and appealing, but you do not have to deal with a living male.

I continued. "Did you hear me on the phone just now? I am going to stay with my friend Queenie after the boys get moved, and I will probably get some work over there. I don't know when I will be back to these parts. So it's best if you start looking elsewhere, sooner rather than later."

Once my words were out, I felt a tremendous excitement. I didn't have the slightest idea what I was going to do. Well, I knew I was going to visit Queenie for a while, but I just made up the part about getting a job. I only knew, for the first time, what I was *not* going to do.

"Bye-bye, Miz Johnson," I said and stepped off the

porch. "Bye, Orval," I said. "I really do wish you all the luck in the world." I blew him a kiss. Miz Johnson stared back at me out of her perpetual misery, but she did lift her hand, like holding up a block of wood. Orval just stared.

I went home and wrote:

Dear Janey,

I have some surprising news. All of Wheat and Scarboro and Robertsville have been taken by the Government. Something big is going to be built here. We don't know what. In any case we had no choice but to leave & they have paid us a pittance for the land truly a pittance. Crops will be ruint and we will be packed up and gone within the week. Walker and Avery are going to cousin L.K.'s near Abingdon and work for him for a while The plan is for them to eventualy buy a piece of land of their own. L.K. has a wife and two daughters to take care of the household and I am not much needed so I am striking out on my own.

I just talked to Queenie and she said I could stay with her for a little while until I got a job so Janey honey I just wanted you to know where I was. Here is Queenie's address be sure to let Dora know.

Love,

Mother

What I didn't tell her was, Avery and Walker expected me to go with them to Abingdon. I had decided I was not going to do that, and I was not going to argue about it, any more than I argued with John L. Keller when I left him. Now that the boys were set on their new place, I decided I had to leave. I just had to. If I spoke to my brothers or thought about it too much, I would get sentimental. I would feel like they were disappointed in me, and they would say my roots were with the family and how would I get two red cents to rub together? And other nonsense. Long ago, I had told Gallatin I was not a runaway person, and I was not. But when a situation became broken before my very eyes, the way it did with John L. and the way it had again now, I was not going to stand around with a pot of glue and try to fix something that had been crushed to smithereens.

I slept uneasy that night, like a schoolgirl before her first dance. In all my days, I had never made a decision without it being tied to someone *else's* life—what they needed from me. This was crazy and difficult, like flinging money in the river, then diving in to find it. I was not going to follow Walker and Avery to Virginia. This was my turning point.

When John L. bothered Janey and I sent her off to live with Dora, I came back to the valley in the shadow of Black Oak Ridge where I was born. I rarely cried.

I kept house for my brothers while they farmed, same as I did when I was a child after my mama died. Now I had to, once and for all, think about who I was and what I wanted out of life.

That night, I dreamed of my sister, Molly, dead now these twenty years. She put on Mrs. Johnson's face like a mask. Through the features of the old woman, she looked at me with eyes gone watery and half-blue with cataracts.

"I can't do it anymore," she said. "I just don't have the strength."

"What do you need to do?" I asked. She tried to take off her Mrs. Johnson mask, but it was stuck to her face.

Then I said, "Don't worry. It doesn't matter." I reached out my hands. "I'll take care of it somehow, like I always do," I said. "We'll figure it out as we go."

I thought all the next morning about Gallatin and

about whether I was being a "runaway person" or not. I imagined him answering me back: "You are not running away. You are being made to leave. It's a perfect opportunity. You are taking a stand on behalf of yourself for once."

"But it's cowardice, not telling Walker and Avery. It's selfishness too." I talked to him as I closed up my sewing machine and packed it in its case. Whether it was going to Virginia or not, it still had to be stowed.

"It's not," said Gallatin. "Not either one." I loved seeing his muscles under the little Arabian vest he wore. He idly juggled a stack of bowls I had not yet packed. "What you call 'cowardice' is just avoiding conflict. And what you call 'selfish,' well, so what if it is? This is your one life, Isabel. How long will you let it happen according to other people's intentions? And really, they will be fine without you."

I had to agree, I could do things besides bake and sweep for room and board like a servant.

"You're still pretty too, Isabel," Gallatin said.

"Thanks." I smiled. I knew I didn't look so old. I had fooled Orval. He thought I was in my thirties. I don't know where he got that. I never gained weight, and my hair was still coal black, thanks to the Cherokee blood in me, though my skin was Irish. The spark had not gone out of me to make myself into something, either. I didn't want to keep on keeping house for Walker and Avery, and I didn't want to marry Orval or anyone. Orval couldn't have married me anyway, of course, since I never got divorced from John L.

"All right," I said.

I packed my flimsy suitcase, the same as I did when I left John L., and took up my Singer sewing machine in its carrying case and started down the steps to the road without telling anybody. I did leave a note on the table so they wouldn't worry. Last week, we had all driven to Abingdon to see where we'd—I mean, they'd—live, and I had planted some radishes and lettuce in an old garden patch out back. I wasn't real sure either one of the boys would take the time to tend the plot, so I asked them to do that and to understand.

I stopped one last time at the hydrangea bush by the mailbox. With spring still weeks away, the big, round poms were dried and brown, but it was possible to see that some of them had been blue and some had been white. The color difference had always fascinated me, and I thought of it as a special plant, but Walker had told me it was just because a dog peed on one side all the time.

"Pissed on, is what it amounts to," I said out loud and pursed my mouth, thinking of the demolition range.

"But without it, you never would be going, so take that into consideration before you curse them," Gallatin said.

So, I left. And I knew that I was seeing everything here for the very last time. Even if I ever came back, this house, these grounds and trees, would be erased. Even the slope of the land might be changed; streams might be gone. I looked and looked one last time. There was a place on the front porch where I had cut my initials when I was a child; all these years, it had been there. I never gave it a thought before, but I put my fingers in the letters and it felt holy.

I am telling you, pay attention every minute. Everything is so fleeting, as you are yourself. Still, I knew this place was permanent in me, would be ever present, like people I loved who had died. The fact of their touch on my life was locked into the grain of myself and couldn't be shook loose. Like when Molly died. I still know the shape of her face, the sound of her voice, the sweetness of her way. I cannot dwell on it without prickling with tears. When Mama died. When Sam died. When Daddy died. When I had to leave Jane. No declaration of taking can steal them from me.

For a while, I just put one foot in front of the other and concentrated on how heavy the cases were and what good blisters I was going to have. And then I started to run over what money I had brought and how long it could last me. It comforted me to know that if there was one thing I could do, it was stretch a dollar from here to kingdom come. I guess I was thinking a little about getting to the bus station and what Asheville would be like. I tried not to think about Walker and Avery or about any aspect of the house that I was fond of. I tried to keep my mind forward. Even though I was all alone going down the mountain road, I was keeping my head up real high and seeing in my mind's eye what my hair looked like, and did I have on enough lipstick?

I was down to the main road now, and on the ridge about a mile away, I could see the tiny cars and trucks moving silently along a silver railing, like someone was pulling them by a thread. I passed a field where huge rolls of chain-link fencing already replaced the hay bales that used to be there. A small fleet of olive-green government trucks had also arrived. The air broke to pieces with the horrible juddering racket of a grader and two bulldozers. I wanted to get away from it as quick as I could. Four men huddled over a blueprint spread out on a tailgate. They were no one I knew.

The dirt and gravel crunched under my soles, one-two, one-two. I started to say my own name over and over to myself—"Isabel, Isabel"—in rhythm with my steps. It seemed now to be the only word left in my brain, and I allowed myself to be sentimental about this person, Isabel. She was little, like a lost child, and deserved to have a fine life, but I was not sure I could give it to her. I vowed not to be sad, swore to myself it was just emotion from starting out. And after that, I began saying "Isabel, Isabel" again, only fiercely this time, and I kept walking, strong and head up, as if I was carrying a flag.

Twenty-Two

Mr. Post

I walked until I got to the Texaco, then hitched a ride with a truck driver to the Clinton Highway. I walked again from there to the bus station. It was attached to a little general store that had been there for years, but I hadn't been down this way for a year or more, and some major changes had taken place.

There was a buffalo tied up outside. I had never seen a real one before, but of course, I recognized it from seeing it on nickels: a bull with a hump. He had a leather collar, and it seemed to be chafing him and embarrassing him both. He knew he wasn't a dog, but there wasn't much he could do about it, on account of a metal cuff around his right front leg, which was attached to a chain anchored in concrete. He only had about ten feet of leeway.

One thing I felt instinctively was that this wasn't the healthiest buffalo that had ever been. He should have had some fire in him, an animal that size. His hair, which was powdered with road dust, was starting to look mangy. Maybe he was underfed or had been whipped. I took a step

177

over to pet him. He seemed so pitiful. I shouldn't have put my hand up so fast, but I was tired and sorry just then for anything that seemed like it ought to be free and wasn't. Startled like that, he yanked his chain and snorted this croupy noise and turned his nasty matted tail to me. He kicked back hard like a mule, and if it hadn't been for my cased-up sewing machine on the ground in front of me, my leg would have been broken for sure.

I started laughing and laughing. I have the worst luck—though in hindsight, some might say I have the best luck, to be so stupid as to try to pet a buffalo and come out un-scathed. I dragged my sewing machine away from the creature's reach and laughed some more at the size of the hole the hoof had made in the case, but the machine itself was undamaged.

Finally, I went inside the store, about to collapse from not having anything to eat since breakfast at six o'clock. I bought some crackers and cheese and an orange drink. Then I went and sat back outside in a row of old theatre seats propped against the store front. The fellow tending the cash register gave me a look. I felt homeless, but did I appear that way too?

The store clerk tiptoed out and stood in the doorway, smoking a cigarette and examining the damage to my case. I leaned back against the building and closed my eyes. I took another swallow of the orange drink and thought about Jeremiah in the Pacific and how I needed to write and let him know what had happened to Wheat, to me. I thought about Janey, safe at Dora's. I should have called to tell her more about what I was doing. They would think I had lost my mind. I would telephone as soon as I got to Asheville.

The clerk sat down next to me and leaned around.

"Are you okay?" he asked. "Sorry about your luggage,

but don't you see my sign?" He pointed to a plaque on the building edge, which read, "Steer clear of the buffaloe. For display only."

"I'm fine," I replied. "My case is not too good, but speaking of miserable cases, that animal is one," I added. "I hate to see him looking so downhearted. I didn't even notice your sign. Why do you have him chained up? He ought to be running loose with a herd somewhere out west. Or at the very least, in a zoo. Isn't there a zoo in Knoxville?"

"I bought him from a Indian in North Dakota. He'll be my star attraction." He scuffed some dust in the animal's direction with the toe of his shoe. "He's a wild thing and has to be restrained until I get him a proper fenced-in spot. I'm starting up a little wildlife farm, you see, for a tourist attraction. There might be a zoo in Knoxville, but people are more likely to stop at something they can see from the road." He framed his hands around an imaginary slogan: "Exotic things: the world as it used to be and the creatures that lived in it."

I would never stop at such a place unless it was also a bus stop and I had to, but I let him continue. He went on like he was quoting from a brochure.

"See, Montana—that's his name—is part of the great American wilderness, and people want to experience that before it disappears."

I started to point out that with Montana tied down, it seemed to defeat the point, but he was ahead of me. Following my eyes, he shrugged.

"I hate to confine him, but how else can people get a look?" He stuck out his hand. "Arthur Post. Pleased to meet you, Miz . . ."

"Isabel. Just call me Isabel." We shook.

"On your way to . . . ?"

"Asheville. For now, anyway," I added.

"Took your property, did they? What exactly is happening over there around Black Oak Ridge?"

"Yes, it was my brothers' land. I was living with them. It's been quite an upheaval for everyone. They are saying it will be a demolition range, but who knows for sure?"

I wanted to change the subject. "What other animals will you have in your tourist farm?"

"Well, Miz Isabel, since you asked. I do already have a few other specimens in my outbuilding, if you'd be interested. Mostly snakes and birds and my monkey. Let me just lock the store up for a minute or two, and I'll show you."

Mr. Post wiped his hands on his dirty butcher's apron and stood up. He looked so happy at my interest, and with his receding fuzz of blond hair and dark-blue eyes, he seemed so much like a needy toddler, I couldn't bring myself to refuse.

"I won't charge you," he said, not realizing my hesitancy was in no way financial. "Consider this a preview of my grand opening."

The outbuilding was a sort of storage shed, full of lawn equipment and boxes of goods and supplies. The health department would have loved to see it, with the white bird droppings on the unopened cases of cornflakes and Spam. The whole place smelled like a wet barn in need of mucking out. There were cages of dime-store parakeets and canaries. Two big birds with orange-and-green beaks the size of hedge clippers had a netted-in space all to themselves. Over in a dark corner, a forlorn little saw-whet owl was huddled up behind some chicken wire, but he couldn't have slept, not with all the racket. And the snakes, in low boxes under the bird cages, must have been driving all of them crazy. I sensed a slow shifting down by my ankles, and an arc of light began to slide over something in a screened-over orange crate. It was golden brown and almost liquid, like a clump of mud breaking up. And then I saw it: a nest of copperheads, four or five of them braided together. I fell away like I'd been hit, and accidentally bumped another box with my toe. A rattler went off.

My blood just about turned to ice. I said, "Mr. Post, I'm not real fond of snakes. You do have some nice animals in here, and I wish you all the luck in the world with your tourist farm. But I better not leave my bags alone too long, and the Knoxville–Asheville bus will be along shortly. I don't want to miss it."

Mr. Post took my arm. A good thing since I was about to faint. "Just right back here's my monkey. Don't you want to see him? He's got his own closet. I don't keep no snakes back there. And anyway, all the snakes are locked up tight. I wouldn't have brought you in here if there was any danger at all." He looked truly concerned, his broad baby's forehead wrinkled up over his eyes.

We stepped around a shipment of brooms bundled like sheaves of harvested wheat, then went along by some large boxes that said Northern Toilet Paper. A beautiful white bird—with a sweeping tail and a cock's comb like fancy red crochet—screamed in my left ear.

"My cockatoo," Arthur Post said proudly. "Got him at the same time as the toucans. My farm will have both North and South America represented."

I looked back at the tropical birds out of their element. Their enclosure was in front of a window, and through the netting and the glass, I could see the layered mountains, dark blue and medium blue and faint blue, like a cardboard picture. I was not at all interested in foreign worlds, except to read about them. Mostly, I wanted to know where I could find a place for myself, a place that felt like home.

Mr. Post opened a door in a chicken-wire cage, and a spider monkey looked down at us from a high shelf. He had watery light-brown eyes, the kind you see on old men in nursing homes. The monkey was sitting up there, pulling on himself. His little thing stuck out brazen as you please, like a stripped twig.

"Mr. Bones! You stop that now!" Arthur Post's pink face darkened a little, and he swatted up at the monkey. "Come on down here now. Say hello proper."

The monkey swung down to his owner's shoulder, then reached with his arm like a fur skeleton to point at the mountains through the birds' window.

"He wants to go outside. That's his signal. Want some fresh air, don't you, Mr. Bones?" The monkey climbed up on Mr. Post's head, leaned over, and looked him in the face upside down.

"Mr. Bones has a good suggestion," I said. I wanted out too. It was like I could actually see that fresh air that Mr. Bones and I needed. I had to force myself not to run for the outside. But I didn't want to be rude.

We picked our way back. Mr. Bones grabbed hold of the toucan's cage and clung there for a minute, like a cat. He screamed at the birds, showing his jagged, razor-sharp teeth.

Once out, Mr. Bones jumped out of Arthur Post's arms and skittered over to Montana, like a wisp of something blown along the ground. For a while, the little animal danced around under the buffalo's legs, which brought the big creature to life. Montana began to haul on his chain, kicking and thrashing.

"Mr. Bones!" Mr. Post called to the monkey like a parent calling down a child he was really proud of. "Now, you stop that right now. You are aggravating old Monty."

The buffalo stamped his heavy hooves and lashed out again with his deadly rear legs. The little creature dodged and wove like a flyweight boxer. He shimmied up the buffalo's leg and sat just behind the giant head. He got his little hand going on himself again, and every now and then, he'd stop and groom deep in Monty's fur. I thought of rag monkeys I used to make out of brown socks and red thread for Sallie and Jeremiah, and I knew I would never make another one as long as I lived. I sure was anxious for my bus to come.

When I finally heard it, I collected my suitcase and sewing machine and moved toward the highway. Mr. Post came over and stood with me. He put his hands in his pockets and rocked back and forth.

"Well, sir," I said, "I want to thank you again for showing me your tourist attraction. Best of luck."

"Thank you," he said. "I'm hopeful, I really am. All this new construction, these new people coming in. Businesses can benefit. We just need to stay up with the changing times." He went to a hand pump a few feet away and pumped some water in a bucket and took it over to Monty. He patted the beast, raising a cloud of dust. The animal didn't seem to object to Mr. Post's touch. The man stood up straight from the water bucket, and his big blue eyes blinked. He really loved all his pets and didn't have a clue in the world that a tourist farm was not the place for a buffalo, or that good intentions toward the creatures you captured didn't make up for what they'd lost.

"Miz Isabel," he said, "I hope you have a nice visit with your friend in Asheville. Course, North Carolina isn't as pretty as East Tennessee, in my opinion, but I've always thought it does a body good to travel."

I looked at Mr. Post one last time and thought about all the people I might or might not cross paths with through the rest of my life. I walked over and gave my suitcase and sewing machine with a hole in it to the bus driver, and he put them in the luggage compartment.

"Wait a minute." Mr. Post ran in his store and was back out in a second, waving a gold-colored magazine. "I just finished this *National Geographic*. Sort of helps me study up for my new line of work, don't you know? But you take it. Something to read on the bus, help you pass the time."

"Thank you kindly," I said. "Goodbye."

The bus pulled away as I was still moving down the aisle, and a mother sitting with her little boy urged the child up onto his knees to look out the window.

"Look, honey. Do you know what that is? That's a buffalo. Can you see his big old horns?"

I moved down past them, way into the back. I had forgotten to get back the deposit on my orange drink bottle, but by the time I sat down, it was too late to retrieve it.

After a time, I took out the *Geographic* and started thumbing through. A piece about Chinatown in San Francisco. An ad for a Packard car with a family in it. Gary Cooper selling Kodak cameras.

I stopped on a picture of a black mountain, the picture so black the ink shone silver in the light.

It was an article about Iceland, which is nearly at the top of the world. It is almost all mountains and glaciers— black mountains from volcano rock and pure-white glacier ice. There's almost no grass in Iceland, almost no animals, I read. No monkeys, no buffalo, no snakes or reptiles of any kind. Cockatoos don't like the cold there. Only mice and rats and reindeer and fish—and sheep, which were brought in and raised for their thick fur.

There was a picture of some people in bathing suits standing in the snow near a hot spring that steamed the cold air white. Apparently, Iceland really wasn't all that freezing, at least not on the coast where all the people lived.

It was a very interesting article. The little arctic island gets dark early every year and stays dark until almost spring. I tried to imagine the sheep and how hard it would be to survive with the sunless sky and the sharp, dark land growing only a few green valleys. The article said people learned to play a lot of indoor games and cards to amuse themselves, and they read a lot. Another picture showed a woman in a handmade embroidered blouse eating a banana, which supposedly grew in a greenhouse right there in Iceland.

And then I read something that really made me stop. It said that women could divorce their husbands just by declaring they didn't want to be married anymore. Two red-cheeked women in scarves, supposedly divorced, were laughing over a hand of cards. When women got married, they didn't change their names, and people were listed in the phone directory by their first name and what they did. I thought it was funny—in Iceland, I would be "Isabel, seamstress" or "Isabel, housekeeper," to show me apart from the other Isabels who taught school or worked in offices. People did have last names. It would be based on their father's name if they were a man and on their mother's name if they were a woman.

I felt a window open in my mind. I sat there and thought how I was Isabel Marthasdottir and Jane was Janeyre Isabelsdottir. Immediately adopting the Icelandic way, I declared myself divorced once and for all from John

L. Keller and fully my own person. And I took back my
original name, Isabel King, at that moment, with apologies
to Samuel. I did not care what was "legal." Sometimes, you
just do what's right, and where I was going, nobody (except
Queenie) would know me, so nobody would care.

I looked out the window of the bus. The sun was going
down behind the mountains that turned green every year.
Now was a time when the land was cold and barren, but
there were brilliant blue skies. I was going to have to move
on from everything I had known and enter a new America,
one with factories and demolition ranges and wild animals
held hostage in tourist attractions.

Was it a consolation to the Icelandic women, to be
divorced so easy and have their own names while they ate
fruit never intended to be grown in their land? Did they feel
that the long-haired sheep redeemed the existence of so
much ice? And I thought it had to, with all those long, dark
days and the black mountain there, reminding you of the
volcano under your feet.

Twenty-Three

Fires

Queenie told me to call her when I got to the Greyhound station, but I hated to bother her any more than I was already going to. It seemed like every prospect I had for the future depended on my old friend. I didn't know what to do about that just yet. Something would turn up, and in the meantime, we would have a good visit, I hoped. I got directions from a man at the counter.

"It's a nice area near the high school," he said. "Just a couple of miles. I'd be happy to call you a cab. You have to go through a tunnel and into the city, and the neighborhood is beyond that."

"I guess I'll walk," I said. "Two miles is nothing where I come from, and it's a pretty day." I didn't add that I had been through many tunnels, in a manner of speaking, places in life where I couldn't see light on the other side. He tipped his finger to his head in a little salute and went back to his newspaper.

I went round the square. It was late afternoon, and spokes of low sun warned me to get somewhere quick before night fell. I was looking for the street to turn onto when I noticed black smoke billowing up in the near distance. A fire truck rushed past me with all the sirens and whistles going.

I stared at the spreading smoke. The people on the street near me began to comment and point. We were close enough to start to smell it. Ever since my mama died at the asylum, I have had an interest in fires. Every time I ran across a blaze, I had to quench my anxiety and see for myself what had happened, see the physical evidence of destruction or survival. I knew I shouldn't do it. When I detoured through an alleyway, I felt a little guilty, realizing I was going to follow another fire.

Fires raised nothing but questions. I don't know why I tortured myself looking at them. Maybe I kept thinking, irrational as it was, that the fires were all related and I was going to find out that my mama had survived after all.

When I was growing up, if you saw smoke in the distance, you had to say to yourself, *Is that coming from the Johnsons' place? Do you think old Mrs. Johnson started a grease fire in her kitchen?* Or if it was night, you might think, *Was it a lightning strike on the Greenes' barn?* Because if it was a neighboring property, my daddy and my brothers and me would go banging on pans and hollering down the valley to wake everybody up and say come help water it down. And you had to know the look of smoke well enough to realize it wasn't just from a chimney.

In a way, it wasn't right to go down the streets of Asheville, letting the smoke smell get stronger and stronger, knowing full well I was just going to gawk and not help. Gradually, I entered a stream of people striding fast in my same direction. We went like it was the opening of a county fair. You could feel the excitement in the body of the crowd.

Somebody said, "With this much of a fire, do you think anybody got caught in it?" And it was like they almost wanted them to be.

A little boy brushed up against me, pulling his mother's arm. "Come on, Mama; come *on.*"

And the woman hustled up, her heels clacking on the pavement, her bottom bouncing. And there were men in suits who ought to have still been at work, and more children, suddenly—boys and girls chattering to each other and chasing about through the skirts and legs of the grown-ups. I almost pulled up short and went back to the bus station. All those kids—I didn't want it to be a school burning or anything. But it wasn't. I was close enough now to see the flames.

Once, in Wheat, I looked up from hoeing the kitchen garden, and it flashed to me that something about the day had gone awry. It was so sudden; I saw a high veil of smoke and heat shimmering, like a dozen giant candles were lit in a row just over the horizon.

I screamed, "Walker! Avery! Fire!" A sour knot rose from my stomach to beat in my throat like a fist. We sounded the alarm for our neighbors' help, then ran for shovels and cutters. We stood fighting that day for our very lives and the lives of our house and our crops. We never did know how it started. Maybe a smoker out walking didn't kill his butt well enough. Maybe it was just a natural event. It had been a real dry year. It was mostly a grass fire; we saw the flames halfway up our north slope. But the wind would bring the fire down to the creek bottom on the opposite side, where we'd planted sweet corn. The ears had grown about three-quarters ready, but we went and cut it all down with scythes and our one tractor, then watched the burning crawl along down through what we'd sacrificed. Fear was the flames would jump the creek, but they didn't, so we saved the tobacco and the house.

What was burning now was a clapboard with a third-story attic dormer, and it was blazing good. It was like a picture-book house on fire. All the windows had bright-orange flags twisting up from inside and plumes of gray smoke in pretty spirals. The house was a box holding nothing but fire, and the question among the spectators was, How long before it falls?

When the fire came to our fields out of the trees, I watched the flames flicker down the hill. It almost looked pretty—the line of the ground started to shift a little and curl. The waves moved forward like bits of sun, licking up the field. From a distance, they didn't scare you at all as you knew they should. Thinking of how my mama died in a fire, I had an urge to walk up to it, but I knew that was not the right way to feel. So it seemed really bad—somehow, the danger was coming from inside myself.

The field fire was peaceful too, like a fireplace with a low roar, just every now and then a sharp pop or a rush of falling wood. But then a piece of flame would run up a pine tree, like a squirrel with red ribbon in its mouth, and it would be horrible, to see a whole living pine standing up in a trailing blaze of flames. The tree would hold up its branches—pitiful-thin branches suddenly—like a black corpse come to life in tattered rags.

That dying would be something alive. Everything smelled wonderful as it burned, roasting corn and the heavy evergreen. I opened my mouth several times like I could swallow it; only, I had to stop because I knew it would kill me if I breathed too much.

A policeman said, "'Scuze me, ma'am," and pushed past me to set up a couple of sawhorses and rope off the area. The onlookers were forced back into themselves and complained. Three fire engines were on the scene, which impressed the little boys in the crowd. A fireman in a black rubber coat was up at the end of an extension ladder and spraying water down on the roof like a gardener watering a bush. A couple of other firemen were busy wetting the neighbors' houses and trees, and as they moved, their hoses followed them like the tails of strange, heavy animals. Every now and then, a little boy would go to the edge of the police line and jump with all his might on the hose to see if he could get the water to stop from the pressure of his feet.

It was all so different from our mountain fire. Any town fires weren't none of our business, my daddy used to say. In Wheat, we would go by some car on the side of the road with its hood up and black clouds pouring out. Other people would be pulling over left and right or coming over on foot to "help" or just to see. Sometimes, a fire chief's car would shove through the traffic, and you would see four or five drivers get excited and take off after the disaster.

"We ain't vultures, and we ain't carrying water on us," Daddy said. "No need to follow a fire."

Still, I couldn't help craning my neck, filled with anxiety and trying to get an answer to the questions from the crowd: How bad is it? How big is it? Is anyone missing? I guess I was no different from anyone else. The fire sirens continued to wail up their octave and back down.

But this time, in Asheville, I was already displaced, solitary. Swept clean first by the Taking, then by my own decisions: wise or foolhardy, the verdict was still out. I stood paralyzed, searching the faces around me.

I looked around for the woman whose house this was to make sure she had not died—the person who, like me, had felt fate wiping the slate clean.

I saw her sitting in a rickety lawn chair over by the fire chief's car. She looked relatively young, maybe twenty-five, and had on a black-and-white uniform and bedroom slides. A man's shirt was thrown over her shoulders. At first, I thought she was dark with smoke, but I took a step closer and saw she was a pretty Negro woman. She had tear tracks down her face, white with salt against her brown skin.

I found I was also curious to see what things she had been able to salvage. My age and on up, you start having a thing or two that's worth the effort to make sure it survives. I had my sewing machine and my daddy's Bible. Most think they need it all—certain clothes and furniture, as well as the baby pictures. Younger folks especially haven't learned—if you've saved yourself, you've saved it all.

I stepped over the rope like it was okay for me to do so, like I was somebody who belonged, a member of the family.

I put my hand on her shoulder and said softly, "Do you need a drink of water?"

She turned to me, breathing hard, her hand to her chest. I didn't wait for her answer. I grabbed the rubber arm of a volunteer fireman nearby. He looked about seventeen. He was squatting on the ground, wiping sweat off his forehead and smoking a cigarette. I grabbed it out of his hand and threw it down.

"Lord God, son," I said. "Don't you breathe enough of that in your line of work? This lady needs water. Do you think you could get her some from that cooler on the back of your truck?"

I glared at him—imagine smoking at a fire. The young fellow brought me a paper cup. I said thank you. The woman reached without taking her eyes off the burning house and gulped the water. The air was foggy with a mix of water vapor and smoke. It had a weight like paste.

Gently, I started to lift her shoulders. I said, "Honey, we ought to move back. It's getting a little thick to breathe, this close."

She stood, and the light lawn chair fell over. There was a wind developing, and it blew away like paper. She let me lead her by her hand—past the trucks, through the puddles of water and ash. I felt like I was leading a child back from the edge of a cliff.

She looked at me with big eyes, the whites of them with little red threads standing out. She reached in the pocket of the man's shirt and took out a key with a piece of string attached to it. She looked at it, holding it out in front of her face like she'd never seen one before.

She said, "They are going to blame me. I work here; I am just a maid and housekeeper. But I have a little apartment here, room and board. The antique furniture, oh my God, it just soaked up the flame like kerosene! The owner, he rents the upper floor to somebody, I don't know the man, but I'm pretty sure it started up there. This is his shirt. I was washing it when it happened. It was wet, and I threw it over my head and ran out; it probably saved my life. Like a fool, I grabbed up the key, like maybe I needed to lock the door, lock the door of a house that's burning down, isn't that something?"

She stopped and looked at me, as if seeing me for the first time.

I waited and she tried again. "He probably left the gas jet on making tea. A little explosion came down through the ceiling, and I ran. He didn't come out. I hate to think he's still in there." She put her face in her hands. "I have a friend—several blocks from here. I'll go over there." She started to walk away.

I went with her. "I am not leaving you yet. Not till I know you are safe somewhere." I had been listening to this young woman talk for a while now. Her refined diction, her grammar, put me to shame.

Suddenly, this woman whose fire I had come to stopped and looked at me. "Do I know you?" she said. "Is there a reason why you're here, standing with me?"

We had gone over several streets and were standing in front of another old Victorian house. I could see this area had been quite the show at the turn of the century—circles of stained glass marked the stair landings, and white wrought-iron benches perched like starched lace under big trees.

"Thank the Lord Wanita and Baby Ray weren't here. Sometimes, she comes and helps me clean." The woman was still getting a grip on things.

I waited. She continued, "That's my friend and my little boy. And again, you are?"

I knew it was no use trying to tell somebody about my life, how I was forty years old and going out in the world for the first time, how I had no plan and only a suitcase of worldly goods and a sewing machine to make a living by. I felt stupid, like a teenage runaway played by an actress who's too old. I tried to think what I could say that would make sense without having to tell a lie.

I just told the truth. "My name's Isabel King. My daddy would roll over in his grave if he knew I'd followed this fire. I am not the type to go traipsing after someone else's tragedy. I have lost my own home in Tennessee, and all I have left is my wits and my two hands. Everything else I had or was is given over to the past. So when I saw that somebody else was starting from scratch like me—I saw a kindred soul. I don't know, did I wonder if seeing you would make me want to turn around and go packing up to Virginia, where my brothers and our dishes and rugs are headed? Or if—or if I just wanted to help you, like helping myself, stand up now and breathe the clear air? This is where I am starting from. It's all been taken away. I choose to see it as a gift. Start from here."

The woman's mouth was hanging open. I looked away down the sidewalk, embarrassed. I was not in the habit of making speeches, but cut away from my old life like I was, I didn't need to behave with normal civility. I felt I could say whatever I really was feeling. All the old rules were gone out the window.

Out of the corner of my eye, I admired the big oaks on either side of the boulevard, each one circled by its own ring of embedded red brick and trimmed ivy. They were pretty and historical, like women in hoop skirts. The whole neighborhood was manicured to a T, with petite stone fences and flowerbeds and shrubbery clipped straight and clean as a knife edge. Where was I? What did I think I was doing?

I mumbled, "Well, I reckon I have overstepped my bounds, and I'm sorry. I'll be getting on now that I have walked you to your friend's house." I put my hand on my sewing machine handle and tugged. The soreness in my shoulder was starting to get familiar.

"No, wait, now." The woman wiped her hand on the tail of the man's shirt and held it out to me. "Wait, Isabel. My name is Claudine. You have been so nice, nicer than most would be. Why don't you come inside and have a cold drink, at least? Letitia won't mind. She's Ray's grandmother *and* my employer, and she's really nice. She's watching Ray for me this morning, as a matter of fact."

Claudine motioned me up the flagstone walkway. She knocked on the screen door, painted a bright blue green and with fancy wooden cutwork all over. A child, about four, barefoot and bare-chested, pushed it open and waved.

"Mama," he said. "There you are." He had hazel-green eyes. Behind him came a white woman who looked to be about my age, but fleshy in soft bundles under her skirt and sweater, and blonde with gray at the roots.

"That's Letitia," said Claudine. "Her family is the owner of the Rock Heaven Motel Court, and this place, the Smithson House, too."

Claudine leaned to pick up the child, and Ray's toes tapped against her hip as she carried him across the porch, which was wide as a street.

"Something bad got all over you, Mama, what is it?" He wiped his fingers across her arm.

"My Lord, what happened to you, Claudine?" Letitia looked at me, puzzled, but, for the moment, didn't say anything, just focused on Claudine, coated as she was in smoke. Had I heard right, that Letitia was Ray's grandmother?

"If you heard the sirens, then you heard what happened to me," said Claudine. "It was that house over on Cumberland where we're staying, cleaning in exchange for my room. There was some explosion upstairs. The fire came right through the ceiling, boards and plaster falling, and I ran out. If only I could have got to my college books and papers, and Baby Ray's clothes, but I'm sure there is nothing left. But my stuff is the least of it; I think the upstairs renter might have been in it. I have to sit down again."

I had been standing quietly by, but now she introduced me. "Anyway, Letitia, this is Isabel King, a lady I just met. She helped me get my wits going again, right as I left the fire. She just got here from Tennessee. And I'm sorry to inconvenience you, but I didn't know what else to do but come on here."

"Claudine, you know it's okay," Letitia said. "We'll figure something out."

Claudine looked at her son. "Have you been a good boy for Granny Letitia this morning?" She closed her eyes. "Honey, run to the bathroom for Mama and get me a washrag." She said to us, "If you will excuse me a moment, I'll just clean my face." She followed the boy down the hall.

"Come on through to the kitchen and sit down. I'll get you some refreshment," Letitia said. "Isabel, would iced tea be all right?" She smiled a warm smile at me.

I said, "Iced tea would be wonderful, thanks."

Letitia went on. "You can leave your things right here in the hall and come on back to the kitchen. We're not open yet." She pointed to the entry, with its black marble floor and fancy patterned rug.

"What is this place?" I asked her.

"It's an old boarding house, sort of famous from the days when all kinds of TB patients came to Asheville. We do tours now, sometimes rent it out for weddings and special events. My family owns it, and I live in part of it. We also own the motel down the street where Claudine works doing other housekeeping. But Claudine is more than an employee. Our families have known each other for decades, and well, we have deep ties."

I could connect dots well enough to know that if Letitia, a white woman, was grandmother to a Negro woman's child, then yes, there were some pretty deep connections. I did not ask any questions.

I followed her through the rooms. I was aware of space over my head, the ceilings being about ten feet high. I caught a glimpse of a crystal chandelier in the middle of a painting of angels swimming through the clouds. To both sides were more rooms, all with red velvet ropes across the doors. There were sideboards and fancy mantels at every turn. This seemed like a residence for fine English ladies and gentlemen. Queenie had told me there was money in Asheville, so I guessed this was some of it.

At the back part of a hall, Letitia opened a little brown door, and we were in an ordinary kitchen. Well, it was ordinary except for a big blue enamel Majestic wood cook stove; we would have died for one like it at the farm.

"Oh my, Mama, you are so dirty," Baby Ray said, still reproaching Claudine as they returned to the room.

"Come here and sit down." Letitia handed the child some saltines out of an old fruitcake tin. He accepted them without a word and began to nibble. His teeth were like bits of white china.

"Please make yourself at home, Isabel." Letitia turned her attention to Claudine. She found a dishrag in a drawer and ran warm water over it. She handed it to her.

"You missed your legs. And here, sip this tea." She gave us both a glass. A bell rang somewhere toward the front of the house.

"Oh Lord," said Letitia. "It's time to open. That'll be the volunteer from the historical society. And the nursery man's coming today with more flats of pansies for the front beds."

She looked at Claudine, who had water running down her calves, then at Ray kneeling in another chair, arranging his crackers. He licked his fingers and dabbed at crumbs on a placemat.

"Dirty I may be, but I have to get to work," said Claudine. "It's my shift at the motel." Both women turned their eyes to me then, and it was like I could hear them thinking.

I said, "I know you don't know me from Eve. I've just been sitting here dropped in out of nowhere, but somehow, you figure I'm safe, not crazy, not a criminal. Somehow, you know I can be trusted. If you have work that needs doing, then here I am."

Claudine and Letitia looked at each other. "Rock Heaven," they said simultaneously.

"Here's the situation, Isabel. I've been taking a break from college," Claudine said. "I go to Bennett in Greensboro, getting my degree in English. I've been working as a housekeeper this semester, making some extra money. I am not in any shape to go into work tonight. For one thing, I need to figure out where Ray and I are going to live."

"Going to college? That explains a lot," I said. "I bet you have quite a story to tell. I know you are not the first to do what you are doing, but surely you are still a rare person, and a determined and brave one as well."

Letitia said, "Isabel, how about this: if you can take care of Ray for a while, I will get Claudine recovered and deal with the business at hand, both here and at the motel. Do *you* have a place to stay?"

"Yes and no," I said. "I have a friend who is expecting me, and I was going to be with her for a while, but my entire life is up in the air. What do you need?"

Letitia looked around the kitchen. "Dishes washed, floor washed, child to be looked after, maybe peel some potatoes, make a salad."

I sighed. "I can do all that. Absolutely."

"If you can stay now, then we will talk more this evening. Stay tonight. I have a room for you here."

I did stay through the afternoon, and when they offered, I slept that night in the Smithson House's next-best bedroom. Letitia unclipped a red velvet rope and let me climb up to a high bed. I climbed a little ladder to get in. The bed was so short, I slept half-propped. On the feather mattress, I sunk, then floated. I laid the sheet across my body—it was starched like a restaurant napkin. I rubbed the tatted lace edge between my fingers and smelled the air and sun from line drying.

Letitia and I had talked. The upshot was, she offered me work at the Rock Heaven Motel, plus a room. Claudine would be going back to school soon, and another person was needed.

"Also," Letitia said, "frankly, there needs to be a white person there. For all intents and purposes, Wanita—you'll meet her—is the manager, but if she needs to deal with anyone, then I have to drop whatever I am doing here and go over. I'm impressed by the kindness you showed to Claudine, so I have a hunch you'd fit with Wanita too. Most people don't want to deal with a Negro woman unless they get to tell her what to do. Wanita will never be able to hold the authority she deserves until times change. But you, you could be the interface." That felt good. She knew I would not act like their boss, just because the world would let me.

"And of course,"—she smiled—"you know how to clean." I had told her enough of my history, being at the farm, then at the laundry in Knoxville, and she'd seen a sample of my domestic skills.

Tomorrow, then, was Rock Heaven, but after all I had been through, this room was haven enough for tonight. There was a canopy over my head. As I fell asleep, I dreamed I was in a clipper ship like the one in *Two Years Before the Mast*. It was really a boy's book and had not been one of my favorites, but apparently, it had made an impression on me. The wind was filling the sail and causing the vessel to move. And in the dream, the wind was my own breath. And I was going fast.

Twenty-Four

Claudine

The next morning, I got up early, found the coffeepot, and had started it perking when the doorbell rang. No one seemed to be around yet, so I opened the door to a fire marshal and a young man in a short-sleeved business shirt and a tie with palm trees on it. The latter handed me a card. It said he was a claims adjuster.

"We'd like to see Miss McQueen," the marshal said. I heard footsteps in the hallway behind me, and Claudine came out in her bathrobe, carrying Ray.

"Yes?" she said, trying to smooth her hair with one hand.

The claims adjuster consulted his clipboard. "Miss McQueen? Do you have any identification?"

"Well, no," she said. "The fire took care of most everything that defines me, including things like a driver's license, but I'm sure that Letitia, the manager of the Smithson House, will vouch for me. I'd really like to go back to my apartment and, if things are cool enough, search to see if there is anything I can salvage. How about if I meet you down there in fifteen minutes? Let me get dressed?"

The insurance man glanced at me and straightened his palm trees. "Well, I guess we could allow that, although at the present time, we are still investigating the possibility of arson or negligence."

I didn't like this young man at all. In addition to his ugly tie, he had a pink chin scraped raw by a too-sharp razor. I was about to ask who he thought he was, allowing or not allowing people to search for the burned-up scraps of their life? But at the last minute, he relented.

"I guess that will be fine. But we will need to make a list of anything you take away. Just meet us down there, *Miss* McQueen."

He looked at Baby Ray. I reached out my arm and shut the door. I heard that "Miss," and Claudine saw me hear it.

"Ray's father is in Europe," she said. "We plan to be married once he's back."

"It isn't none of my business, honey," I said. "You are a woman after my own heart, a woman who tells the truth and lets people like it or leave it. Back home, girls who had babies out of wedlock made up married names and invented no-good husbands that nobody ever met. Amy Herndon, when she showed up in church one day toting a two-month-old boy after a long absence, announced that her name was now Mrs. Daniel Anderson, and Daniel was with the First Infantry. *Miss Amy* could never be a mother in our community the way *Mrs. Daniel* could." But I was in no position to criticize, especially since, inspired by the women of Iceland, I had retaken my own maiden name.

After Claudine dressed, I volunteered to go with her while she scouted the premises for things she recognized. Ray came along and reached up to take my hand.

The ground was still wet and smoldering. Claudine stepped around a Frigidaire burned down to black, then over the charred top of a wringer washer. Seeing things destroyed always made me think about how they were made in the first place. How did a rock get to be a sheet of metal that became the side of a refrigerator, for instance? I have seen a seed cracked open and pointing a green finger at the sun and seen that wind up a flower. Nature was one thing; industry, invention, and things off the assembly line were yet another.

"Do you see anything?" I asked Claudine.

She was picking her way through the mess, both hands clamped over her mouth like she might scream, then she took them away to speak.

"This is my bureau," she said, yanking on a drawer. The heat had swelled it stuck, so she put her foot against the base and tugged harder, careful to avoid the big scabs of burned paint with sharp edges. The drawer pulled loose and fell on the ground, along with its contents of clothing, or what was left of them. Heat had turned the material the color and texture of Bible parchment.

"This is Baby Ray's." Claudine picked up a garment, and I could faintly see the design of cowboys and bucking broncos, sheriff stars and boots.

"My pajamas! Let me see!" He ran forward, but I grabbed his arm.

"Stay out of there, honey. There's dangerous things in there." I picked him up.

The workmen were still ducking in and out of the front doorway. Every now and then, you could hear a board fall, followed by a shower of plaster and ash, like someone was pouring sand. The smell of the air dried out the lining of my nose.

"Here's your shoes too, Ray." Claudine's voice filled up with tears. "And look at this." She moved to a warped wardrobe nearby. It had been pretty once, inlaid in places with some carved gold-painted wood, but now the doors hung loose, and the clothes inside were scorched and drenched. She touched what looked like a child's party dress. It fell apart when she touched it. A net underskirt had flamed to a tight frazzle of brown plastic filaments, and the lace collar was crisp as toast crumbs. She moved to another ruined piece. "My wedding dress—my wedding dress that I was saving."

"You'll get another one, a better one," I comforted her. The white satin had turned a rich brown gold, and the waterlogged train dragged it down. Claudine started picking off sequins like they were berries and putting them in her pocket. She tugged on a piece of lace across the neck, and it came off like a paper ripping. Pearls crackled off like a tiny row of firecrackers.

"We have no clothes," Claudine said. It was like she was telling a joke. "Baby Ray, we have no home. I have lost all of my research and my writing, and we have no clothes."

"Let me tell you a story," I said. "Not to mean your own situation is not dire, but it's good to realize that tragedy doesn't have to be fatal. We had a fire on our farm. Two days after the mountainside and our corn burned, we were able to go out and walk through the cinders. The air still smelled smoky, and every now and then, we would come across a hot pocket, some little spot in the ground that was still smoldering a little, so I would pour some water on it and Walker would rake it out. You go out there in that wide-open space that had been close green air and rustle of sound, the horizon blocked by the tall corn plants, and it feels real strange, harvest come too soon. We got hot, even though it was still cool. Walker was sweating and wiping his face with his sleeve. It stung me, the energy we'd put on the crop, and now it was like sweat dried away into the air—nothing to show for our efforts but exhaustion. And the money we needed but wouldn't get, always in the back of our minds. All that mattered. But then we looked at the burned ground and smiled at each other. It was clean, somehow, when you had to start over, no matter the reason. I'd felt calm, looking up the half-bald hill. And in several weeks, the ground was lying under a new growth of velvet green, including little sprouts of leftover corn, like the fire's joke. And suddenly, there's hope for next year. You know the ground is richer than ever with mineral ash."

Claudine smiled. "Thank you, Isabel. I can see the hope in all that, but to tell the truth, I can't think straight enough yet to look on the bright side."

I looked at what lay before us, before Claudine, and did not share my thoughts further. I did want to help her see the bright side, but this was not exactly the same as what I had told her about the field fire. When a house burns, it's a different case. It's not clean or helpful to nature. It's just a mess, with a slimy film of water and soot everywhere and a rotten stink starting to set in. Oftentimes, nothing burns long enough or deep enough to disappear. There's just a world of blackened, distorted shapes torturing your eye into remembering the things that were, and you have to pitch in and clear it all away and decide what to do next.

I thought about this place I had landed in, this Land of the Sky, as they called the town, and my big idea to start a sewing and alterations business, with Queenie's help to set it up and get some clients going. But I couldn't bring myself to walk away without at least offering to fix something I knew I could. I put my hand on Claudine's shoulder.

"I can help you with that last," I said. "That you don't have any clothes, you said. Sewing is a thing I do. I could whip up a couple of dresses for you. Make some shirts and pants for Baby Ray."

"What?" Claudine wrinkled her forehead and turned toward me, the ruined wedding dress still shredded in her fists.

I repeated, "I do sewing. I can run you all up a couple of outfits. Maybe that will take a little something off your mind. Seems like you're going to have your hands full figuring out the rest of this."

"That's really nice of you, I'm sure. But we'll manage. There are secondhand stores and church basements for people like me." She half laughed.

I said, "Haven't I taken my meals the last two days free on account of you and Letitia? Didn't I sleep in that fancy bed last night? On account of the kindness of strangers. Dressmaking won't be that much of a payback."

Claudine showed her seed pearls and the scorched cowboy pajamas to the man with the palm-tree tie. He waved his dismissal. "Is that all you've got?" he said. "No dishes or anything?"

"I was a maid here, sir, no dishes of my own," she said. "There is nothing here now that I care to save," she said. She ran her finger over the spindle of a chair leg and then scratched her forehead, leaving an ash mark. "It's all yours."

The man clutched his clipboard and stepped over some charred planks and linoleum remnants.

"I still have questions for you," he said. "This fire might not have been accidental. Don't leave until I say so."

Claudine made a mouth behind his back, then looked me in the eyes.

"You don't know me, really," she said. "I am in

graduate school, and I intend to stay there, and I intend to teach." She paused. "I don't give up. I just keep hoping that if I keep on doing what I know I can, the time will come when it'll all feel perfectly natural—not just to me, but to everybody. When my mother hears about this, she'll say it's a sign that I ought to be with Thomas, I ought to be in my own home raising Baby Ray and taking care of a husband. But I have other plans, and I will not let this change my mind. My professor has a copy of my first five chapters. I'll just have to reconstruct what I've done since. Fortunately, a lot of my notes and research are at my carrel at the library."

I barely understood a lot of what this girl was talking about, but there was something about her I believed, the same way I knew, the day before, sitting at Letitia's table, that the two of them believed me and believed in me.

"Reconstruct. Now you're talking."

Claudine turned to the man with the clipboard. "Here's where you can find me if you need me." She gave him the address of the Smithson House and turned on her heel. I followed, admiring the flowers all the way, thinking how nice it was that they were there to look at, and I didn't even have to grow them.

I asked Letitia did she have some old newspapers. She did. I taped pages of the classifieds together and spread them on the floor.

"What in the world is going on?" Letitia stood in the kitchen door with some blouses and a skirt and dress draped over her arm. She had had the same concern I did, how to dress Claudine, and had pulled out some old clothes of her own. The woman had a good heart; only, Letitia weighed twice what Claudine did, and it would be a shame to put such a young woman in such an old style too.

"Are those some things you could part with?" I asked her. "If they are, I could alter them to fit Claudine. Making new out of old is a specialty of mine."

I told Claudine, "Lie down here, now."

Claudine smiled. "On the floor, on the newspaper?"

Ray squatted nearby to watch. "Oh, Mama, you're a paper doll."

"Baby Ray, do you have a crayon I could borrow?" I asked.

He ran and got me a red one, and I drew his mother's outline on the newspaper. "Your turn, honey," I told the boy. "Lie down here. This is the way I make all my patterns," I told him. I gave him a hand up. "Now, Ray, if you can find some scissors, you can start cutting out your paper-doll self."

Letitia got busy cutting the seams on one of her old suits.

"You can leave on the buttons and just rip the zipper opening on one side," I told her. I was getting comfortable. I took my shoes off and pinned a piece of newspaper to the back of what used to be Letitia's gabardine skirt. I began to remake it for Claudine.

Twenty-Five

Rock Heaven

The three Negro women who did the laundry with me at Rock Heaven were Wanita, Emogene, and of course, Claudine, until she would leave again for college. The Monday morning I was supposed to start work, Letitia took me over early and gave me the key to a room.

"It's not much, I know, but maybe it will do until something better comes along."

"I appreciate the opportunity," I said. "I did not expect to fall into work so soon, so I am grateful."

"I really need to get back to Smithson House," she said. "Claudine is off today, but the other women, Wanita and Emogene, will be here shortly, and they will show you the rest, which I am sure will be things you have already done and won't take much getting used to. Get them to take you around, look at the old draperies in the units so you can think about making those new ones like we talked about. And, oh, tell them you need a uniform."

"All right," I said. "Thanks." I strolled around to the inner courtyard and watched a family pack suitcases in their station wagon. The man and woman sat for a moment in the front seat, studying a map while the children bounced in the back. What must that be like? I had never been on a vacation in my life.

I explored until I saw a door that said Laundry / Staff Only. Inside was a pile of sheets in a wad by the washing machine, so I just started getting them ready for the tub. That's what I was doing when Wanita and Emogene came in wearing their seersucker uniforms and white crepe-soled nurses' shoes. They put their lunches in a little icebox in the corner and hung up their sweaters. I kept putting sheets in the washer. I could feel them looking at each other behind my back.

"Hello," I said finally. "I'm Isabel."

Emogene was broad and solid, with ironed hair that came down on either side of her face, hard and flat as a pair of shingles.

"I'm sorry, ma'am, but this is a staff area. There is a warshing machine for guests out by Unit Number 5. You know, where the ice machine is? And the Coke machine? That's where it is. It costs a nickel." I had assumed Letitia had told them I was coming, but she hadn't.

Wanita stood listening. She's the one Letitia told me was the real manager of Rock Heaven. I thought she was beautiful—very dark, with narrow features. She was dignified and would have looked striking in a long satin dress on a stage.

"My name is Isabel King," I repeated. "Letitia hired me. She gave me a room to stay in instead of full pay, and I am going to make some new curtains and bedspreads for all the units." I paused. "And I guess I am going to help with the usual housekeeping tasks. So I hope it is okay that I came in here and started processing these bed linens."

Emogene spun in a circle and confronted Wanita. "That Letitia! I love the lady, but she don't tell us nothing. I got three friends been wanting to get on here, and now she goes and suddenly hires a white woman?" She cocked her head back at me. "You just getting out of prison or something? Why you want to work here?"

Wanita stepped in. "Well, Emogene, you act like that, *nobody's* going to want to work here. Now, I know you got you some manners, but they sure are hiding right now." She reached to shake my hand and introduced both her and Emogene. "Pleased to meet you. This is unexpected, I admit, but we can always use an extra pair of hands."

I looked at Emogene in particular. "You can blame Claudine as much as Letitia for my being here. Did you hear what happened to her?" They had not, so I explained about the fire and how I met her going by as it happened.

"I came from a little place north of Knoxville, Tennessee," I told them. "I was keeping house for my brothers, but the government took everyone's property in our valley. They are building a big facility, some kind of a demolition range to help with the war. We were not told the particulars. But when all this happened, I decided to strike out on my own. I was coming here to stay with an old childhood friend until I got on my feet. Walker and Avery, my brothers, are in Virginia now. I guess they feel like God picked them up in a whirlwind and set them down again a hundred miles away, as it happened very fast."

"Where the rest of your family?" asked Emogene. "Why don't you go stay with them?"

Wanita opened her mouth at Emogene's tone, but I waved my hand. "It's all right. I have a son in the navy, and my daughter is living with her older sister. I left my husband, so it's just me now." I added, "I didn't tell my brothers ahead of time I was leaving when the government moved in, so they might be pretty mad at me, but it just seemed like the right time to make a break. Anyway, I sure don't want to upset any more people or take away a job if you think it would be unfair to someone else, so let me know right now and I'll just march back to Letitia and tell her."

I waited, but I saw that my words had calmed down Emogene. She still had to get used to me, but her attitude released. Now she knew I was a woman with a complicated past. She also saw that I would not be arrogant with her or hold on to Letitia's offer unless I was allowed to by them. I had put the decision in their laps. The two women looked at each other. Emogene shrugged.

"Well," Wanita said finally. "Looks like you know what you are doing with them sheets. Just keep on with it, and I'll check back. What room Letitia put you in? I'll put a couple of uniforms on the bed for you."

That night, in my room, the full impact of what I had done hit me for the first time.

I was tired of leaving places and never staying, and now it looked like I was going to be staying in a place where people were not intended to stay put for any length of time.

If for any reason Letitia got tired of me or did not like my work, I might find myself once again on the bus, looking for the next fire. Of course, I could always go to Virginia, to Walker and Avery. They would have to take me in again. They would act like it was a favor, and they would have to discuss why I'd felt it was necessary to leave without telling them or helping them move. I was tired. I needed this to work, at least for a little while.

Twenty-Six

Queenie

Dear Janey,

     I am now in Asheville, North Carolina, a place I never expected to be. I started off to visit Queenie, but got off the bus and followed a crowd to look at a house on fire (I know—where else would a fire be except in ASH ville?) and I wound up meeting the woman whose life had just burned up. She has the sweetest little boy. We started out just helping each other, me making her some new clothes and her introducing me to Letitia, who runs a motel. Letitia hired me, and I am staying in one of the units. It is its own little apartment, with a table and kitchenette and a bed, and I do the laundry for the place and replace the sheets and clean the rooms. I am making curtains and bedspreads, too, and get paid extra for that. So far it is working out good. I reckon I can stay here until something better comes along, which it will. I hope you are doing fine in school. There is a phone in the office. If you get a chance call and leave a message and I will call you back. Here is the *number. You know Janey, the next school vacation you have, maybe you can take the bus over here for a visit. I can get you a rollaway bed. We could take a taxi into town and go to the movies and out to eat. You know I have never been a city girl, but I may learn to like it. Did you know Ava Gardner stayed here for a day or two? I heard she is from North Carolina. Well let me know if you would like to come for a visit. I miss you.*

I love you,

Mother

I had not seen Queenie for six or seven years, though Knoxville and Asheville were just hours apart and we had written letters back and forth for years. So, I approached her house with some anxiety, wondering what she would think of me in person. Would she judge me as old and worn? Would our personalities still fit us to be friends? Yes, she had invited me to come. She was the only person in this town that I had history with, so I wanted it to go well.

Queenie taught English at Lee Edwards High School and lived in an old Victorian house just off Montford Avenue, a home very much in the class of the Smithson House Museum, actually. The front porch was deep and shaded, with large baskets of hanging ferns. I twisted the doorbell and could hear it *bringgg-bringgg* just on the other side.

And then there she was, just the same cute, outgoing person, only with lots of character now around her eyes and her blonde hair, which she wore in a bun now, streaked faintly gray.

"It is you!" She was laughing to see me and leaped to give me a hug before I could get in the door. "Isabel! I can hardly believe you're standing right here!"

"I can hardly believe it either! I already like Asheville, though, and your neighborhood is so pretty and peaceful."

"Come and catch your breath!" She took me by the arm and led me into her kitchen. There were plates and a cake on the table, and I smelled coffee brewing.

I took in everything all at once—the style and quality of her clothes, her health and appearance, the size and decor of the rooms. Everything quite a few steps above how we were raised. A general feeling of affluence and ease. There was a picture of her late husband above the fireplace mantel. He looked like the lawyer/banker he had been, but I thought that if Queenie had married him, he must have been a good person. He had died of a heart attack a few years ago, leaving Queenie to rattle around alone in this big place. He had made sure his wife would be well provided for, but she was still relatively young and they had not had children. She would not sit still and be a widow with nothing to do, and she had returned to teaching. This all seemed right for her, and I knew Nancy, if she were still alive, would be proud if she could have seen where Queenie's education and her good marriage had stationed her in life.

"Sit down! I will show you around this place in a little bit, but first, let's have a bite of cake. I bet you have been through the mill the past few weeks, and I want to hear all about it." She cut slices for us both.

I was still feeling ungrounded and mostly homeless and very low down on the social scale, compared to where Queenie had landed. But she was my oldest friend in the world.

"You are sweet to make apple stack," I said, taking a bite. "It makes me feel right at home."

And it really did somehow bridge the gap of years and the strain of being cast out of Wheat and Black Oak Ridge, and I was able to look her in the eyes and give a smile—not a smile without fatigue and sadness, but a smile.

"Didn't you get in a couple of days ago? I thought you would come here. Where were you? Here—have your coffee the way you like it." Queenie handed me the cream, and again, I felt a lift in my heart, to be with another person who knew my ways and preferences and had some care about my comfort. She had remembered how much I whitened my coffee.

"I've ended up staying at a place called the Rock Heaven Motel. Do you know it?"

"Oh, no! Oh, Isabel, of all places! Well, we'll have to remedy that! But then, you must have seen what happened to that house on Cumberland, that terrible fire everyone is talking about. I have not been by to see the ruin, but I read about it in the paper. I just made the cake and then spent the morning grading essays."

She pointed to a pile of papers on one of the dining chairs, and I reached to take up the top theme, titled "The Women of *Silas Marner*, including the Author."

I knew the novel well. Its plot and themes—an innocent person accused of theft and driven from his community, lost wealth, miserable marriage, the search for happiness—were quite familiar.

"I first got George Eliot from your own mother's hand," I told Queenie. "And I am thankful for it, as ever I was for all Nancy did for me. Poor Silas. There is nothing new under the sun, I say, if I am tempted to feel sorry for all that has happened to me in recent times. How do your students like the book?"

Queenie laughed. "They don't, for the most part. It's been on the required reading list for decades and doesn't seem to connect, although, of course, there are always a few, like the girl who wrote that one, who are bright and eager. It makes teaching rewarding, but I only wish I could say I had anything to do with her insights."

"I would love nothing better than to sit here all day and read what your students have written," I said, and I laid the essay back on the pile. "But back to the fire." I outlined for her how I had seen it and stood watching it, and how I was drawn to Claudine and her misfortune and straightaway got myself a job and a room. And then I spent some time telling her all that had happened in Wheat and how the government overtaking had changed all our fates. She had many questions about this family and that person and where they had gone. Eventually, she returned to the present and to how I had met Claudine.

"Isabel, it is just like you to pitch in and help anytime someone is in need. And you, in the circumstances you are in, it's just amazing. But I will drive you back, and we can pick up your things and get you settled in here, and then we can make a plan for your next step. Come on upstairs; I'll show you your room."

I followed her, but I was already thinking and talking. "Queenie, I know we had said I would stay with you until I got back on my feet, and I did think that would take a few weeks, and I am looking forward to catching up more with you on our lives. I'd love to hear more about your teaching. But for now, it looks like I can stay at Rock Heaven and do some work for them and not have to take up your guest room."

Queenie acted like I had not spoken. She opened the door and showed me the suite, dappled with sun coming through the hemlocks in her yard. It was elegant and peaceful, and for a moment, there was nothing I wanted more than to curl up and nap on the cool white coverlet.

"Mother made that," Queenie said, referring to an appliqué quilt at the foot of the bed. "She was not that much of a seamstress, so I value what of hers I inherited."

She turned to me. "Now, of course you are going to stay here. I won't have you staying at that nasty motel. I just want you to get some good rest, and in a couple of days, we can talk about your future. I have already spoken to some of my colleagues at Lee Edwards, the high school, as well as to some women I know at the Presbyterian church, and we've got quite a brainstorm of ideas going on your behalf. We'll have you a position in no time in a nice household, one where you will be appreciated and not worked to death."

Queenie's guest room was beautiful, and my friend, so well meaning, had obviously been worrying about me. But it was not sitting right with me, despite her good intentions. When we were children and I had lost my mama, I relied on Queenie and Nancy, but there was a lot of water under the bridge since then, and I did not want to be anyone's charity project. I did not want Queenie saving me from "the nasty motel" or putting me in a position she deemed suitable with her own standing in the town.

"Queenie," I said. "I don't think you understand. I know it's sudden, but I think it will be fine, this job working at Rock Heaven, doing some sewing for them, some laundry and cleaning—"

"But—"

"No, wait, I don't mind it. They are going to give me a place to stay and a small salary."

"Isabel, it is no trouble to me! Don't you know I have been looking forward to having you here? You can see I have this old mansion totally to myself since Stanford died; it will be wonderful for us both."

"Don't think I don't appreciate this offer." I started back down the stairs to the entry foyer. The longer I stayed, the more tempted I might be to accept. "But for the first time in my life, I am truly on my own, making my own way, and I think I should try that. This job is a gift horse, and I am not going to look it in the mouth." We turned to go back into the kitchen, but I stopped and put my hand on her shoulder. "I tell you what. If it doesn't work out, I will come on here. Knowing that you will take me in if need be will be such a reassurance."

"But, Isabel." Queenie wrinkled her forehead and looked toward Sanford's portrait. "Honey, maybe you haven't thought this through! I mean—" She struggled for a way to say what she wanted. "I am aware of all the people who work there. All the housekeepers are Negroes."

I stood very still. "Yes, I know that, Queenie. I met the women who are working there now. They are nice people. One of them is even about to graduate from college with a degree to teach English and history. She is quite refined and could surely discuss *Silas Marner* with the best of us."

I backed up from her and looked at the cake on the table, my mama's recipe. "Do you think I am so proud that I would not take the job because I would be associating with Negroes? Queenie, I have worked for nothing or next to nothing all my life and always had to be beholden to people on top of it all. If I went to work for some society friend of yours, I would be 'Queenie's old childhood friend' more than I would be myself, and I would constantly wonder if I was up to par for them. There are no strings on me now, and I rather like it that way; I can behave how I want and leave if I want, and the fine people of Asheville can like me or not."

Queenie came to me and took both my hands. "Isabel,

we have been friends our entire lives, and I don't want us to stop now. But sometimes, it seems to me you are holding yourself back. I hate to see you do that. You do not know this town; if you get started at that place, you will get known as a certain type of person. It will make it harder for you to do better things if the opportunity arises, which it will."

"It may look like servitude to you, or it may look like I am associating with the wrong type of people—or rather, the wrong color of people." I was holding a lid on my temper now and was on the verge of not measuring my words. "I am sorry if you are disappointed in me or would be embarrassed by me, but I am through with putting my spirit into someone else's definition of proper."

I set my mouth. Queenie was silent and just looked at me, her eyes big. She was not used to me speaking up to her.

I said, "Queenie, I am tired, and all this is new, and I don't want to fight with you. I guess I better go now."

"We can talk about this later on, perhaps."

"Perhaps. Thank you for the cake and coffee." I opened the front door.

"Let me give you a ride."

"Thank you, but I'll walk. You are right about one thing. I need to get to know the town."

"We'll be in touch." Queenie stood at her open door as I walked to the street. I smiled a little smile at her, but after that, I did not look back. It struck me that for the first time, our roles were reversed. I was in a position to teach Queenie something, not with a book in my hand or with academic information. Maybe she would learn by just watching her old friend, right here in her own town, live in a nasty motel and wash sheets with Negroes.

In my mind I knew she was standing there watching me from the steps of the banker's house, but I moved forward, and she got smaller—and smaller still.

Twenty-Seven

Wanita

I had a chance to work with Claudine off and on for a few months before she returned to college. The more I knew her, the more impressed I was by her. And we became friends, for all that she was just a little older than Janeyre and I was of her mother's generation. With me, she talked freely of what she was studying, and I could respond freely from what I had read and thought.

There we were, cleaning rooms together, and I was commenting to her about *Little Women*, which I had somehow missed in my earlier reading but had found at a rummage sale, and she was telling me about a paper she was writing on two sisters, abolitionists from South Carolina named Sarah and Angelina Grimke.

"Not from South Carolina, surely," I commented. "That must have been quite unusual, especially before the War between the States."

"Yes, it was. Angelina, in particular, saw a connection between the plight of women in general and slavery. She was one of the few Southern women of her era who could see what was going on around her." Claudine shook two pillows down into crisp new cases as she spoke.

"Why do you do that?" I asked her.

"What do you mean? This is the way I always put on the pillowcases," she said.

"No, I mean, why don't you just talk properly with Emogene and Wanita the way you do with me? You would never discuss the history of the abolition movement with them." These questions had been on my mind since I had met her. I continued, "It would probably be good for them to improve their knowledge, as well as their grammar and speech. I know when I was growing up around country people, my friend Queenie and her mother, Nancy, encouraged me and corrected me in my talk. Not that I don't lapse back into bad grammar when I speak. Especially when I am stressed. And I probably still have what many would call a hillbilly accent, but I did—I do my best to improve myself."

"I don't know that the people I grew up with would see it that way, Isabel. I *do* lapse back and talk like they do where my mother lives or down on Eagle Street. If I didn't, I would get such looks. I might not even have any friends left." She broke into a bitter affectation: "Lordy, the way dat Claudine like to tawk white. She done raised herself up, been to that college! She think she too good to be 'sociatin' with the likes of us reg'lar niggahs." She added, "It is bad enough and lonely enough to be a black woman in this world. To cut myself apart from my community by virtue of my education and my speech—well, sometimes it's just another level of lonely I can't bear to ask of myself. So I speak their language and try not to get too much above my raising, at least in my heart." We pushed the linens cart out into the courtyard and locked the door.

"That's interesting," I said. "It's a good thing I have

gotten used to being alone, because I don't fit anywhere anymore. Not in educated society, not out in the country on the farm. I know too much to be in the one place, but not enough to be in the other."

Claudine stopped to press my hand. "I like you, Isabel. Let's not give up—agreed? We have to remember that there are others in our same boat, and that education, however we happened to have gotten it, is a good thing."

"All right," I said. "I am not as young as you, though. And even if I was, whose role model would I be? Not like you—you already know."

"Stop that! You are plenty young." She grinned. "I'll be going now, got to get my Baby Ray. My mother's got him today."

Claudine was as good a friend as I'd ever had; she became more to me in six months than I could have believed. I watched her, watched how she fought to hold her head high, how she kept pushing. I rarely saw Queenie, Queen Elizabeth, anymore. Her rarefied atmosphere did not suit me, and she was my past. When Claudine was through with her college course, she stayed on at Bennett as a teacher. She was certainly a mentor to me, if that label can go from a young person to an old, so it was only right that she encouraged other young women.

The day after Claudine left, Letitia called me to come and see her.

"Isabel, I want to promote you to manager. You'll get a raise."

"I appreciate it, but I also feel strange about it. I feel like Wanita ought to have it."

Letitia looked at me and I looked at her, both of us already knowing that was true but that it could not possibly happen.

"How about this, then?" I said. "I will take the title, but just half the raise, and you give the other half to Wanita. Nobody has to know that she and I are comanagers. How about that?"

It was not much, I know, to manage a group of housekeepers at a motel, but as my formal education had ended when I was nine, all in all, I was pleased about it. I wrote to Janeyre and Jeremiah and Walker to let them know. And I did not tell them about the arrangement I had made concerning Wanita.

Twenty-Eight

War's End

1945

I had been working at the motel for three years when the atom bomb was dropped and the war with Japan ended.

We heard it first on the radio, then we read the newspaper the next day. Even though I studied between the lines and tried to conceive of the fire and the radiation and how many tons of TNT it was equal to, it was hard to feel it. I thought back to when I had first arrived in town and met Claudine at a fire where a man had just died. They said he had been trapped upstairs in the house. I had tried to feel something, but the idea of it was not enough to raise my emotion. Even if I worked to picture it in my head, all I could manage was, *Well, I hope the smoke got to him before he knew.* I had never met him or even seen him. I just knew I was *supposed* to feel shocked. And even with my mama, mostly I just thought of my own loss, not her suffering. I was supposed to have a mother, but there was a fire and my mama was gone.

With the atomic bomb, you knew that a great many people had died, and died horribly, but the full truth of it was not conceivable in our minds. Like everyone, I was glad the war, with all the grief and deprivation it had caused, was finally over. People rationalized it, said the Japanese were crazy and that the emperor of Japan might never have surrendered otherwise. I read that Germany had been working on this weapon as well, and I joined in the relief that the US had developed the bomb before they did, if bombs had to be invented at all. Anyway, the killing was ended for now, and Jeremiah would come home.

Still, there was general ignorance in addition to general elation. Soon, there came another revelation: the bombs had been built in East Tennessee at Clinton Engineering Works, eighteen miles west of Knoxville, with "secrecy so great, not even the workers knew of their product."

My emotions went all over the place to hear of it. So that's what it was. I felt a simmering anger, the kind where you know you could speak and speak and it would do no good, so you are silent. All the words stay behind the glass of your resentful expression. Wheat and Scarboro, Elza— the little towns by Black Oak Ridge. I felt affection growing for my own town, Wheat, that I'd never had when I lived there. We all grew peaches.

Wheat was only the name of a man, the first postmaster. I see him like a figure from Currier and Ives, tall as Abraham Lincoln, only with a shock of blond hair. We were a bunch of naive country people, as blink-eyed and innocent as any the US government could find without leaving the country. They would have had to go to some *National Geographic* place to find people they could take advantage of, people more raw and trusting, but they would not have been able to make them leave home without going into international negotiations. All they had to do with us was say, "Leave." And all we had to do was say, "Thank you, sir; glad to oblige."

I could not keep on with this attitude, carry around this kind of disgust, any more than I could live thinking about John L. and myself every day. Any mourning I felt for Wheat and Black Oak Ridge had to come to a close. What the place had been and what it was now might as well have been separated by hundreds of years.

One funny thing was, I found I was a minor celebrity in the world of Rock Heaven. Though I kept saying, "I knew nothing about it; I was no more aware than you," Emogene kept telling people that I was from "the bomb place," as if my small connection made me as interesting as a nuclear scientist.

I had started taking little evening walks after the work of the day. Not too long after the news about Hiroshima and the unveiling of what had been done in Black Oak Ridge, I found myself going down McDowell Street. It wound down to the railroad tracks. If you went left, you could go to Biltmore, where the pretty depot was, as well as the village and church erected by a rich eastern railroad baron to accompany his castle and estate just a few miles away. Instead, I turned right to Swannanoa River Road, where there were warehouses and little car repair places, a few barbecue joints, and shanty houses.

It was not the best part of town for a woman walking alone. I knew it was possible I would be approached as dark fell, but I was in a brooding mood and kept on. It comforted me, somehow, to be near the river, to smell the brown water and know it was moving, traveling through. I wanted to be near something that appeared to have a simple, definite purpose. What was more basic than water? I focused on the current, but when I explored down to the edge, I saw that someone had dumped an old stove over the bank. It had caught tires and paper trash that had also been deposited in the stream.

I planned to turn back toward town, but I kept going down the road, past the ruin of an old icehouse. It obviously hadn't been used in years, and the red letters on the side had faded and then been overpainted with graffiti. It was no more than a shell, with big, open bays that used to hold sliding doors, and a splintered porch running the length of the building. I heard sounds coming from inside, and I quickened my pace, fearing an animal of some kind. Instead, two teenage boys came out, disheveled and panting, and one of them, slim and blond, buckled his belt. The other boy, darker, stockier, saw me first and grabbed his friend's arm.

"Not yet; wait!" he said.

I averted my head and walked faster to let them know I was not a threat, but they darted back inside. There were secrets everywhere, and I did not know whether any of it was wrong or right. I would let events glance off my mind and spirit and hope that in the long run, the world would lean to the good.

I reached in my purse and took out a little metal can. I pinched some of the contents between my fingers and put it in my cheek. I had secrets of my own. In recent months, I had begun to dip a bit of snuff. Never while I was working, so no one knew. I felt my pulse begin to slow as I massaged the shredded tobacco with my tongue and the bitter juice sapped my mouth. I sighed. It began to drizzle rain, but I did not bother to put up my umbrella as I walked home.

Jeremiah wrote me that he would be docking soon in San Diego. He had mustered out of the navy and wanted to visit everybody before he decided on any future plans. Did I think he could stay for a couple of days in Asheville and see me? I could get a rollaway bed, so I said yes, of course, I would love to see him.

We had a nice visit and didn't talk about John L. at all. He seemed satisfied that I at least knew I had made a big mistake back then, a mistake he had warned me about. Dora and I had agreed on one thing, and that was that we would not tell him about what had happened to Jane.

As for the things that had happened to him in the war, those events might have been covered over as well. He made it seem like one big, happy adventure, told about the places he had gone to—Oahu and Mindanao and the Marshall Islands—and showed me pictures of his ship—he called it "Elsie," after the letters *LSI* on the side of the hull. He brought me a photo album with wooden covers that had palm trees engraved on it, and a silk handkerchief that said *Hawaii* and was painted with a hula girl in a grass skirt. I treated him to dinner at a local restaurant, and he ordered both hamburgers and chicken and biscuits while we talked about his future. I had nothing in the way of help for him, either job leads or money in hand, and he already knew he did not want to go to Abingdon and work on Walker and Avery's new farm.

He stayed long enough to apply as a chef at the Grove Park Inn, a magnificent stone resort frequented by wealthy visitors. I went up there with him and stood on the terrace and looked over the golf course while he filled out a form. I thought of many things—of Sam saying he had come here with a friend when he had really come to sell his carvings, of my own attempts to secure work in "nice" places and being rejected because I didn't look or sound the part or have the education. The golf course, bright green and

clipped year-round, made my eyes narrow. It was a lie—
everything was not neat and pretty. Oh, you could look into
a box here and there and pretend it was. The Grove Park
Inn was such a box, I decided, watching a tiny figure on the
grounds below tilt his leg and pose. He was dressed natty as
a fashion ad and swung the club as if the arc it drew was a
clean boundary to keep the world right. I lifted my head into
the wind and breathed.

Jeremiah came back to me across the high lobby with
its enormous fireplaces. There was a saying carved into the
granite, inviting people to return. Jeremiah was smiling; he
was optimistic.

"They're nice people," he said. "But they say it might
be awhile. Maybe it will pan out. We'll see. I just need to get
some cash flowing! I can always reenlist if I don't hear back.
But in the meantime, I'll see what else I can find—don't
want to put all my eggs in any one basket, hoping."

Finally, he went on to see the folks in Knoxville. He
could not sleep on my rollaway and wait for the gears in
Asheville to turn in his favor. Dora and J.C took him under
their wing. Of course they did. He went back to work in
their store, only now he had a much larger and more important role. As he had been a cook in the navy and had
worked himself up the grades into facility management, he
knew all about ordering staples and green groceries. He
began helping them with their advertising, which brought
in new customers, and he could talk to the housewife
shoppers and restaurant owners about food and recipes.
J.C. was not getting any younger, and by taking on Jeremiah,
Dora had secured the future of their grocery and mercantile;
that is, she had once again made a decision that would
ensure her own survival to her best advantage.

When November rolled around that year, she was happy as a clam, with Janeyre and Jeremiah, both of her babies, back in her fold and the war over. She decided we should have a family reunion.

Twenty-Nine

Family Reunion

1946

*D*ora sent out invitations with little RSVP cards that Janey return addressed in her round hand, with circles instead of dots over the *i*'s. In typical Dora style, the reunion was to be *big*. It would be a two-day event, with a welcome lunch and movie at the Princesse Theatre in downtown Knoxville, which had been bought out for the family that afternoon. The next day would be a reception and photo session, followed by a sit-down dinner under a tent on the lawn at Dora and J.C.'s home. Her dining room had a table for twenty, but she needed room for one hundred, Jane had said. I didn't know that our family had expanded that much, but apparently it had. Jane's note, at the bottom of my invitation, said there would be a three-piece band and catered food.

It had not taken long for several cute little girls to set their caps at Jeremiah, and he had picked out one to accent his future at Dora and J.C.'s Grocery & Mercantile. The young lady would be run by the family at the reunion, which was noted to be especially in Jeremiah's honor, returning safely from the war as he had. It was expected that they might announce their engagement at the party. All in all, it was quite a to-do Dora had planned.

If it had been three years that I had worked in Asheville, it was also that long since I had seen my brothers. Walker and Avery were doing well in Abingdon. After their initial disapproval and concern about my "leaving them," as they put it, they had settled in on their new ground and even looked at the situation of the government's overtaking the Wheat property as a blessing in disguise. Good things had happened as a result of the government Taking, things that never would have happened if they had been left to make their own decisions.

Though their acreage was smaller, it had been quite productive, and Avery had found a new calling raising bluetick coonhounds, which he sold for a pretty penny to hunters and would-be gentlemen who admired the unusual gray-blue coat and sweet temperament of the breed. Walker and I had been exchanging letters and talked on the phone at birthdays and Christmas. I made a special call to him about the reunion, and he agreed to come through Asheville and pick me up so we could go together.

"Avery is reluctant to leave his dogs," my brother said. "That's as good an excuse as any for him to miss Dora's party, her little chivaree for Jeremiah." Walker went on to say he had a surprise for me and that I would see what it was when he came to get me. "You might as well hush," he said. "You are not going to wheedle it out of me ahead of time. This is something I want you to find out about in person."

I had made myself a new skirt for the occasion and

bought a pair of open-toed shoes with Cuban heels. They were red and matched the skirt, but I immediately regretted my decision. It was probably better to just be yourself and not try to branch out into a flirty new style if you were over forty, but I had not taken my own counsel. Now I felt that everyone driving by was staring at my feet as I stood on the corner by the Rock Heaven sign, waiting for Walker to arrive. I had had the forethought to ask Walker if he still drove the old Ford truck I remembered, and he snorted.

"That ole jalopy? I got rid of it as soon as we got to Abingdon and bought a real car, an Oldsmobile. It's white, with a Virginia plate."

So I was looking for an up-to-date sedan. I started smiling when I saw it turn the corner and pull toward my curb, and then I noticed that there was another person in the car. So much for surprises, I thought, but I kept my good face going. It had been hard, at first, to tell it was a second person, because she—yes, it was a she—was slid over in the front seat and so jammed up against Walker's hip and shoulder, there was no daylight between them. And then I noticed that the woman, plump and big-boned though she was—well, twenty-six was my generous estimate of her age; she could have been younger.

"You old devil, you," I said out loud to the automobile, but then they were both out of the driver's side and around the bumper to greet me.

"You look mighty nice," said Walker, hugging me and taking in my outfit from head to toe.

"I love your shoes," said the girl, and I did believe she was sincere the moment she said it. She had short blonde hair topped by a navy-blue tam-o'-shanter cap. There was a little pleated scarf tied around her neck, but that did nothing to distract from her hourglass figure, packed rather alarmingly into a sweater and close-fitting skirt.

"Isabel, I want you to meet my wife, Laurey," said Walker, who seemed to be a jumble of pride and nerves. He was certainly in as high a mood as I had ever known him to be. He nudged the small of Laurey's back to get her to shake my hand. Which she jumped to do, at the same time twinkling the little diamond on her left hand before my face.

"My goodness, this is astonishing!" I said, admiring the ring but meaning the whole turn of events. "When did this happen?" I looked at Laurey, then at my brother. "The only thing that could amaze me more is if you told me *Avery* got married too!"

"Well, the wedding was two weeks ago," said Laurey. She cast her eyes at Walker. "Can I tell the story?"

"Yes, but let's do it as we go," Walker said, picking up my bag and putting it into the trunk beside their own luggage.

It was a four-hour drive to Knoxville, but by the time we pulled up in front of the Princesse Theatre, things were relatively clear.

Laurey and Walker had met at a fruit-and-vegetable stand owned by Laurey's father. Walker had to pass it going from his new place into Abingdon proper, and Laurey was working there.

"I never saw a man need so many apples," she laughed.

"And him never having made a pie in his life," I added.

"It was her personality, so bright and cheerful. Just made me want to come back. I did get a cider press, though. And then brought a jug back to Laurey at the stand for her to taste. And then finally, one day, I said to her, 'Are you this nice to all the customers?'"

"And I said, 'Just the good-looking ones,' and so the next thing you know, he had invited me to go in with him to make and sell cider from our apples with his press."

"Walker! Couldn't you have been a little less eager?" I commented.

"Well," said Laurey. "It wasn't really all that fast. First, he invited me over to his house to see the press—it's a very sweet little place, but it really needed a woman's touch—and we spent the evening in his kitchen with the radio on, making cider. And I straightened out his silverware drawer, and that was our first date."

"And then one thing led to another as the weeks went by," Walker said.

"It certainly did," Laurey said. "We started selling lots of cider."

"That's not what I meant," Walker said. They both started laughing.

"And what about Avery? Is he living there at the farm still?" I had to ask.

Walker spoke up. "The kennels are out behind the house, and they are quite nice, with running water and electricity, and a little kitchen and storage area for the dogs' food and supplies, so we just added on a room, and he seems to be quite happy out there."

"He comes up for supper most nights," Laurey was quick to add.

"She's a wonderful cook," Walker said.

"I'm sure she is." I leaned up to the front seat and put my hand on her shoulder. "Well, I can hardly believe it, to have a sister-in-law after all these years. I'm happy for you both, and I am happy for myself too."

"You will have to come and visit us soon," Laurey said.

"I'd love that." We were driving through downtown

Knoxville. It made me think of John L., and I got a twist in my stomach. My eyes darted around as if he might be nearby.

I knew the chances were slim for that, but it was the last thing I wanted.

"What has Walker told you about our family?" I asked Laurey.

"Not much," she said.

"You'll see for yourself. No need for me to poison the well with my commentary," Walker said.

"I'm pleased with it so far," Laurey said, and she smiled at me.

The Princesse marquee was lit and had been made up to read:

WELCOME KING FAMILY REUNION
WELCOME HOME JEREMIAH

I put on a little lipstick and stepped out bravely.

Walker caught up to me. "What do you think of Laurey?" he whispered.

"I think she's a peach, and I think you are a terrible old rascal who has been very lucky to rob a cradle. Why didn't you tell me about all this sooner?"

"My head's been spinning. Isabel, she's not a gold digger or anything like that. She doesn't care about my age." His face started to fall.

"Wait, wait, I can see that! I'm only playing with you. I think it's great; really, I do."

"I never thought I could be happy, really happy, but I think I might be."

I squeezed his hand. "Be happy, then, honey. Be happy if you can. Now let's go see what mischief the rest of our family has gotten into the past few years."

We went through the double doors and into the lobby, which was hung with crystal chandeliers and had marble floors.

"It reminds me of France in here, the churches," Walker said, glancing up.

And then, down the branching stairway from the mezzanine, came Dora, followed by Janeyre, both of them in cocktail dresses.

"Here come the beauties," he added and drew his bride to his side. Laurey, in her plain country best, was to them like a plump dove to redbirds. She cast her eyes down, but Walker held her tighter. She drew herself up a little, and her own arm went around his waist.

Dora was in her prime now, full-figured without being heavy, and our Indian blood showed in her strong features and creamy tan skin. Her thick black hair was perfectly coiffed. She stood back, running her eyes over me head to toe, and kept looking at my fancy red shoes.

I took a step to her, and she took a step to me. "Isabel, I'm so glad you and Walker could come." A puzzle mark appeared for a split second between her brows as she glimpsed Laurey, but she would deal with that later. I wanted to love Dora, but it is hard when you know a person doesn't really care for *you*, and that is just the way it had been, and ever since she had taken in Jane, things had been no better. She put one hand on my back and brought her cheek close to mine for the space of a second, and then the duty of any affection between us was done.

My thoughts went very fast and seemed to focus on how I was shod: *You shouldn't have bought them—worn them—I love these shoes—I don't care—who cares what Dora thinks?*

But then I heard, "Mother, oh, Mother. You're here!" and spun to Jane. We took each other in our arms, and it was real; time and distance melted—we had not changed our essential bond.

"You look lovely, honey!" I let go of her, and she twirled in a float of lavender silk and chiffon. I could hardly believe this was my own child, nearly grown, lovely as a fashion model and with not a trace of our hardship in her face or bearing. My stomach still hurt, and I could not tell if it was because she had had it easy in the years since we left John L. or because she had not.

A few hours went by very fast. We had to pin on name tags, which we found laid out on a side table, and then sign a guest book. I did not want to put down Rock Heaven Motel as my residence; I just wrote "Asheville."

Coffee, tea, and finger sandwiches were served at the concession stand by waiters in white coats, but I could not eat anything. There was Jeremiah, who I had recently seen, in his navy dress whites, and his new fiancée, Sammie, a gum-chewing young woman with an imitation Ginger Rogers pompadour and a too-loud laugh. I tried to get a read on her character but drew a blank.

"Her father is a Methodist minister," Jeremiah said and pointed him out. He was conferring with Dora. I did wonder the degree to which she had orchestrated Jeremiah's relationship. We watched as Dora led Sammie's father to a very elderly woman with heavily rouged cheeks sitting in one of the velvet throne chairs by the entrance to the darkened theatre. She was stroking a fur muff, but then it moved and I saw it was a tiny lapdog with a pronounced underbite.

"Who is that, Jeremiah?" I asked.

"That is Great-Aunt Eliza, our daddy's aunt," he said. "Have you never met her? Dora tracked her down a couple of years ago and brought her to live in a nursing home here in Knoxville. Remember, Daddy used to say Dora took after her?"

"Now that I think of it, I guess I met her once, when I was a child. Daddy used to say she had gone off, married money, and gotten above her raising. How old must she be?"

"Ninety-two, I think," he said.

"There seem to be some others here I don't recognize. Are these folks really members of our family?"

"Dora says they are. A lot of them are Dixons, from Daddy's side, apparently."

"Well, that explains something. I wouldn't know them much, though I'd certainly be interested in meeting them. What about Uncle John and our mama's people from Tellico Plains? Where are they?"

"The Cherokee people, you mean? I guess Dora couldn't find them."

"Or didn't want to."

Jeremiah nodded as if he understood that, but just then, Sammie motioned to him with a cock of her Ginger Rogers head, so I waved him on.

Then I was reunited with Sallie. Dora and Jeremiah had not seen their sister for years either. Was she that same little girl who had come to my arms when I went to care for her family during the flu epidemic? She was here all the way from Akron, Ohio, with one of her teenage sons, who had driven because she didn't know how. My stomach ached more. This time, it was absolutely because Sallie had had it hard. All her sweetness was scarred by a pain that showed in her slow voice and careful choice of words. All her blonde prettiness was coarse now, her clothes not the right quality or style—even I could tell it. She was wearing a big crucifix necklace and kept touching it.

"Well, Sallie, honey, how are you?" I said and held on to her, our shoulders touching. I should have brought tissues in my purse. I needed them constantly.

"I'm good," she said softly. "I had to get divorced, but the Church helps me. It don't approve of divorce, of course, but even Father Joe—that's my priest—understood I had to. The one good thing that I got out of my marriage, besides the kids, is that I converted." She told me about her work at the Goodyear Tire Factory cafeteria, so I told her a little about John L. and the Rock Heaven, and we locked eyes and smiled at our sad pasts. Our relationship was on a new level then. She introduced her son. I could see he couldn't wait to get out of here, either to get away from all of us or just to go smoke.

Jane kept coming back to me to see how I was doing, and it was good to know that she considered me the most important person in the room. But at last, she came and took me by the arm.

"Everyone is going into the theatre now," she said. "Dora is going to make an announcement, and then the movie will start."

"What is the movie?" I asked.

"*Thirty Seconds Over Tokyo.* It has Spencer Tracy and Van Johnson. Dora thought it would be good to show something with a military theme, in honor of Jeremiah."

"By the way, where is J.C.? I haven't seen him yet."

"Well, you know he's shy and likes to stay behind the scenes. He's probably up in the booth with the projectionist or in the back of the concessions area, managing the food."

I took a place, with Jane on one side and Walker and Laurey on the other. There was a giant pipe organ in the theatre, left over from the 1920s. Even though Jeremiah had been in the navy, an organist played "Wild Blue

Yonder" while everyone filed in. Then Dora stood on the stage with her hands clasped in front of her. She looked across the space of the auditorium and waited for silence.

"It does my heart good to see all my family here today," she said. "I hope most of you will be able to stay tonight and then for our photo session and dinner tomorrow. As you know, both of those events will be held at my home. But now, I want to take time for us to celebrate the other reason for our coming together: the end of the war and the safe return of my baby brother, Jeremiah! Jeremiah, come on up here."

Everyone clapped, and out of the corner of my eye, I could see Walker and Laurey tapping their palms. I suspected Walker was thinking of his own war—twenty-five years is barely enough time to let some things lie in your mind before you can look at them without falling down into a heap.

Jeremiah bounded up the steps to the stage, saluted to the increased applause, and said, "Some of you know this already, but I'd like to use this opportunity to introduce my future bride, Sammie Wilson!" He motioned to her, and she scurried to join him, holding a bundle of small American flags. She pursed her lips and glued them on to Jeremiah's cheek, all the while rolling her eyes out to the crowd, as if urging them to enjoy her little public display of affection. Finally, she stood up straight and began throwing her flags into the audience.

One landed on Laurey's lap. My new sister-in-law stared at it as if it were an errant bird; maybe it would go away in a minute. But it did not.

"And thank you, Dora, for putting this event together," Jeremiah was saying. "Those of you who live in the area, don't be strangers. Come on in to our mercantile, where I am the new supplies manager!"

At this, Dora returned to center stage. "Yes, he is, and J.C. and I are delighted to have him. And now, let's settle back and enjoy ourselves awhile with the feature presentation, *Thirty Minutes Over Tokyo*, just for our own wonderful family!"

The movie opened with the sound of whistling bombs and marching feet. Walker twisted in his seat, and Laurey looped her arm in his. I was distracted at times by the sight of the handsome Robert Mitchum playing poker, his fingernail flicking the edge of his cards, the dimple in his chin moving as he spoke. Van Johnson and Spencer Tracy had never done much for me, though naturally, I rooted for the pilot, Captain Lawson, the Van Johnson character.

I didn't notice Walker again until the planes were in the air on their way to Tokyo. The camera was right in the cockpit and in the turret gunner's space. The audience was flying with them just feet above the water. The city was on the shore ahead. It was so real, I reached out and touched Walker's hand, which was covered with sweat. As soon as I did, he said, "Excuse me," and stood in a crouch to inch his way to the aisle. He fled up the theatre carpet to the lobby.

Laurey and I looked at each other in the shadowed light cast from the screen. The plane had crashed in the ocean, and an injured Captain Lawson and his crew made their way to the beach.

"He'll be okay," Laurey mouthed to me and reached across his empty seat. We held hands until we knew everyone in the crash was still alive.

When the film was over, the lights came up and everyone clapped and waved flags again. Dora came onstage and said that if anyone needed directions to her house for the dinner tomorrow, Jane would be in the lobby to hand out slips of paper with a map on it. Dora scanned the extended family spread below her, her eyes lingering here and there. Her gaze passed by Laurey and me, her face as blank as the surface of the sea.

"I'm going to find Walker," Laurey said.

"Good; I will go say goodbye to Jane," I responded.

I watched my daughter from a distance. She was so beautiful, so sweet with everyone. The true princess. It probably was for the best that Dora had completed Jane's raising—I could never have done this well for her, and she certainly deserved the best. As long as she still loved me and we were keeping in touch, I could feel all right about it, couldn't I?

She smiled as I approached her. "Did you like it?" she asked. She put her hand to one side of her mouth and whispered, "J.C. had to buy every seat to get the theatre for the reunion."

"Oh my, he and Dora certainly did something special for us. Did J.C. ever come down from the projection booth? I still haven't seen him. The movie was very good. The whole evening was nice, but it's a lot to take in. I feel like I'm in the middle of a circle and everything is a blur, going round and round. It's been so long since I have seen people, and some of them I have never met, ever. Well, maybe tomorrow I'll have a chance."

"Where are you staying?" she asked. "I wish you could have stayed with me, but Dora said no, so many people were here, and she didn't want to show any favoritism."

Dora could give whatever explanation worked, I thought. Then I said, "We are in a motel here in town. My manager at the Rock Heaven, Letitia, helped us arrange it and got us rooms for next to nothing. So we're fine." I changed the subject. "What do you think about that development? Your uncle with a girl, at long last? And about Jeremiah and Sammie too?"

"It's amazing and unexpected, but I am in favor of love, whenever and however it occurs."

"You are exhibiting wisdom as well as beauty, I'm glad to see." We hugged deeply. I breathed her for a moment and wrapped my hands on the fine bones of her shoulders. It was amazing and unexpected that she should be my offspring.

"I have missed you so much," I murmured.

"Me too. I'll see you tomorrow."

"Yes, tomorrow. Good night."

The dinner the next day went well, though I felt like I was in a play. It was a beautiful setting, in Dora's back garden. The tables had white linens and full place settings, and vases of colorful zinnias backed with fern. Dora sat at the head table with Jane, Jeremiah, Sammie, and her father, the minister. There was an empty chair next to Dora for J.C. Something had happened at the store, Dora said, and he had to go down to see about it. Sammie's father offered grace, and we all got quietly to work on our crab cakes, salad, and coffee. Jane waved at me from where she sat. When a member of the waitstaff came by to refresh the drinks, I saw it was J.C., bald and a little stooped, looking worse than I'd ever seen him and wearing a white apron.

"Why, my goodness," I said. "J.C., how are you? I haven't had a chance to talk to you, and I know you are responsible for this shebang in a major way. Aren't you going to sit down and eat? I hope everything is all right at the store."

"Some boys broke a window," he said. "It's all taken

care of. And as for this event, I will sit if Dora makes me," he said. "But I'd really prefer to be up and doing, making sure everything goes along good."

"Why, it's wonderful," I told him. "Dora seems very pleased with it all." The shadow of some happiness went across his face. "We are all very pleased with it," I added.

To tell the truth, it was too formal, a bit too stuffy. Dora had given our family a veneer we didn't really have, sat us down like paper dolls at a pretty tea party. Overall, the family group was much smaller than yesterday. Many of us had not been able to afford an overnight stay or had to travel back to be ready for the work week. Or we did not like to have our picture taken and deal with all this fancy commotion. Sallie and her son had gone back to Dayton; the Dixon contingent had not been able to take more time off from work and had disappeared back to their lumber mills and forges; Aunt Eliza and her muff dog were re-ensconced in the nursing home.

Walker and Laurey and I were having a nice time. We had let our guard down, started to relax, when I noticed a stray dog had wandered into the yard party. It smelled the food, no doubt, and was hoping to find a piece of bread or was longing for some friendly soul to toss it some scraps. It was a scroungy collie—thin, with dirty, tangled fur. If the poor thing hadn't been so hungry, it probably wouldn't have had the audacity to enter the gathering. And then there was Laurey herself. She seemed unaware that her presence as Walker's wife, his new little country wife, was received by Dora with barely veiled hostility. But she was just being herself.

And so she fed the dog things from the banquet table. "Oh, look," she said. "I could not show my face to Avery when we got back home if I sat here and ate chicken while that poor collie sent me starving looks. C'mere, come here. Good girl," she said. She used that high baby tone we all do when we speak to dogs.

The collie slunk through the tables to Laurey's side. Odor indicated it must have been in a garbage heap somewhere. Its fur was matted, and it sat watching Laurey's face, catching in its mouth every tidbit that was offered. I looked up and saw Dora drop her napkin and rise from her chair, her jaw set and her finger beckoning to me. My eyes darted to Jane. "No, no," she was mouthing, and it seemed she wanted me to make Laurey stop or make the dog go away.

Dora kept motioning to me, so I followed her away from the tables to the back door of the house and into the kitchen, where J.C. was supervising the help as they cooked and prepared the plates. I turned to a man frosting a three-layer cake, bits of whipped vanilla frosting sticking to his fingers.

"That looks beautiful," I said. "I can't wait to taste it. Thanks for all this work you're doing."

"Yes, ma'am," he said. His eyes flicked up for just an instant, but Dora was right there. He looked down again at the cake.

"Isabel!" Dora said. "Pay attention to me, please!" She gripped my arm and swiveled me into a pantry. J.C. turned his head and pretended he didn't see what she was doing.

Dora put the edges of her teeth together and said to me, "That little hick wife of Walker's is disrupting the re-union! He is your brother, so I would appreciate it if you would speak to him, or to her, and stop this inappropriate behavior immediately. I will not have her feeding a mangy animal like that off the table, turning our gathering into a barn, a humane shelter."

"Dora, Laurey is just being kind! I'm sorry if you object to that! I'll ask her to take the dog somewhere else and feed it."

"That would be excellent." She closed her eyes, as if looking at me caused her to have a headache. "I am trying to create a nice event here, something tasteful. I don't want it ruined by some poor little white-trash floozy that none of us have ever met before. The nerve of you both, bringing her here."

I felt the skin prickle all over my body, and I resisted the urge to slap her—an urge, I realized now, I had had since she was five years old. I clenched my fists and was about to speak when Jane stuck her head in to see what was going on.

"Is everything all right?"

"It will be," I said. "I just needed to say that, unfortunately, Walker and Laurey and I have to leave early and won't be staying for dessert."

"What's wrong?" Jane held out her hands, first to me, then to Dora. But I could not bring myself to attack Dora, even verbally, in Jane's presence. Dora clamped her mouth shut. You could practically see the steam rising off her, though. Jane knew it, knew I had done something to get Dora riled.

"Don't leave; why must you leave?"

Walker, at that moment, appeared and added himself to our conversation. "Isabel, Laurey has gotten sick. I think we had better clean her up and get on home."

"I hate this, Jane, but I guess we better." I gave my daughter a quick hug, then reentered the garden party to find that the tables around ours had cleared out and Laurey was half standing, dipping her cloth napkin in a water glass and brushing at her skirt. Immediately, I could smell that she had vomited. Other guests were covering their noses and mouths; no one was eating their food.

"Oh my, I am so sorry." Laurey was wavering on her feet and could not let go of the chair. "I have never had crab cakes before. I guess, with all this excitement, they must not have agreed with me. Give me just a second, and I will clean up after myself."

But it was already being done. Dora came after me, only to see the stray collie lapping at a disgusting puddle beside Laurey's chair.

"*Get out!*" Her fingers rigid against her face, Dora screamed the words.

I took one of Laurey's arms, and Walker took the other.

"Can you make it to the car?" he asked his wife.

"Yes, I think so. I ruined everything, didn't I?"

"No, you didn't. It's just one of those things that can't be helped." Walker spoke to me over Laurey's back. "Isabel, how can we be kin to such a person?"

We got Laurey into the car, but she wasn't done yet. She opened the door, leaned, and threw up again on Dora's curb. I gave her a tissue, and she wiped her mouth and said, "Don't leave her. I could never face Avery if I did."

At first, I thought she meant Jane, who came halfway down the drive to call to me, "Should I go with you?" but Dora was at her shoulder and grabbed her hand to pull her back. I could see Jeremiah behind them both, but he was going to be of no use, as Ginger/Sammie was clinging to his arm and gaping at the spectacle we had created. And then I realized that Laurey meant the collie dog; don't leave the dog.

Walker took a sharp breath, hesitated, but then he called it. "Come on; come on, then. Let's go."

And weakly, Laurey managed, "Here, girl; here. Don't stay with these people." Moving quickly and low to the ground, the creature approached, and Walker opened the back door and it jumped in, on top of me. And so I rode back to Asheville, sharing the seat with a stinking collie.

"What a fiasco," Walker said finally. We had been silent for miles, except for the sound of the dog panting.

"I'm all to blame," Laurey said. She was feeling much better by the time we hit the North Carolina state line.

"No, you're not," I said, and it was true. I did not fault my new sister-in-law, though I wanted to cry for all that Jane and I had not been able to say to each other in such a frantic leave-taking. And as for Dora—well, her name bore a dark cloud over it now, and for sure, there was much unfinished business between us.

Thirty

Gary

1948

*D*ear Mother,

       Thanks for inviting me to visit you, but I can't come just now. Secretarial school is going well, but I have a secret to tell you. I had been waiting for an opportunity, but then I didn't get to when things sort of fell apart at the reunion. You must promise not to tell Dora. Do you remember at the reunion, when I said I was in favor of love, whenever and however it is found? Well, I am engaged! His name is Gary Archer. He actually is from Jefferson, N.C., but he lives in Knoxville now. I met him at his cousin Norma's party. Norma is in secretarial school with me. He was in the service for nine years. He is very smart—he was a pilot and was in the Pacific during the war. He wound up in Hollywood after that and worked for an aircraft corporation. He understands all kinds of things like thermo- and aerodynamics and air-conditioning. He is tall and has blue eyes and a real good sense of humor, which is *important in life, don't you think? As you can tell, I could go on and on about him.*

Dora has met him, but she doesn't approve of him because he is twenty-nine. She says, "You were just a little slip of a thing when Pearl Harbor happened." She says things like "experience levels. You're just past being a baby, and he has a high experience level; that is why this is not a good idea." She tells me that when I was in elementary school, he was fixing to enlist. I was learning to write cursive and he was learning to grade runways. She tells me we don't even like the same music. (Dora bought this big organ now, I am learning to play it. The organist from The Princesse is my teacher; you would be amazed). Dora holds music against Gary too! She says people need to know and appreciate the same songs. All the big-band songs are what Gary likes, but I am learning mostly classical and hymns. When I say, "Dora, you like Glen Miller," she says, "That is because Gary and I are the same generation, and honey, that means he is old!" However, J.C. is fifteen years older than Dora, so she does not have a leg to stand on. J.C.'s favorite song is "If You Knew Suzie Like I Know Suzie." But mostly he likes church hymns, ones like "There's a Church in the Wildwood" and "Old Rugged Cross." I am learning those to play for him.

I figured out that Dora's main objection to Gary was that she didn't want me to just settle for love. I know she thinks, deep down, that love wears off, while property and money do not. She would never admit that.

You would like Gary. I hope to introduce him to you soon.

Love,

Janey

I put the letter in my apron pocket, intending to answer it as soon as I could figure out what to say. But in the meantime, one of the girls came to say the draperies in 117 had been stolen, apparently gone home with the last occupant, and I had to make some new ones. I can only imagine the horrible curtains they must have had at home if they needed to take those old things. I thought I had time to deal with Janey's news; it certainly explained her receptivity about Walker's marriage and Jeremiah's match: *"I am in favor of love, whenever and however it occurs."* I was not going to be as severe as Dora, ever, but I did hope this Gary might be a passing fancy. Janey was so young.

So the weekend went by, and we were plenty busy on Monday, with lots of people checking out. I had to go to the bank and make a deposit, and then we had to call a repairman to fix two of the ice machines. The hours went by fast. No sooner was the key in my door that evening than my phone began to ring. I fumbled the lock open and ran for it. You know how it sounds the same every time, but sometimes there's a hysterical edge to it? You feel it's more important than usual. And sure enough, it was Janey, calling me from the road. I could hear cars whoosh past in the background.

"Mother, hi, it's me."

"Well, hi, darling. This is a surprise. I was fixing to answer your letter. I have been thinking hard about your new development."

"Well, yes. There is another new development. That's why I called."

"Well, honey, what is it?"

"Mother, Gary and I are going to get married. I want to come by and see you first, though, since you have never met him."

"Well, yes, I understood from the letter that you had gotten engaged. I was hoping to talk to you about it beforehand, but of course you can come by. I'd been hoping you would, and of course I want to meet your—your young man." I tried to stay really calm.

Jane started again. "Well, actually, Mother, what I mean is, well—I mean we are going to get married right *now*. We are eloping. We are driving to Myrtle Beach for it and will have a little honeymoon while we are there."

Her voice was so pleasant, but the word *eloping*, though I knew it, did not ring a bell at first. She might as well have told me the two of them were going to skip down the beach. When it finally registered what she was saying, I drew in a sharp breath.

"Oh, honey, is this absolutely necessary? Do you *need* to get married?"

"Well, no; we don't *need* to. I'm not expecting, if that's what you mean."

I was silent. I felt her turn and pause, and frantic whispering took place on her end.

Janey continued, "I am sorry you have not been able to meet him before this, Mother. Once you know him, a thought like that would not occur to you." A degree of coldness had crept into her voice, but what was I supposed to think?

"Well, Jane, I would love to meet him. It's just that, honey, I am hoping you will not make the same mistake I made. You haven't known him but a couple of months. Please now, why don't you wait just a little longer? Finish your school, at least. There is no reason to rush into anything."

"It doesn't feel like rushing. I know this is right, and really, we are trying to do the right thing now. Dora was ready to forbid me to see him; we couldn't go on in secrecy."

"When will you be here?" This conversation needed to happen in person.

Voices muffled as the receiver changed hands. I heard the soft smack of a kiss.

"Hello, this is Gary. I know this is sudden, and not exactly the right way to introduce myself, but I just want you to know how much I love your daughter! And I am really looking forward to getting to know you. But we'll be there in about an hour, and I apologize for the shock and suddenness of this."

My face tightened. I did not want to accept any "apology," but neither did I begin ranting at him. This was not the best idea I had ever heard. Though Jane was legally old enough to make up her own mind. *You, you man!* I thought.

"We'll see you in about an hour, then."

"Yes, ma'am." He laughed nervously.

"All right." I hung up, which was rude for me, to not say good bye, but I didn't care right then.

I changed into a clean dress and put on lipstick, then took a broom and did a little sweeping by the office, just to put my nervous energy to use. I didn't want to do anything where I'd get dirty again.

In an hour, just as the man had said, a white Pontiac drove up. Jane got out, dressed in a navy-blue suit and wearing an orchid corsage. All the ease she'd had with me at the reunion, the restoring flow between us, was gone. I had so much needed to bridge the wound of our separation, but what I felt from her now was an alert energy. I realized she was nervous to see me.

I hugged her and shook Gary's hand. I felt like a stick

figure: formal, as if Dora had momentarily possessed my body.

"How do you do?" I said to my future son-in-law. "Pleased to meet you." Which was a lie. "Let's go around the back, to the courtyard," I said. "We can sit and chat." I took Jane's hand. "Mr. Archer, I hope you don't mind, but I'd like to speak to my daughter privately for a moment."

"Please call me Gary. And I just want you to know—"

"You might as well call me Isabel." We passed my little room, my motel room. I ignored the fact that he was trying to say something. "Why don't you wait here?" I said to him. "We'll be right back." I turned Jane into my door, then waved at Wanita, who was pushing her linen cart down the walkway. I knew I was frowning. Wanita stopped and put her hands on her hips and wrinkled her brow.

"What?" she mouthed.

I closed my eyes and held up one finger. The gesture told her, Later, I will explain later. Just a minute or so. Wanita nodded.

I closed the door. "He's so wonderful," Jane said immediately.

"Honey," I burst out. "You may think you are on a trip to Myrtle Beach, but that is not where you are ultimately going! You won't be able to get out of this so easily if it doesn't work out! I know! Please, let's just think for a minute."

"Mother, I love him. He really is a good man. I know he loves me." She came to me and put her arms around my neck. "It will mean so much to have your support. I wish I had Dora's too, but maybe that will come in time."

My heart was in a knot, but there was not one thing I could do to pull her back from the edge, so I just hoped for a soft landing. I asked what worried me most.

"There is one thing I need to know. Is he a drinker? I absolutely cannot condone this marriage if he is."

Jane put her hands on my arms. "I know what you are getting at, Mother, and he is nothing, nothing like . . . well, you know. I can't say he doesn't have a beer every now and then. But it's nothing he does on a regular basis. It's not something he has to do. He is just so smart and has such a great future. Once you get to know about him, you'll see."

Oh, Janeyre, what have you done? I thought. Out across the parking lot, by the road, the neon sign blinked off and on. *Rock* and then *Heaven. Rock Heavennnn.* It could have been the name of a hymn, or it could have been an off-color joke about what our guests did behind closed doors.

"What does he do, then?" I asked. "This great future you are talking about?"

"His job is secret; he can't tell me what he does. It's with Clinton Engineering Works, where Wheat used to be!" There was a note of pride in her voice.

"Where Wheat used to be? You mean he works for the people who obliterated half of Anderson County, the people who built the bomb?" My knees went to water, and I sat down on the bed.

"Yes! I told him you lived there before, and about Grandaddy's farm and all that, Mother. It's just another one of the reasons why it's all so perfect! It's like we were destined for each other. It's all coming back around."

"But, Jane, of all places!"

"Mother, I know this is a shock to you, but Gary and I couldn't stand to be apart any longer. I called Dora and she won't talk to me. She turned the phone over to J.C. I know they think I have been ungrateful for all they have done for me. I hope you don't think that too." A partial smile edged onto her face. "Do you know what I did to make my escape? I told Dora I was going to spend the night with Norma. Gary's cousin? You know I am not the type to lie, so it was hard, but Dora wasn't suspicious. To her, I probably still seem about thirteen."

"For once, Dora and I see eye to eye."

She blinked past that comment, just kept on delivering her tale while she checked herself in the mirror, straightened her blouse under the jacket. "Our story was, we planned to go to dinner and a movie, so it would be late and I would stay over at Norma's. I packed a little overnight bag. It's good Dora didn't get too curious. I had some brand-new underwear and a negligee in there, and some other things." She giggled and looked out the window at Gary pacing in the courtyard.

"What about all your things? How will you get them?"

Jane said, "Well, when I left, in addition to bringing my train case, I had dressed in a triple layer of nylons, slips, blouses, and skirts. I looked about five pounds heavier than usual, but Dora always says everyone looks thin and young to her. She didn't notice." She continued, "I packed up a lot of my other shoes and jewelry and clothes in a few boxes and put them inside my closet. I taped an envelope to one, and in there, I had a note to Dora and postage money so she could mail things to me.

"I don't know," she said. "Maybe she will, if she's not too mad. If they don't get here next week, maybe you can call her for me."

To think that Dora would do anything because I asked her to was beyond discussion. Knowing what she knew about John L., if this did not work out, she would find a way to turn this back on me, say the apple didn't fall too far from the tree. As if it were clearly an issue of learned morals or of not being able to "resist."

"I think we should go back outside," I said. "Enlarge this conversation with the other party involved."

Gary stood up as we approached. I knew I did not look friendly. How could I?

"I just want you to know." Gary swallowed. "Isabel, I intend to take very good care of Janey! I have a great job lined up with the Atomic Energy Commission, the Clinton Engineering Works. The pay is excellent, if I do say so myself, and I've secured a little house right down the road from Y-12—I mean, right down the road from the plant where I will be working. It's a very nice place, and the house too. The town has everything we could want. It's practically brand new," he added.

"I know about Oak Ridge, the Clinton Engineering Works, you say, and I certainly know where it is located. Jane said she told you where we are from. Everything there is built on the ruins of other people's lives. My family had a farm there going back to the seventeen hundreds!" I did not bother to measure my words.

Gary's eyes widened, and he looked helplessly at Jane. I knew I had a hostile tone, but I couldn't help it and didn't care.

"I will come after you if you don't treat her right, and don't imagine I make idle threats."

The couple came together, and Jane linked his arm. She actually looked calm now.

"Mother, I have no doubts. I am ready to be with this man for the rest of my life." The two of them looked at me and waited. I could see Wanita watching us, slowly wheeling her cart down the sidewalk on the opposite side of the courtyard.

When I was nine, I stood in a field watching my mama leave. There was a great emptiness around me then, and I felt the same now. But this time, I knew better than to try and hope all could be restored. The problem was—had always been—how to come to terms with a thing that was out of your hands.

I was slowly seeing how Jane's situation might have played out. If she had not eloped, it would have gotten complicated, with both Dora and me on the same side for once, trying to talk her out of it. Then, after we finally relented, as we would have, there would have been all the preparation: with dresses, cakes, and guest lists. I had no money to help her, and a fancy party put on by Dora and J.C. would have shot my nerves. A planned wedding would have been a burden, no doubt, but this helpless feeling was nearly as bad.

I sighed. "Honey, I love you. I just want you to be happy."

"I am happy! So happy, Mother! So will you give us your blessing?"

"Honey, 'blessing' is not the right thing to call what I am wanting to offer at this moment. What I can say I have in my heart is the beginning of an acceptance of this and a wish for your happiness and welfare. Maybe an honest blessing will come in time, but this is so new and so much is unknown right now. But I do thank you for stopping to see me; I know you didn't have to." I looked at the man, tried to start getting used to his looks, figure out what my daughter saw in him. I couldn't see it yet.

Jane looked relieved. "Well, we have to go now. A minister is expecting us in Myrtle Beach. Listen, I will call you once we get settled; give us a week or so."

I walked them to the car in a daze. Kissed Jane, shook Gary's hand, looked him in the eye. I did not want us to be adversaries. But things did not seem real just then. They waved at me as they drove away, and I walked back to my room and unlocked the door. A trickle of sweat ran down the middle of my back, and I just wanted some restoring breeze. I leaned against the doorjamb taking deep breaths. Wanita's cart was down at the corner, and as soon as she came out to exchange towels, she saw me and scurried over.

"What's going on? You don't look too good! I saw you from a distance. Who those people? You most never get visitors." She put her hand on my arm. "I hope nobody died."

"No, nobody died, although I thought *I* might. It was my daughter, telling me she is eloping with that man, that older man you just saw! You know, Wanita, this upsets me to no end. I cannot convince myself that she is seeing straight. But she claims she is in love, not pregnant, and is going to a church right now. They came for my blessing."

"Well, mercy, is that all?" Wanita stamped her foot and laughed. "If that happen to me, I would say my prayers be answered! Here your daughter is *telling* you and axing you for a blessing! I got three grands from my daughter, all with different daddies. She never told me nothing, just waited for me to notice she was getting big! If I had me a son-in-law, I'd be dancing right now! With them three babies, why you think I have to work like I do?"

Wanita bumped my hip. "Anyway, *you* remember! You can't tell 'em nothing when they young!"

"I don't know how it was for you, Wanita, with the men in your life. My second husband, Janey's stepfather . . . it was a bad marriage. He was a damaged person, perhaps he was. And my daddy, the way he treated my mama . . . it drove her away from the family. How do you tell them, how do you tell your girls . . . ?" I didn't quite know how to put it. Things had worked with Samuel, despite the way the formation of our relationship had raised eyebrows. But it took years for us to bring it about. On the other hand, the passion that had drawn me to John L. seemed so distant, a false treasure buried now in anger and ice. It had been a horrible mistake. "How do you tell your girls that feeling good is not worth the pain you have if it turns out wrong?"

Wanita's face went soft. She thought for a while. "Men and women coming together—most times you can't predict which way it will fall once the fire burns down to steady. Work out fine or go up in flames—I've had both and learned from both. Maybe the good side is only how it strengthens you, makes you wiser. That pull is too powerful for a young body. They has to learn the hard way, the same way we did."

Was I stronger from having loved? I was not sure. Love had been a disappointment to me, a disappointment in so many ways. It still hurt to think maybe John L. never really loved me.

"I pray Janey will be all right," I said. "After what I went through with my second husband, my own view is, being in love can be like a disease. It binds you up around the middle and affects you all over your body. You can't get a breath deep enough in your lungs. You can't remember if you ate or not, and you lose weight. Your heart hurts like your ribs are wire. You can't concentrate on anything—your brain works like a sieve."

"Yeah, I 'member that," said Wanita. "You go round hoping people won't notice your body glowing like a furnace, and if you have been with your lover, you are sure people can tell all the things you did."

"There are things I never told Janey, things she needs

to know but won't listen to now. She is a woman like me, and a woman who is part of me. And when I think how we fall for love, think how we rate the experience so high, I have to shake my head. I hope she won't regret this."

Just then, one of our tourists pulled up to his room in his car, so Wanita and I had to stop and smile at him. It broke the spell of our talk.

"Hi. Good evening. Everything all right with your room? Good."

Wanita turned me around and pushed the wings of my shoulders toward the bed. "Now listen, go have a little lie-down, I'm come check on you later. Don't worry so. It will be what it is."

She shut the door behind me. I sat down on the bed and examined the spread and the matching curtains. I had washed them twice, but they still smelled of smoke from all the travelers before me who had been in this room. The fabric was heavy, nubbed bark cloth, olive green with a large tropical fern print. If I washed it much more, it would be limp and faded and fall apart.

When I married John L., I made a dust ruffle for our bed out of eyelet. I thought it looked so elegant and bridal. But after what happened with Janey, I thought about that bed, and the blunt thought came to me: what is lace but cloth with holes? I'd been a fool, and Janey and I both paid a price. If I hadn't dared to want him in the first place, dared to think he was an answer to something I was seeking, none of it would have happened.

I lay down on the tropical ferns and squeezed my eyes shut. Religion seemed to be leaving me as I got older. I went to church with Queenie from time to time at First Pres-byterian, but mostly it was to keep a minimal connection in honor of our past together. The Presbyterians didn't get too hysterical about Jesus and seemed to welcome inquiry, up to a point. When I was a girl, God was an old man's face looking down kindly from His spot in the center of the ceiling. His long beard hung down like Spanish moss. I never told anyone about this notion of mine, that God, sweet as He was, was not all that useful: He was a freak, a head with no body. He couldn't even fly like the angels did. Mostly, He just sat there, issuing commands and judgments.

I felt so, so tired. I curled up on my side and took out one of the pillows and wrapped myself around it. When Janey was a little girl, we used to sing back and forth as she fell asleep. I would sing, "London Bridge is falling down, falling down, falling down. London Bridge is falling down, my fair lady." And she would sing back to me, "Iron bars will bend and break, bend and break. Build it up with silver and gold. Silver and gold. My fair lady." I was tired and needed to cry, but unless I went to the movies to watch something really sad, the tears would stay concreted in my chest.

I did not know what to do with the information I had now. Love might be a kind of disease. In fact, I know it is, because you can get over it and go on with life if it doesn't kill you first. I wasn't in love with Samuel, not like that. My Lord, he started out as my brother-in-law. I liked him well enough, but the liking just got more permanent, more comfortable. I do think he cared about me, in a fond and convenient way, but he loved me more as time went on. I was in love with John L., in love hard, but it faded fast into pain. It was a sickness I barely survived.

Well. It was bad enough that Janey was running off to get married, but it was just sinking in that the place she was going was Oak Ridge. I peeked up at the ceiling to see if God would return in my time of need to give me an idea.

But He was just a stain on the plaster. I pulled the cigarette-smelling spread over my legs and drifted toward sleep.

I went to bed upset and mad, but when I woke up, I boiled water for Sanka on my hot plate and resolved to start my daily work as reasonably as I could. But as if to demonstrate that the chaos in my head was going to show itself one way or another, Emogene came thudding down the walkway, her nylons scraping together under her uniform and her massive bosom shuddering with each step.

I unlocked the front office and said good morning to a gentleman buying the daily *Citizen* out of the newspaper machine before I gave her my attention. Emogene was wearing her agitation like a jacket and could hardly stand still.

"What in the world—"

"Miz Isabel, you come on over to 214 right now! I knowed those two soldiers was bad news soon as they checked in—and those were just young schoolgirls with 'em, don't tell me they wasn't! Well, they have tore that room to pieces! There ain't no just *cleaning* it! You gonna need a carpenter, a painter, and lord to goodness, you gonna need bleach! There is blood on the sheets and towels and in the tub and on the shower curtain . . ."

"Emogene, is there . . . is there a *lot* of blood? Should we call the police?"

"Miz Isabel, you come on and see for yourself."

"Emogene, if I have told you once, I have told you a hundred times, stop calling me 'Miz.'"

I had no choice but to put my daughter's life out of mind and take care of the business in front of me. The blood was not so much as Emogene said, incidentally. Though I do think that there was a very fine party in the room, and innocence was probably lost that night. But yes, there needed to be a carpenter and a painter. And bleach.

Catherine Vance

In a couple of days, the mail brought me another letter having to do with Jane. So I came round again to the matter of her marriage.

Dear Isabel,

I know you are surprised to hear from me, but I have some terrible news. (I tried to reach you by phone, but who-ever answered the phone at that motel where you work ap-parently never delivered the message.) Janey has eloped with a man nearly twice her age. I think she is living with him in Oak Ridge.

I am sorry to have to tell you this, and you may hold me responsible, but she is an adult in the eyes of the law, no matter how much we still see her as a child. And to think that J.C. wasted all that money for her secretarial course. I had high hopes for that girl.

I had met the man, and while I objected to his age, I consented for Janey to go on a couple of dates with him, as he was able to give the reference of his older sister, someone I knew from the Women's Business League.

However, I did not follow up on my suspicions the night in question, and for this I do fault myself. She was chattering away, saying she was going to the movies with her friend (turns out this "friend" was the man's cousin) and would be spending the night at the friend's house since it was a late show. As soon as she left, I felt something was wrong. I thought I had never seen girls so excited over just going to the picture show. I couldn't put my finger on it, but it was in the air, like the time a salesman talked up a blue streak, all friendly, while he unloaded his merchandise, and then overbilled me. After J.C. and I had dinner, I was still feeling uneasy, so I went straight upstairs and found a box of her things, ready to mail, and a note telling me of her tragic plans. She called from a pay phone later that evening, I think they were in a bar, it was so noisy, but I was too upset and had to give J.C. the phone.

There is no way to help the child now. She has made her bed and she will have to lie in it. You know, J.C. would have given her a full-time job in his store, right alongside us and Jeremiah. She would not have had to work a hard day in her life if she had stuck with us. I know when we were growing up, Grandaddy, your daddy, thought that anything that did not make calluses wasn't real work. Handling dry goods and money does not raise blisters—that is true—but it is nothing to be ashamed of. Who knows what kind of life this Gary Archer has. When we were first introduced, he was still "looking" for work! I don't know what will become of our Janey. I am sorry to have to be the bearer of bad news.

Dora

I screamed a little with my hand held over my mouth and rolled my eyes. It was because of Janeyre and what she had done. It was because of Dora and her smug superiority in telling me something I "didn't know" and her ridiculous sense of propriety in society. I screamed, too, because I had not learned—after all that had happened to me and to the ones I loved in my life—I still had not learned to accept that things will be the way they be, as Wanita put it. There were regrets and guilty feelings I could not ignore. I found I still wanted to have the power to make things happen the way I thought they ought to. I, too, had high hopes for that girl, but in a different way than Dora.

I ripped the paper in two, in four, and again—rip, rip, rip, a snowfall over the trash can—and then I went for a walk.

Thirty-One

Bish

I had called Letitia to tell her about the wrecked room, and she said she trusted me to spend whatever I needed to get the place fixed back up.

"But, Isabel," she did say, "from now on, get a driver's license number, even if a person pays in advance. Such is the way the world is going." I promised I would.

Then Letitia said, "As far as getting someone to do the repairs, just ask the girls. Wanita and Emogene both have lots of people they can recommend. There's always somebody looking to pick up a little extra work, usually somebody related to them. But they won't steer you wrong."

Wanita said she would get her Uncle Bish, who did odd jobs now but had been the maintenance and handyman at Highlands Hospital before it burned. Fixing up tables and beds would be a piece of cake for him.

I had not even come out of my room the next morning when Wanita knocked. "Isabel, Uncle Bish, he's here—over by the laundry, ready to go."

"I'll be there in just a minute."

I drank my coffee and ate a piece of toast, and I was on my way, but first I heard the banjo music, a strumming that quickened my pulse and my feet.

A coincidence, probably some musician traveling through, doing a show here in town, I thought. But an image was clear in my head: the last time I saw my mama at Ryan's Point Insane Asylum, there had been a man sitting on her bed. I had lingered in the doorway and watched his agile fingers and wondered, *What is he doing here?* My mind went much further now than it had when I was a child. That familiarity had to have meant something. But I noticed that I did not care. I did not care that the man was black, though it worried me, thinking of the disapproving reactions, then or now. It would have been disastrous for them both if they had been discovered. Also, I did not care that my mama was married, or whether the musician was. Whatever it had been between them, I was not shocked, and indeed, I hoped my mama had found some joy and companionship before her death, especially as my daddy had offered so little in that regard.

I rounded the corner, following the music, and he was sitting in one of our green metal porch chairs, the banjo on his lap and a toolbox by his feet. He stood as I approached. Our eyes met. There was a column of air between us, and we both wavered, trying not to fall into it. Though it was years ago, I felt certain. Still, until I moved to Asheville, I had not known black people, and I had only seen the banjo player the one time. I didn't want to make a terrible mistake of identity, the kind that can be so insulting to their race, so I was silent, but Bish was looking at me the same way.

Wanita felt the mystery and had a wrinkle between her brows as she introduced us. "Isabel, this here is Bishop Truman, my uncle, come to fix 214. Folks calls him Bish."

"I think I know you . . . young lady," he said.

He reached out to shake my hand, and I took it. He was still a handsome man, now in his sixties probably and with gray hair. But those were the supple hands of a musician and craftsman and the shapely arms that had caught my attention when I was eleven.

"A bit of time done passed," he said. "But I recognize you. I surely do. You look like her too."

"What now, Bish, you already know Isabel? You must be joking on me, for sure!" Incredulous, Wanita's neck was out of her collar. She turned to me with suspicious eyes and placed her hands on her hips.

"Who do you look like?" she said.

"I look like my mama, Wanita. Don't you? Look like *your* mother too, I mean?" I didn't want to be cranky. "I wouldn't say I know Bish exactly, but our paths crossed once. Ryan's Point, in Knoxville."

I had named it, and he shook his head yes. "My mama was there," I told Wanita. "It was an insane asylum."

"I see," Wanita said. It was uncomfortable for everyone, so she turned to Bish. "That the hospital that burn, and then you come over here and work for Highlands, and it burn?" She was laughing now. "Maybe we're gonna get an investigation going on you, see where you keep all the matches. Every job you has, the place burn." Her voice changed, and she looked back at me. "Your mother in that place, you say, Isabel?"

"It's a long story," I said. "I'll tell it to you sometime."

"A lotta things is a long story," Bish said. "We got some talking to do." He pointed his finger at 214. "But first, let's get this job done." He stood and picked up his tool carrier, and we went to discuss the work, leaving Wanita gaping.

I'd heard him sawing and hammering all the next day and knew he had completed the job. I had an envelope of cash ready in my apron pocket.

"He said he'd be by around noon. When he shows up, you can either pay him, or tell him what more he needs to do to get it right," said Wanita. I noticed she'd collected her curiosity and shut it back away. Apparently, Bish himself had told her enough, as she did not ask me any more questions about my mama. As for myself, I had nothing but questions.

I unlocked 214 and looked around. It was clean as a pin. There was the smell of new wood, and I saw the table he had made. As we had discussed, it was a block piece in the cabin style, simple and solid, and when I put my hands on it, it didn't move. Good. The new bed frame was also complete and waiting for a replacement box spring and mattress. He had cut out the two holes in the wall and put in new drywall and sealed the edges. A coat of paint and new linens, and the room would be better than ever before.

At lunch, I took my sandwich and sat by 214. He came right on time. There was a paper sack under his arm.

"Everything look all right?" he said. "I didn't see no paint, but give that mud another day to dry and I can finish up that wall."

"It looks just perfect." I handed him the money envelope. "I appreciate it. Let me know if that is acceptable." He did not look inside. We had not discussed his fee, but my intuition was that he already knew I would be eager to do that part right. I found myself thinking that since he was a black man, it was more than fair, but immediately, I realized that was society talking in my head, and I shut that voice down. I wanted to give him what would be fair in anyone's book, and I hoped he thought that I had.

"Do you have time to pull up a chair for a few minutes? I haven't thought about anything else but my mama and Ryan's Point since I saw you here the other day. I thought there were some things in life I was never meant to know or find out about, and I had accepted that, put the past near forgotten in some corner of my brain. But now I see it truly would be a sin to have you right here before my eyes and pretend there was not the connection there is. So, just tell me whatever you can or want to, and we can go from there."

He stared into the distance for a long while. Finally, he said, "If it seems odd to you that I am setting here now, believe me, it is even odder to me. I am from this town, and when I was a very young man, not even out of my teens, I followed a gal over to Knoxville, 'specting she and I would settle in together, and I would never see Asheville again. Well, we did settle in, for about a year. But my eyes was too big for my stomach, you might say, like is the case with mos' boys, so she kicked me on my way. But I stayed around Knoxville, playing music and doing jobs, like I still am."

One of our guests passed by just at that moment, his room key in hand. "Good afternoon," I said. "Everything all right?"

"Just fine," the man said. He pushed his mouth into a purse and slowed, looking hard at the two of us sitting with our chairs drawn up together.

"As I was saying about the work you did," I said to Bish, a little overloud, and the man went on.

Bish continued. "Time came I started working at the asylum. I did all kinds of things: maintenance, repair, kitchen, even some things qualified as nursing. A lot of the people in there, they *was* crazy, but crazy from the meanness that had been done to them, and I understood that. I seen too many of my own people come just that close. But one reason I stayed on was 'cause of this."

He patted his banjo. "I used to play on the streets of Knoxville. I got a happy response, sure, a little change in my hat, sure. But in the asylum, I got gratitude. Gratitude. And I think I took it then as a kind of calling, a kind of healing I could do with my music. That's why I stayed at the place. And I got paid reasonable for the work I did, the maintenance and such."

"My mama loved music," I told him. "She loved to dance, and my daddy frowned upon it. Even as young as I was, I know it must have been a blessing and a healing to her to have your sounds in her ears."

Bish nodded. "I guess I musta been there about five years by the time your mother got there. I was thirty-seven years old. I had seen a lot, and the new ones come in. You size 'em up, see how they gonna treat you, see what their problems be and how they gonna act, see how careful you need to be. Right away, I saw your mama, and I knew there was not a thing wrong with her mind. I could see her wheels turning, see her eyes looking back at me, axin' me to recognize she was a person with wits. She should not have been there."

He picked up his banjo and started strumming softly. "At that time, I was a lonely man, and she was a lonely woman. In the asylum, the reg'lar rules of the world do not apply." He picked on, tapping his foot and moving his head. He sang it a little: "The reg'lar rules / of this ole world / they just did / not ap-ply.

"What else you want me to tell you, Isabel? Martha, your mama, was not a reg'lar woman anyway, and I was lucky to meet her." He looked at me. "She talked a lot about you, about your brothers, told me how she hated to have run, but had to. The thing so funny, so sad, we used to talk about is—she ran to keep from going crazy and wound up at Ryan's Point, sane as God."

I listened to his flowing melody. The sky had darkened, and I could hear thunder in the distance. The trees were shushing in the wind, and I felt bands of cool air twining around us; I could tell their edges from the warmer air.

Finally, I said, "What about the end?" I did not look at him. "My family got a letter; she was about to get out. My Uncle John had gone to a lawyer . . . we heard there was a doctor who understood she should never have been taken there. It all seemed just about ready to turn around."

"Yes. I knew about that. She was excited about that." He stopped playing. "You know, she worked in that laundry in the basement of the building. At night, they lock all the doors. It was about five o'clock in the afternoon; she was still in there washing, but they had already lock the door. The fire was on the first floor. She, and the other women, was down there. They could not get out, and they could not come up the stairs 'cause the fire done block them in."

Bish inhaled slow and held it. Then he took the paper bag and unrolled the top and handed it to me. "I been having this since then, took it from under her pillow. You keep it now."

Shaking, I reached inside. I pulled out photographs, one of Dora as a babe in arms with Sam and Molly, one of me and Walker and Avery. There was something else soft underneath the cardboards. I lifted it to the light, gasping. It was a blouse just my size. I had made it all those years ago, black and white stripes, with hand-turned buttonholes that had taken me forever. It's always good to do your best work. You never know if—or how—or when—it'll all come back around.

Thirty-Two

Dora Revisited

The funniest thing was getting another letter from Dora with an entirely new tone. You would think she had never written the other one—the elopement letter, as I called it—all upset and dismissive of what Jane had done.

By now, it just amused me, the way Dora needed to have the upper hand and frame a story in the prettiest way, or the way that made her, Dora, look best. And then inform me of developments, and thus put it up that her bond with Jane was deeper than mine, and that Jane was confiding in her and not in me. And so forth. And so on.

Dora could do and say what she wanted. I was content enough about Jane, though I still felt wary of her husband. I knew they were settled in at Oak Ridge and things seemed to be happy and stable. She told me she had written to Dora, too, and that she and J.C. had driven over to pay them a visit. Everyone was apparently reconciled, and I was glad. I did not want Jane to be burdened by estrangements, and if she was going to be independent from Dora, at least that meant that we were now free to begin a relationship truly on our own terms.

But Dora's letter! Now that all seemed to be going well, you would have thought she had orchestrated it, predicted it. But for sure, she wanted to bask in it and claim her little piece of fame because it all was successful beyond anyone's expectations.

Dear Isabel,

I just wanted to touch base with you to let you know that J.C. and I have been to see Jane and her wonderful new husband, Gary. Despite our initial concerns (because of Jane's youth, of course) I thought you would like to know how well it has all turned out. She and Gary have a brand-new, three-bedroom home right there in Oak Ridge. It's such a cute little community, all planned out in such a perfect way, so modern. Gary is an important engineer with the Atomic Energy Commission; can you imagine? I can see he makes a fine addition to our family. He has a maturity that will be good for Jane. His sister, the one who is president of the Business League here, and I have gotten to be good friends now too!

Jane is keeping busy with housework; the place is immaculate, and she has selected lovely Danish blond furniture for the rooms. It undoubtedly cost a fortune, though Gary can well afford it. They introduced us to their neighbors: the people on one side are from New York, and the people on the other side have just arrived from New Mexico. They were involved with the bomb program in Los Alamos; it is sort of hush-hush.

Gary treated us to dinner at an Italian place that just opened up. J.C. had never had pizza before and loved it—poor dear, it takes so little to make him happy. But in any

case, I think you can relax, knowing Jane is in good hands.
And who knows? Maybe we will have some new little ones
to enjoy soon!

Dora

And it was true—Jane and Gary did have a little girl within a year, and another one three years after that. And Jane asked me to come and live with them there in perfect, modern little Oak Ridge. And as for what Dora thought about that, I never asked. I didn't care to know.

Thirty-Three

Where I Stand

1950

That Saturday, one March long ago, when my mama left me, I thought spring was going to be coming. Instead, the world had tilted more than it was supposed to, and I got thrown beyond some of the innocent years I was expecting.

My mama had pushed me aside and shouted for me to not follow when she vanished into the tree line by the Clinchfield tracks. She dropped her plow lines in the field and got astride the mule and ran away from the family. It seems her body finally had to follow her thoughts and go.

A child does not see this coming. Only later, much later, could I grasp it.

Queenie's family's farm was about a mile away, across the footbridge on the other side of the creek. We went back and forth all the time and made a pleasure of chores by doing them together. I see those times through some rose-colored glasses. I overthink the sweetness, the way you do when you remember ordinary things as a last moment of

The Before. We were making lunch for my daddy and my teenage brothers, Walker and Avery, and then I went to see my mama in the field, and she left me. She just left.

Most people can't mark the end of their childhood— that is, there's not an absolute event for it on the timeline of their life. Normally, you might turn and see it disappearing behind you, almost visible, like the wake of a boat showing where you've passed. Sometimes there is a ceremony, like a graduation, or an awakening with a lover, and you might *say* that was the end of your childhood, but it really won't be because you kept on acting like a little fool for years afterward.

Eventually, a person has to take responsibility for who they turn out to be, but trauma makes it harder. It takes years to realize it can't always be someone else's fault. As my life flowed on, all I ever wanted was for my life to get clean and smooth, like a piece of white satin when you run your hand over it. Eventually, I realized it was never going to be that way. I was just . . . I was going to have to hold steady, no matter what befell. That was to be my life accomplishment.

And so, here I am now . . . I knew it was going to be different, but this place, Oak Ridge, is as foreign to me as Egypt. There is a hard smell in the air, something metal, and an odd silence instead of birds. Land features, buildings, people—everything I once knew has been reduced to the thin sepia of ancient photographs and dreams. Sometimes, I think I made up that old life in my head, or else it was a fairy story I read one time about a girl living on her daddy's farm in a place called Wheat.

I am country-looking and plain, late-middle-aged now. Most people would not give me an extra glance. I do not have the authority or presence to make listeners raise their chins and nod. But I have always had intuition and a sense of the true. I am someone to pay attention to, but I do not know how to get anyone to take notice.

Seeing Oak Ridge was not like a return home after many years, one where you find the old schoolhouse torn down, or the vista of a familiar pasture covered over with asphalt. Oh no. It's all, all gone. The only thing left to look at by way of mourning is some tombstones leaning this way and that. Our little cemeteries look pitiful, stranded as lost islands in the government complexes where stuff called uranium is processed. I thought about people I'd known, no more than names on these graves now. In my mind, they seem to be walking around bewildered, saying, "Atom bomb? Atom bomb? I had me a peach orchard in this valley."

What do you do when you come home and there is no home? When all you have left is your body and your spirit, and you know that is as fragile as a leaf hanging on in its season?

Just tell it, I told myself. Just tell it as best you can, and let them make of it what they will.

Thirty-Four

Oak Ridge

A week before Easter is when I arrived. Jane had been offered a secretarial job ("a wonderful chance to make extra money") just in the past month. Her call for help ("what if you came here to live and took care of Joanna and Susie for me?") came at just the right time. Rock Heaven had changed hands and lost its name; it belonged to a national chain now, and they brought in a manager from Raleigh. Only Emogene stayed on. I could have looked around in Asheville; Queenie continued to say it was high time I found myself a real place to live and got a different occupation. She started to say "a nicer job," but she stopped herself.

It's always been hard for me to say no when I was needed. So I rode the Greyhound back, back "home."

Janey was there, waving yoo-hoo, her hand over her head, standing beside their black Pontiac sedan. It was a new car, of course.

"You look pretty," she said as I came off the steps of the bus. She sounded surprised about it. Thank goodness I had put some lipstick on at the last minute. I was wearing my suit with the matching gloves and my hat with the veil. I knew I could look good when I tried. A half century and still only a thread or two of gray in my hair, and I guess I always would be slim. Usually, I wore housedresses and aprons, though; you would never pick me out of a crowd.

Little Joanna, four years old but smart as a whip, hugged me, then wrinkled her nose.

"I smell dirt with sugar in it."

It was my Blue Rose snuff—I had had a pinch on the bus, and I knew I was going to have to be careful about using it from then on.

"Now," Janey said, "is that a nice way to say hello to Grandma Isabel?" She cut her eyes at me. Janey hated that I had not totally quit snuff. It reminded her of the old country life—it did me too, which is why I took comfort in it on occasion. She referred to it as my "nasty habit."

"Why don't you just smoke, like normal people?" she'd say.

I got settled in the back of the Pontiac and opened my purse. "Looky here what I've got." I shook a pack of marshmallow chickens at Joanna. "We can share them with little sister when we get home." But when I went to hand the treat to Joanna, Janey reached over the seat and held out her hand.

"I'll hold on to them until later," she said, taking them. She looked at me in the rearview mirror. "It'll spoil her supper if she has them now."

Some of Dora might have rubbed off on Jane, but only some. She was attractive and had finished her business course by mail after she and Gary got married. Though I had been skeptical at first, her marriage to Gary seemed to be solid. His job paid fine, and he was mostly a teetotaler, and of course, they had the two beautiful girls. But her time with Dora had made its mark in ways I was just beginning to notice. I had made sacrifices for Janey, and I had assumed she knew it. Maybe she did, deep down, but there was a surface to her now. The coming days would allow us to get to know each other again, learn each other's natures.

We drove through Oak Ridge, the government-built offices and stores sharp and about as interesting as new cardboard boxes, and with yellow parking lines painted around the curbs like spokes of sunshine in a drawing.

"Over here you can see Y-12," Janey said. "That's where Gary works, and where I'm going to be too." She sounded so happy. The plant was a little below us in the valley, and when I saw the flat roof of it sprawling out for acres in its concrete ugliness, I did not know at all where I was. I did not believe it when I reminded myself that this was where uranium was processed now, and that my daddy's farm was bulldozed underneath it all.

It was a blue, sunny day with a light breeze. "Look, Mother," said Janey. She pointed. It was nothing but a little island of green with crooked tombstones and a fancy monument or two sticking up from the ground. "There's the cemetery of your old church."

"Can we stop for a minute?" I asked. We had already passed the preserved graveyards of several other churches, forlorn pieces of the past now stuck to the coattails of the modern world like burs.

Janey pulled the car into the Y-12 overlook picnic area pavilion, and we got out and walked over.

"I guess that is what is left of Step Creek," I said. I referred to a gully lined with concrete that ran along one side of the cemetery. "Step Creek used to be a very special place; it had stones in it that had fallen into a formation like stairs. You could go down in the hollow to the water and walk between upper Step Creek and lower Step Creek. The water flowed real slow; it made a clear skin on the stones as it came down. We used to baptize people on the steps in that water." It all used to fit together, the church, the creek, the trees, the gentle graves.

Janey listened, but I sensed her impatience. My daughter is full of the future. She is a secretary for the Atomic Energy Commission.

"Where was the church, Grandma?" Joanna asked, jumping over a bunch of tacky plastic poinsettias that had blown loose from a vase. She looked up with her earnest little face. "What happened to it?"

"They tore it down, sweetheart. All this property used to be my old town. The church, now, was just a white wood building with a peaked roof, not even a cross on top. There was a door in front and three windows on each side. Now this pavilion is here." I flicked my hand out to the picnic tables bolted to the concrete slab. The place before my eyes seemed less real than my memories.

Janey crossed her arms and raised her brows. "That little old church was cold as ice, is what I remember," she said. "And the benches were hard. Fortunately, time marches on." She turned and looked with satisfaction over the complex below us.

She made the past sound so bad, as if we'd been backward on purpose. I resettled my hat, feeling shabby and out-of-date. Janey was wearing a narrow skirt with a slit in the back and a fitted sweater. Folks tell her she looks like Audrey Hepburn.

"Well, we better get on home." Janey shook her car keys.

We piled back in and drove on. Everything was going away in patches, claimed by housing developments, by the

Manhattan Motel Court or an Oldsmobile dealership. These boundary areas twinged my soul, gave the illusion things might still be saved. I managed to recognize some farmland on the Pellissippi Road at the edges of the Oak Ridge preserve, saw the gate to the Greenes' pasture with the distinctive giant holly still rising beside it. Now it's a scenic feature beside the parking lot of the New Dixie Diner. I can't tell you the strangeness there is in recognizing a tree and feeling sorry for it, as if it were a person I knew that used to be free and was now enslaved.

"Here we are," Janey said as she swung the car into their driveway.

Janey and Gary's house looked like a loaf of white bread with a green door. There were three bedrooms, one bath, and a garage. They had set me up in a little room just off the kitchen.

"This is where you will be," Joanna said, pulling me by the hand. "It used to be my room."

"You are so sweet to let me have it," I told her. A picture of Humpty Dumpty sitting on his wall had not yet been transferred out, but otherwise, it was fixed up very much like the maid's room in an estate, with its narrow bed, dresser, lamp, and small closet. I did not mind in the least. I knew I was not in charge here, and was happy to keep a roof over my head and be useful.

Later, Gary prayed at the dinner table, "Thank you for bringing Isabel here safely to help us." I was in agreement. And that is how I came back to Oak Ridge.

It was on Good Friday, just a few days after I arrived, that Janey opened the door to a man carrying a briefcase. This struck me as odd because it was obvious he was selling something, and Janey had always hated door-to-door salespeople. Maybe it was because I was here now, and she had practiced opening the door to her home by letting me in.

When we lived with John L., she hid from the Jehovah's Witnesses and the Fuller Brush man. The Jehovah's Witnesses could be annoying, and she didn't want to face them and be rude, so I always did it. But the Fuller Brush man, with his kitchen gadgets and his odor of vanilla, made her panic.

It used to baffle me, her reaction, but after I knew what John L. was up to, showing a child what her little mind was never meant to see, it made sense. Those "free" letter openers he gave out with the handles in the image of a man in a suit, they were awful to Janey. Only looking back did I comprehend her shrinking back as the man pulled things out for us to look at.

"Here, honey, this is for you." It was just a letter opener. I didn't know why she had screamed.

So you could have knocked me over with a feather when this man—this Bible salesman—came unannounced up the walk, gripping his black leather case, and she let him in at once. She swung the front door back against the wall, and there he was, taking up half the space of the springtime sky. Maybe it was because there was a Y-12 holiday and Gary was home (Janey felt safer). In any case, he was selling religious material, and since it was Easter week, she relented.

We were about to color eggs with the children, and the kitchen counter was arranged with four teacups, a dozen eggs, a bottle of cider vinegar and the McCormick food colorings—red, blue, yellow, and green. The young man adjusted his tie with one hand and stood up straighter.

"Good afternoon, ma'am," he said, and sure enough, "are you and your young 'uns about ready for Easter?"

He shifted his case, possibly so his sweaty palm could breathe, or maybe to remind himself, and us, that the thing was not as light as it should be this late in the afternoon.

He had carefully combed, light-brown hair and pale, unlined skin. I saw Janey look at him; he was not a threat like the Fuller Brush man. But to me, he had a slight hardness of expression. I first attributed it to tiredness. Then I saw his alert marketer's eyes with their too-eager shine, like the clear glaze on a doughnut.

"Well," said Jane. "Come on in and sit down, and we'll take a look. Let me get my husband."

The next thing I knew, the whole family was sitting straight-backed on the living room sofa while this salesman, this whippersnapper, offered a prayer over a six-inch-thick Bible storybook, which Gary and Janey had just bought. Yes, to everyone's surprise, he sold it to them. It was almost like surgery—you wake up and say, Has any time passed? What has just happened to me?

The book had a picture of David slinging a rock at Goliath stamped in gold on the simulated calfskin cover, and it was filled with glossy pictures and paintings of Old and New Testament scenes. The spine of the book cracked from newness when I lifted it off the coffee table, and it opened on Daniel in the lion's den. Daniel was young and blond and right with the Lord, and his smooth brown chest was open to the snarling animals while faces peered into the pit from above.

Gary sat forward, tapping his heel to soothe the baby riding on his leg. He had been working in the yard, and there were grass stains on his white socks. Janey's fingers were clasped prim in her lap, and she was listening to the young man's prayer:

"Lord, bless this family as they read and continue to

learn about You and Your Word, and be with them and
with us all this season as we remember the great love You
showed us by sacrificing Your Son and having Him rise
again. A-men," he intoned.

I cracked one eye, like a cat stalking a bird. Why did
they let this go on? But then I saw that Gary was doing it as
a favor to Janey. She groped for his hand as the prayer was
said.

The young man finished; the sale was made. He shook
Gary's hand, then shook Janey's and kept shaking it.

His false etiquette was like something Scarlett O'Hara
would have approved of in a Confederate officer. He and
Janey both galled me to no end. He patted Susie's head and
grinned at Joanna. He looked at me and gave a tiny smile,
then looked away. I blinked. When I opened my eyes, there
was an empty space in the air and a green afterimage probably only I could see.

"Sweetheart," Janey said to Gary. "Thank you." She
kissed him and ran her hand up one sleeve of his undershirt.

He sighed and resettled his wallet in his back pocket.
"I'm going to finish the yard now," he said. Pulling a small
pruner and a pocketknife from his pants, he headed for the
back door. The Bible storybook remained, gleaming alone
in a puddle of sun. Susie braced her hands on the coffee
table and stared at it, as if it, too, were a visitor.

Janey smiled at Susie and Joanna, then cleared her
throat and turned to me. "Easter's not just baskets of
goodies, new patent-leather shoes, and the Easter bunny.
It's serious, and I think we ought to keep a focus. It means
something, and the children need to learn."

"You don't have to explain Easter to me, Janey," I said.
"Let's get back to business." I winked at Joanna.

Janey ran a panful of water and dropped in the eggs. She kept this pan only for boiling eggs, because, she said, the calcium in the shells chalked up the stainless steel, and she didn't want to ruin *all* her pans. Next, she took out her measuring spoons and tapped some vinegar into the cups.

"It stinks! My goodness, it really does!" Joanna held an egg to her nose and kept sniffing.

Janey scowled at her with a teaching face. "Is that all you can say? Didn't you listen when we talked about what day is coming on Sunday?"

"Yes, I did," said the child. "Jesus rose." She paused. "Up into the sky," she added.

"What can I do to help?" I asked. Behind her head, I could see the doorway to my little room. It was clean and quiet in there, and my clothes were hung up or put away in the dresser, which Janey had lined with fresh brown paper. I was a boarder, like I always have been, and it was a place like the others, a place I could, but couldn't, call my own.

"Get a candle stub," Janey said. She poked at the eggs with a slotted spoon. "Joanna can write her and Susie's name on some of these before we dye them."

I rummaged in the drawer she pointed to and helped Joanna print her name on the white surface of the egg. It was invisible, but then we dipped it and out came the letters.

"Aaaah, Joanna," the child breathed. A miracle it was, her name on an egg.

That night, Janey turned the pages of the Bible storybook while the rest of us listened. She turned the volume around and showed the painting of the *Last Supper* by Leonardo da Vinci. Joanna and I didn't touch—we had purple thumbs. Janey had worn gloves for the dyeing.

"They don't look happy," Joanna said, looking at the

disciples. In the picture, no one was eating, and the robed men were peeking warily around the table. "Don't they like the food?"

Next came a picture of the crucifixion by an artist named Velázquez—"Don't show her *that*," said Gary, flipping the page away from the nailed feet dripping blood. Finally, we turned to the Resurrection. I didn't like the picture of the empty tomb, Jesus in his glowing bedsheet with marks on his hands and a phony, lifted expression. I thought of the salesman, when Gary handed over the five-dollar bill. But I admired the white lilies that lined the path. They looked normal to me, as real as any you could find in the supermarket during Lent.

I didn't want Janey to know how skeptical I was about Easter. I had, after all, taught her what she knew of salvation. I was skeptical of myself being skeptical. But when a point of view is so widespread, you start to think it's only you, being uneducated or maybe not bright enough to understand the mystery of it all. And so, the readings ended, and the children went to bed.

Sunday came. Gary and Janey went to the Cumberland Presbyterian Church in Clinton, which is a denomination she got from Dora and J.C. and was the same as being Baptist, as far as I was concerned. But the white lilies were lined up in the foyer, which satisfied me, and Susie and Joanna were darling in matching lilac dresses, with lace-edged socks and new Buster Brown shoes. Janey and Gary were a perfect couple, for all the world elegant and attractive as Princess Elizabeth and her dashing Philip. I wore my gray suit again.

The minister said some unremarkable words, though you couldn't tell it by the congregation. Everyone clasped their hymnals and seemed to listen with all their heart. Maybe it was just me, being new and with an outsider's eye.

I thought about Easter, how the minister seemed so sure it had saved us all, and how heaven was the home we should want. I thought of the mystery of my life, and my parents and children and grandchildren, and how I had returned but not returned to the place I was from. Sometimes, we just have to keep on with life as best we can, and it is strange how optimistic I am, despite the way it all turned out, because what do I know? What do any of us know?

Everybody sang "Thine be the glo-ry ri-hi-hi-sen, con-qu'ring Son," then went home to eat ham and go on Easter egg hunts.

We all had a very nice afternoon. On Monday, I stayed with the children while Gary and Janey went to work at Y-12; that is, they went to work at a bomb factory that sat on top of Daddy's old pasture. They did it like it was the most normal thing in the world.

Acknowledgments

I will be eternally grateful to D. Ynes Freeman and Tod Tinker of Balance of Seven for their belief in me and in the power of women's quiet stories. Thank you, Georgina Key, for steering me in the right direction and for your amazing editing job. Dr. Nyri Bakkalian offered historical perspective and gave me hope this novel could be viable outside the region where it is set. Cindy Childress gave structural advice and encouragement when I really needed it. Appreciation to Eben Schumacher for the cover art.

I want to thank Vicki Lane, Elizabeth Lutyens, and others associated with the Great Smokies Writing Program in Asheville, North Carolina, for their affirmation of Isabel's voice and adventures. *The Great Smokies Review* was the first place to publish a piece of the story.

I have to shout out to my writing group in Houston. We sustained each other through Covid and beyond. Thank you for offering validation for my stories. Tanya Terry, Brooke Summers-Perry, Stefanie Fercking, Sandy Schnackenburg, Robin Leonard, Mike Sheehan, Corin Bauman, and Nicole Moore-Kriel—yes, you guys. Love also to Jamie Portwood and the folks at Writespace Houston.

And those strong women in my family who rooted for my success—Jean Vance, Susan Bennett, Lauren Agrella-Sevilla, and Elise Agrella-O'Rourke—you have my heart always. Also naming my Encore friends, especially Sondi Wise, who never lost faith in me or Isabel. My cousin Scotti Jencks, now gone, read early drafts and urged me to "get on with it." And finally, to the memory of my grandmother, Kate Kearney Little Kyte, who was the main inspiration for Isabel. Sometimes, you just have to keep on and do the best you can.

About the Author

Catherine Vance was born in Oak Ridge, Tennessee. She holds an MFA in creative writing (fiction) from Washington University in St. Louis and was a recipient of the Dobie Paisano Award from the Texas Institute of Letters. She now lives in Houston, Texas, where she teaches creative writing for Writespace Houston and has recently completed training to be an interfaith chaplain.

In her time off, Catherine can be found dancing in her car or expanding her knowledge of Spanish or Arabic. Connect with her and learn more at CatherineVance.com or on Instagram at @bluemtns2sea.

CPSIA information can be obtained
at www.ICGtesting.com
Printed in the USA
LVHW081229190323
741932LV00027B/1217